FEAR THY NEIGHBOR

Books by Fern Michaels

Books by Fern Michaels (Continued)

The Godmothers Series:

Far and Away
Classified
Breaking News
Deadline
Late Edition
Exclusive
The Scoop

E-Book Exclusives:

Desperate Measures
Seasons of Her Life
To Have and To Hold
Serendipity
Captive Innocence
Captive Embraces
Captive Passions
Captive Secrets
Captive Splendors
Cinders to Satin
For All Their Lives
Texas Heat
Texas Rich
Texas Fury
Texas Sunrise

Anthologies:

In Bloom
Home Sweet Home
A Snowy Little Christmas
Coming Home for Christmas
A Season to Celebrate
Mistletoe Magic
Winter Wishes
The Most Wonderful Time
When the Snow Falls
Secret Santa
A Winter Wonderland
I'll Be Home for Christmas
Making Spirits Bright
Holiday Magic
Snow Angels
Silver Bells
Comfort and Joy
Sugar and Spice
Let it Snow
A Gift of Joy
Five Golden Rings
Deck the Halls
Jingle All the Way

FERN MICHAELS

FEAR THY NEIGHBOR

ZEBRA BOOKS
Kensington Publishing Corp.
www.kensingtonbooks.com

ZEBRA BOOKS are published by

Kensington Publishing Corp.
119 West 40th Street
New York, NY 10018

Copyright © 2022 by Fern Michaels.
Fern Michaels is a registered trademark of KAP 5, Inc.

All Kensington titles, imprints and distributed lines are available at special quantity discounts for bulk purchases for sales promotion, premiums, fund-raising, educational or institutional use.

Special book excerpts or customized printings can also be created to fit specific needs. For details, write or phone the office of the Kensington Special Sales Manager: Kensington Publishing Corp., 119 West 40th Street, New York, NY, 10018. Attn. Special Sales Department. Phone: 1-800-221-2647.

First Kensington Hardcover Edition: April 2022

First Paperback Edition: May 2023
ISBN: 978-1-4201-5426-9

ISBN-13: 978-1-4967-3717-5 (ebook)

10 9 8 7 6 5 4 3 2 1

Printed in the United States of America

FEAR THY
NEIGHBOR

Prologue

Ohio, 2010

Alison tossed her cap and gown on the dresser, then plopped down on the narrow twin bed pressed against the wall. Sharing the room with three other girls didn't allow for privacy, though tonight she was alone in the room for the first time since she came to live with the Robertson family almost two years ago. As soon as Mr. Bloomenfield placed her diploma in her hand, she'd glanced toward the bleachers, hoping Mr. or Mrs. Robertson were there to show their support. Tonight of all nights, her high school graduation, and not one member of her so-called foster family bothered to attend.

She'd hurried out of the auditorium as soon she received her diploma. A grad night celebration with her fellow classmates was not happening, because she did not have any friends. She started Madison High in the middle of her sophomore year, which had made her stand out like a sore thumb. Add in her living conditions and all the popular kids *and* the dorks did their best to avoid her. Alison heard the slurs, the hateful comments made as she stood by her locker waiting for the halls to clear so she could hurry to class without facing her tormentors.

Tears streamed down her face when she thought how stupid it'd been to hope the Robertsons would surprise her with an impromptu graduation party, a gift, or even a card. She didn't belong here. In four months, she would turn eighteen, no longer a responsibility of the state of Ohio. Alison Marshall planned to leave at 12:01 on her birthday.

She used the thin blanket to wipe her tears. With the entire summer ahead of her, she knew her misery would continue if she stayed. A plan began to form—while not impossible, she could only achieve it if she used her brain. Patience would be required, something she had plenty of. Always on the outskirts of the families she'd been forced to live with, she'd learned early to blend in, not make trouble, and do as she was told, yet there were times when that had been nearly impossible. She'd done what any kid would've done if they'd been in her shoes.

She would sneak out of her bedroom window during the night, searching for something better than what the state provided. Her first attempt at escaping the system happened when she was nine. This happened so many times, she'd forgotten exactly how many foster homes she'd been placed in. A few of them were okay, but most of them sucked. The only reason the foster families took her in was for the money from the state.

She'd learned that the hard way and lost what little innocence she'd had in the process.

Planning her future would require discipline, another attribute she'd learned the hard way. *Do as you're told, and no one gets hurt.*

Those days were about to end.

Emboldened at the idea of making a life for herself, Alison sneaked into the communal closet, where she hid the cash she'd earned babysitting and working part-time at the local pet store. She counted eighty-nine dollars and forty-three cents. Not much, but it was enough to pay for a bus ticket anywhere but here. The bus station was open twenty-four hours, though she was unsure if there were buses leaving tonight. At daybreak, she would hitch a ride downtown, purchase a ticket. She didn't care where she wound up; just thinking about a new life cheered her up. A graduation gift to herself, she thought. Yes, this is exactly what she would do. The heck with waiting until she was eighteen—she would leave now. The Robertsons wouldn't report her missing, because they were greedy. They'd want to continue to collect money from the state for as long as they could.

The three other girls she shared the room with, all younger than her, would probably tell someone at school, and from there, the authorities would be called in. Maybe they would search for her. Maybe not; either way, it didn't matter. She'd made up her mind, and she smiled to herself. This was the last night she'd spend living under the rules of the state. With this thought in mind, she drifted off, content for the first time in years.

She dreamed of parties and unknown people with

blank faces. Animals, lions, bears, and giraffes with human features chased her down a school hallway while her female teachers danced with each other. Lockers opened on their own, schoolbooks flew out the windows, and desks clung to the ceiling. Startled when her English teacher curtsied, then asked her to dance, Alison bolted upright in the bed, her heart racing. Sweat dampened her face and her hair. It took a few seconds for her to shake off the silly dream. She laughed to herself at the insane images in her dream; then, a creaking sound startled her. She sat up, inching toward the wall, pulling the blanket up to her chin.

"Who's there?" she called out.

Waiting for a response from Charlotte, or Pamela, her two youngest foster sisters, she raised her voice. "This isn't funny," she said. "I'm gonna turn the lights on, then kick your ass."

Nothing.

"Sarah?" She was foster sister number three. She was fourteen, street-smart with a mean streak as wide as their room. It would be like her to try and scare the crap out of her, especially tonight. Sarah did horribly in school and was resentful of Alison's good grades.

Alison waited a few seconds and scooted to the edge of the bed. She let the blanket drop to the floor. She stood, quietly easing across the room to flick the light switch on. The second she touched the switch, a hand grabbed her arm, yanking it so hard, she winced.

"Don't say a word."

Cigarette smoke permeated his breath, his mouth so close to hers she could swallow the air he exhaled. Fearing this moment, knowing what was about to take place because he was not the first, she raised her knee, aiming for his crotch. The sharpness of her knee gouged his most sensitive area. He released her arm, giving her a millisecond to wrench out of his grip. Standing as close to the door as she dared, the room in almost total darkness minus the hazy glint of moon that shone between the heavy drapes, Alison touched the door, the wood rough against her hand. Fumbling for the doorknob, she felt the rusted brass graze her palm. Hope filled her with a power force. She yanked the door inward only to feel the bulk of his weight slam against it, her arm caught between the frame and the latch.

"You're hurting me!" Alison cried out.

"Shut up," he growled. "You think you're smart, don't you?" He eased the bulk of his weight off the door, freeing her arm. Ripples of hot pain pierced her forearm. She knew it was broken. Clenching her teeth, she pushed away from him, but he was too fast for her.

Grabbing both feet, he dragged her across the dirty linoleum floor. Her head hit the corner of the dresser, the sharp edge slicing into the delicate skin on her temple. Warm blood oozed down her face, the coppery scent gagging her.

"Stop!" she screamed through gritted teeth.

Wicked laughter spewed from his mouth. "I'll stop when I'm finished, you little bitch."

Straddling her, his knees pressing on her thighs, he used one hand to hold her wrists above her head. Tears rivered down her face, mixing in with the blood from her head wound. With his free hand, he ripped off his belt, the metal buckle hitting her chin. More blood, pain, and rage provided enough adrenaline for her to yank her arms free. She heard the swift sound as he ripped open his zipper, knowing what was next. Through her blood-drenched vision, by the dim light from the moon, Alison was able to see the table between the two beds. The extension cord on the lamp, snaking across the linoleum, was within her reach.

She yanked the cord, and the lamp smashed onto the floor, also hitting the iron bedframe. Quickly she reached for a large piece of glass, feeling its sharp edge. Before he realized what she'd done, her adrenaline pumping, she jammed the broken glass into the soft spot in the center of his neck.

His body limp, stunned, he touched his neck. "I'll kill you!"

She pulled the shard of glass out of his neck and stabbed him again, and again and again.

Pushing his heavy body aside, she wiped the blood from her eyes, took her wad of money from the pillowcase, and crawled out the window.

The words *never again, never again* kept rhythm with her steps as she ran down the sidewalk. Amid angry tears and unrelenting pain, Alison promised herself she would never let another man touch her again.

Chapter One

Tampa Bay, July 2022

"The tourists are gone—I'm ready for a change," Alison Marshall told her manager at Besito's, one of the finer Mexican restaurants in the city.

Pedro shook his head. "No, you can't leave now. I'm already shorthanded as it is. We'll liven up soon, the locals will turn up."

"Sorry, Pedro, but it's time for me to move on. I've worked the last two seasons here. I told you when you hired me I was a drifter," Alison explained. She needed a new scenario. She'd been in Tampa Bay long enough. The tourist season was over, and the big tips didn't come from the locals eating free baskets of chips and salsa on Taco Tuesday. One might earn twenty bucks in tips, *if* they were lucky.

At twenty-nine, Alison was footloose and fancy-free. She liked being self-sufficient, able to pick up and go whenever the urge hit her. She had no family, no close friends, and had never owned anything except an old Jeep she'd paid cash for three years ago in Tallahassee. No attachments suited her perfectly.

"You're leaving me in a bind, Alison. I can't give you a good reference," Pedro told her as she folded her clean BESITO'S work shirt along with her bright green apron.

"Fine. You'll find someone else to take my place. Put an ad on your Facebook page. Trust me, you'll have your share of applicants. I don't need a reference from you."

Pedro, all four hundred pounds of him, shook his head, his black hair sticking to the sweat on his forehead. "Then go," he told her as he wiped his forehead with a dirty rag.

"Nice knowing you too, Pedro." Alison left her shirt and apron on the counter by the register. She had no hard feelings toward her manager; she knew it was time for a change.

She waved goodbye to the empty dining room. "Later," she said as she walked to her car. Her rent was paid up, so no strings there, either. Renting an efficiency apartment weekly suited her nomadic lifestyle. Living on the seedier side of Tampa Bay had its risks, but for two hundred a week, she hadn't worried about them. She carried a .22-caliber pistol in her purse with five extra clips, all legal and necessary for a woman in today's world.

Once inside her one-room apartment, she neatly packed her clothes into her battered luggage, took her two pairs of extra shoes from the small closet, and grabbed her toiletries bag, stuffing it inside with the rest of her worldly belongings.

Alison took the three Diet Cokes out of the mini refrigerator and placed them in her small cooler. She took one last look around the modest space that had been her home for two years.

"Yep, it's time to hit the road."

She filled the cooler with ice before stopping by the office to return her key.

"You goin' already?" Bert asked, brown spittle staining his white beard. He reeked of stale cigars and whiskey.

"Time to move on," she said. "Take care of yourself."

Bert nodded. "Always do." Alison had a snarky reply at the ready but kept it to herself. Bert was who he was—an old drunk with a half-ass job that gave him free rent. Not unlike herself, minus the drunkenness and cigar smoke.

She pulled into a convenience store and filled her tank, then purchased a few snacks for the road. She kept a sleeping bag, a flashlight, and a set of jumper cables in the Jeep just in case. Always be prepared for the worst, a lesson she'd learned after spending her first seventeen years in foster homes. After graduating high school early with honors, she took a bus from Ohio to Georgia with nothing but the clothes on her back and the money she'd managed to save from the part-time jobs she'd held during high school. She spent four years in Georgia, had a number of jobs, saving every cent she could, living in hostels, cheap hotels, and sometimes the back of the twenty-year-old van she'd bought. It was hard work, saving as much as she could, until she returned to Middletown, Ohio, on her twenty-first birthday to search for the family of the man who'd sent her running. Since she was a legal adult, the state of Ohio no longer controlled her. She spent over a month searching for any information about the foster family whose son had tried to take her life. Alison spent hours at the local library, searching obituaries online. Information from the local police provided nothing, though the lies she'd told about her reasons for wanting such information might've been why she'd been unable to get answers. Knowing he was no longer a danger, and that possibly her fears about his family were irrational, she put the nightmare back in a place where her dark memories resided, and left Ohio once more.

With 12,000 dollars saved, she rented a room at a local boarding house in Georgia and found a job at a Frisch's Big Boy. She spent six years there, working as a waitress. When she'd had enough of Georgia, she'd said her goodbyes and headed south to Florida.

Alison liked the warm weather, though she didn't care for the humidity in the summer. However, she loved the laid-back lifestyle. She'd stopped in Talla-hassee but didn't like that remote area so then headed to Tampa Bay, where she found a place to live and a job. Now she was on the move again.

Driving south on Interstate 75, she figured she could head for the Keys, where no one would care where she was from or who she was. These were her thoughts as she drove at a steady pace along the interstate. She checked the gas gauge and saw she was down to a quarter tank. The Jeep was a gas hog. She pulled over at the next exit, and after parking her Jeep, she went inside a Circle K convenience store and bought a large coffee and a map. She gassed up, then pulled to the side of the parking lot to look at the map. The closest city was Fort Charlotte. She would stop for the night, rest, then head for Key West first thing in the morning.

As she was about to pull out of the parking lot, she heard a cry. Stopping, she eased the Jeep toward the pumps, where she thought the cries were coming from. Turning off the ignition, she got out of the Jeep and walked toward the sound. What she saw broke her heart—a cat with two small kittens, the mother cat stretching to find food in the nearby garbage can.

"Oh, sweet girl, look at you." Alison bent down, careful not to startle the cat. While she'd never had a pet, she'd worked in a pet store in high school and so knew a little about momma cats and their kittens. "You're hungry, huh?" Momma cat meowed loudly and took a couple steps toward her. Alison spoke in a soothing tone—at least she hoped—so she wouldn't frighten her. Momma cat came right to her, snaking around her legs, the two kitties meowing for attention, too. Without giving it another thought, Alison scooped up Momma cat and her kitties, opened the passenger door of her Jeep, and sat them in the seat. She petted the kitties, and they meowed even louder. Gently closing the door, she returned to the driver's seat. "Okay, girls, we need to find supplies."

Decision made, she took the Tucker's Grade exit to Highway 41, driving down the old state road, searching for a cheap place to stay that allowed animals. She

spied an older place to her right—the Courtesy Court
Motel, a typical L-shaped building, single story. She'd
seen many old places like this in her travels. A sign in
the office window read LOCALLY OWNED, PETS WEL-
COME. This usually meant cheap rates. Since it was the
middle of summer, the July heat kept most local folks
indoors or swimming if they were lucky enough to
have a pool or had the time to spend a day at the beach.

Alison parked next to the office but left the Jeep
running so she could keep the air on for the cats. "Be
right back," she called over her shoulder, even though
she knew they couldn't hear her.

The motel, painted a bright orange with a green
flat roof, was probably built in the early sixties and
stuck out like a sore thumb. Each room had an old
iron chair and side table beside the door. Hardy fox-
tail ferns flourished in yellow pots on either side of
the entrance. A bell jingled when she stepped inside
the air-conditioned office.

An older woman with snow-white hair, sapphire
eyes, and an apron tied around her thick waist greeted
her. She smiled, wiped her hands on her apron, then
took a pair of eyeglasses from the desk. "I was bak-
ing—can you believe that? In this heat. I swear, I think
this heat is frying my brain. Now, what can I help you
with?"

Alison couldn't help but smile. It should be obvious
to the woman, but maybe she offered other services besides the motel.

"I want to rent a room for the night," Alison said.

"Of course you do," the woman said. "Just you?"

Alison nodded. "And my cat."

"Okay, just sign your name here." The clerk pointed to a large leather-bound visitor guest book with an alligator embossed on the front. "What kind of cat do you have?"

"Just an old stray I picked up. That's it?" Alison asked while signing her name.

"Yep, nothing fancy here, but fresh linens, good mattresses, and cable TV. We don't have Wi-Fi, so if you're looking to play on your computer, you'll have to try the Holiday Inn further down."

"No, I don't need Internet." Alison didn't have a cell phone or a computer. They were useless since she didn't have anyone she wanted to speak to. If she really needed to search the web, she used the library.

"Then it's thirty dollars a night plus ten bucks for a pet deposit. And we only take cash," the older woman explained.

Alison took a twenty, two fives, and a ten from her wallet, handing them to the woman. "Thanks. So I guess you're going to give me a key."

"Of course. As I said, this heat has fried my brain." She removed the key from a drawer to room number two. "This is close to the soda machine; there's an ice bucket in your room if you need it. Ice machine's next to the soda machine in the breezeway."

Alison took the offered key. A real key—no key cards to scan here. She liked this place already.

"Checkout is at noon," the lady told her.

"I'll be long gone by then, but thanks," Alison said.

"You're welcome. I'm Betty. If you need anything, just buzz the office. We do have telephones in the rooms."

"I appreciate that."

Once Alison was inside her Jeep, she pulled away from the office, parking in the space reserved for room number two. She shut the engine off, then went to the back of the Jeep for her luggage, dragging the old black case behind her. The key slid easily into the lock; then she pushed the heavy metal door aside, startled when she saw the inside of the room. Alison had stayed in a lot of dumpy motels in her day, and nothing surprised her. Until now. The room was immaculate, with nice wood floors, the furniture modern. The chair and table with a lamp would be a nice place to have a meal. The bathroom had been updated, too. There was a modern shower, with a removable shower head that appeared to be brand new. Little bottles of shampoo, conditioner, and soap were arranged neatly on the counter next to the sink. A tiny green box held a shower cap, mini sewing kit, and three Q-tips. She hadn't seen this kind of stuff in the dumps she'd stayed in throughout the years. She had her own toiletries, but she'd use what they provided, since she'd paid for them. Never one to waste a dime on anything, she was ever conscious of her finances.

She went back to her car and carried the momma cat and her kittens inside the room. She placed them on a pillow from the bed so they had a soft place to rest. Once they were settled, she took a paper cup and filled it with water. "I know you need more than this, so I'll be right back." She rubbed Momma cat between her ears. She wasn't sure what kind of cat she was, as her coat was a multitude of colors. Each of the kittens was a replica of their momma. The dollar store wasn't that far, so Alison raced out before the cats ran after her.

Thirty minutes later, she returned with milk for the cats, wet food, and three disposable litter boxes, along with three food dishes and one large dish for their water. She poured a generous amount of milk in the water dish, then added wet food to the smaller dishes. Momma cat practically inhaled her food, while the kitties nibbled at theirs. They all lapped up the milk, then returned to their pillow. Unsure if Momma cat was still nursing, Alison kept an eye on her. The kitties had to be only five or six weeks old.

Once they were nestled together on their pillow, Alison unpacked the few items she needed for her stay, but wasn't quite ready to call it a night. She found the TV remote next to the bedside table and clicked on the National News Network. The country was in turmoil; nothing new there. She flipped through the stations, stopping when she found a local news station. The anchor spoke about a mango festival in Matlacha Pass, the festivities beginning at eight o'clock tonight. Alison figured she'd scope it out, as she had nothing better to do. Lying around the motel would bore her.

The animals were sleeping, so she left more food out just in case, plus filled the milk dish again. Without giving it further thought, she took a quick shower, then changed into a pair of white shorts and a navy striped top. She slid her feet into her secondhand Birkenstocks. Her long blonde hair was wet, and since it was too hot to use a hair dryer, she pulled it into a ponytail. Checking herself out in the mirror, she decided she could pass for a local. She considered herself a Floridian. Her skin was tan from visits to the beach when she'd had an occasional day off from Besito's. Her bright blue eyes were those of a survivor who'd seen too much too soon in life. Already she had crow's feet, something a woman her age shouldn't have, but too much time in the sun, hard work, and the burdens she carried hadn't helped the aging process.

Inside the Jeep, she looked at the map, calculating Matlacha Pass to be about a thirty-five-minute drive. As she drove along Pine Tree Road, she thought about her drive to the Keys, thinking it might be fun if she'd made a few pit stops along the way if there wasn't too much expense involved. She'd take a few of the pamphlets she'd seen in the motel office and see what southern Florida offered.

The drive was uneventful. She drove to Matlacha Pass, where loblolly pine trees flanked the two-lane road. Mangroves thriving in the salty coastal canal waters acted as Mother Nature's fence, preventing her from viewing the homes behind them. As she neared the bridge to the island, she saw a post office, a CVS, and a Publix grocery store. Approaching the old wooden swing bridge, she saw dozens of people fishing. She saw an old sign naming it the "World's Fishingest Bridge." She slowed to a crawl to get a closer view of the folks with yellow bait buckets, large casting nets, and various types of rods and reels. Some wore white rubber boots, others were in sneakers, and a few in flip-flops. Some were tanned, others as red as lobsters. Alison guessed the latter were tourists. As soon as she reached the bridge, she, along with four other vehicles, drove across the wooden slats at a snail's pace. The *thump thump thump* of the tires scared her, as she was unsure of just how sturdy the old boards were. As soon as she crossed to the opposite side of the bridge, she looked in her rearview mirror, watching as the wooden gate slowly opened to allow a fishing boat to pass through. She'd never seen this side of the Sunshine State.

A small, rusted sign about a mile past the bridge read WELCOME TO PALMETTO ISLAND, even though it was still a few miles ahead. Driving at the thirty-five mile per hour speed limit allowed her to glance at the unique shops along the way. There was an art gallery painted aqua blue with purple trim. The Blue Crab Bar and Grill was painted red and pink, with a giant sign in the shape of a blue crab. A tiny chartreuse building housed the Rainbow Row ice cream shop. Alison found it all colorful and unique as she continued her drive. Reaching a fork in the road, she had the option to turn right onto Dolphin Drive or go left onto Trafalgar Avenue. She opted for Dolphin Drive simply because she liked dolphins. To her right, she was surrounded by canals, more mangroves, and palmetto trees. There were also cabbage palms, or swamp cabbage, trees she remembered seeing in Tampa. She wasn't sure of the names of the various types of palm trees, though it was more than obvious Palmetto Island's name suited the surroundings.

Alison drove slowly down the stretch of road, surprised there was no traffic, no scooters or bicycle riders, no tourists as there had been at Matlacha Pass. Reaching the end of Dolphin Drive, she again had a choice to go right or left. This time she took a left onto Loblolly Way. About a dozen upscale homes faced the Gulf of Mexico. She could see a strip of beach in front of the houses. Unsure if this was a private beach, she made a U-turn, hoping for a sign, anything to indicate whether the area was off limits to the public or not. Desiring the feel of the warm sand on her feet and the briny salt water against her skin, she pulled into the parking lot of a souvenir shop. There were no cars, so she assumed the place was closed for the day. She grabbed her sunglasses from the visor, along with her small cross-body bag that held a bit of cash and her gun. She placed the .22 under the seat, confident she wouldn't need to carry a weapon for a stroll on the beach. Locking up the Jeep, she walked across the parking area to the main road. Seeing a grassy path between two houses, she made her way to the beach.

There wasn't a single soul on the beach, so this had to be a private area. She kicked off her shoes, letting the salty water caress her feet. The warm breeze blew her hair away from her face. For a minute, she closed her eyes, imagining what it would be like to live in a house right on the beach, a dream she'd had since leaving Ohio. Before she was caught, she retraced her steps back to the path.

"This is private property."

Alison stopped. She turned around to see where the voice was coming from.

"Up here," came the voice again.

She looked up and saw a man standing on the deck of one of the houses.

"Sorry," she said, hurrying toward the main road.

"Wait!" the man said.

Frightened, she bolted toward the road as fast as she could. Alison heard footsteps behind her as she sprinted across the parking lot to her Jeep. Heartbeat racing, she unlocked the door. As she swung the door aside, a hand grabbed her. She whirled around to face the man from the deck.

With forced bravado, she spoke. "Don't you touch me again, or I'll blow your frigging head off!"

The man stepped away from the vehicle, both arms high in the air. "I didn't mean to scare you."

"Then what the hell are your intentions?"

"I saw you on the path between my place and the Dubois house. I was going to show you another way to get to the beach without trespassing on anyone's property."

Shaking, she held her ground. "Sure you were."

"Next time you come to the beach, take Dolphin Drive all the way to the end, turn right at Loblolly Way. There's a parking area—it's hard to find if you don't know it's there. It's not a private beach." He stepped forward, holding his right hand out to her. "I'm John Wilson. I own the bait and tackle shop. I was about to head to the shop when I spotted you."

"So you could chase me down, scare the crap out of me?" She shouldn't have spoken of her fear. But it was too late now. She gave him a once-over. The man was probably mid to late thirties. Dark eyes, dirty blond hair, built like a brick shithouse. Not bad looking, probably just an overgrown beach bum in need of a shower. She waited for him to continue.

"I didn't mean to," he explained. "Most islanders know their way to the beach. I assumed you didn't live around here; that's why I called out to you. When you ran, I didn't want you to think I was some kind of weirdo."

Alison shook her head. "Too late for that," she said.

"Sorry, I'm outta here," he said, then walked away while giving a half-hearted wave.

So far, her first impression of Palmetto Island was not a good one, as John Wilson had spoiled it for her. She cranked the engine of her Jeep, revved the accelerator, and peeled out of the parking lot. On Dolphin Drive, she stopped at the four-way stop, unsure if she should return to Matlacha Pass or drive down Trafalgar Avenue. Deciding on the latter, she drove slowly, continuing to check out the local shops. She passed Terri's Diner, a nursery, and a large marina. She pulled into the marina's parking lot so she could turn around and was surprised when she saw John's Bait and Tackle across the street. Okay, so he owned a business. At least that's what he wanted her to believe. Didn't give him the right to chase her down. He could be a serial killer, for all she knew. Alison was tough, hardened by life, but a strange man chasing after her in an unfamiliar area still had the power to frighten her.

No longer enthused at the prospect of going to the mango festival, she backtracked, heading back to Pine Tree Road. Maybe she'd stop at the Rainbow Row ice cream shop. She checked the clock on the dash. 7:33. As she drove back, the bridge was opening for another fishing boat. Possibly a shrimp boat; they all looked the same to her. She waited in traffic for ten minutes and watched the oncoming traffic grow bumper-to-bumper. Once the bridge was lowered, she carefully crossed the wooden slats, relieved when the paved road was beneath her tires again.

Alongside the road, people were setting up tents and tables, and from somewhere, loud music blared from speakers. Apparently, the festival was off to a late start. She pulled over to the shoulder where other vehicles were parked, careful to lock the Jeep before heading in the direction of the music. Laughter, an occasional shout, and an outboard motor could all be heard in the distance. Alison felt the vibes of the small community come to life. Where were all these folks when she'd driven through here half an hour ago? She walked to the bridge and inched her way through the throng of tourists. Several boats below were decorated with flags— skulls and crossbones, some with gold flags with red lettering, though they were too far out for her to read. Another boat had a flag with a white star encircled against the black. She leaned in closer, hoping to get a better look. She couldn't read what the flag said, but it looked evil, out of place. Probably someone with nothing better to do. This place must be a gathering spot for boating clubs. Maybe. She watched the boats for another five minutes, then headed back to her car. This wasn't much of a festival, she thought. She'd expected lots of mangoes.

"Hey, wait up," a familiar voice called out.

She turned around before John Wilson had a chance to grab her by the arm again. "Are you following me?" Certain that he was, she turned her back, running to her Jeep. Unlocking the door, she reached under the driver's seat for her gun. Spinning around, she faced him, though this time, she dangled the loaded gun from her hand. "I'll ask you again—are you following me?"

John took a few steps back. "Are you nuts? You can't just . . . have a gun in broad daylight."

She rolled her eyes. This guy was a real jerk. And dumb. "No to your first question, and yes, I *can* have a gun in daylight, darkness, and any time in between. I'm legally licensed to carry, so in the future, you might want to consider what could happen if you 'bump' into me again. Which I don't believe for one frigging minute. You're following me. I want to know why."

"It's a coincidence," he said.

"Bull. I don't believe in coincidences. Now, tell me . . ." She raised her right arm, gun in hand, her finger on the trigger. "Why are you following me?"

"Look, lady, I ain't following you. I just hitched a ride on a pal's boat. The festival's off to a late start. I wanted to tell you to hang around, if that's what you're here for."

Alison lowered her arm to her side but kept her finger on the trigger. "Okay. So first you chase me off the beach, follow me to my car, practically yank my arm off, and now here you are, asking me to stay for the festivities. I don't know where you came from, but where I come from, men like you usually get the shit beat out of them for stalking a woman. Or arrested. I can't decide what would best suit you." She looked at him, her eyes trailing from his dark eyes to his dirty feet encased in a pair of worn Nike slides. He wore faded blue shorts and a white T-shirt that had seen better days. She looked at his hands. Rough, callused, with dirt crusted beneath his fingernails. If he owned a bait shop, business must be incredibly slow. He looked like a homeless person. No, that was an insult to the homeless. John, if that was his real name, was definitely weird.

He held both hands up. "Hey, I'm leaving, so you can put your little safety net away. No harm, no foul, okay?"

Alison didn't believe him for a minute. "Sure, just remember if I lay eyes on you again, if you just so happen to be anywhere near me, I will make sure you don't follow me, or any other woman. You getting this, John?"

He took a step toward her. "You know what I think?"

"I don't care what you think. Leave me alone or I'm calling the police."

"I was about to tell you, you're a real ballbuster. I know your kind—power hungry for control, all that feminist garbage. You're not worth the effort." He turned to walk away and then stopped. "Folks like you don't belong on this island, so you'd best leave now. While you still have a chance."

Alison got in her Jeep and cranked the engine, backing up slowly so she could follow John. Hanging her head out the window, she spoke in an intimidating tone. "Threaten me again and I'll use my 'little safety net.' And next time, I won't hesitate." And she wouldn't. Tough as nails, living on the streets, in places not fit for an animal, she'd fought to stay alive her entire life. Nothing had changed.

"You'd better leave," he said again, then pointed his index finger at her head.

Alison knew when it was time to move on. No way would she give this piece of garbage another chance to frighten or threaten her. She raced down Pine Tree Road toward her motel, stopping at a drive-thru on the way. She put the sack of food next to her. As soon as she spied her motel, she breathed a sigh of relief. Before she forgot, she removed the gun from beneath her seat, placing it inside the fast-food bag. With her food, purse, and keys in hand, she had to juggle a bit to get her room key into the lock. Pushing the door aside, Alison felt grateful for the little room, even though it was just for one night. Her new pals were still sound asleep, and she didn't disturb them. Who knew how long it'd been since they had a decent meal and a roof over their furry little heads?

Removing the gun from the paper bag, she placed it on the table while she ate. When she finished, she crumpled her wrappings into a ball, tossing them into a small wastebasket beside the nightstand. She peered out the curtains. It was dark. Glancing at the clock, she saw it was only nine-thirty. Wanting to grab a few of the pamphlets she'd seen in the office, she used the phone to call Betty.

"Courtesy Court Motel, Betty here."

Alison smiled. "It's Alison Marshall, room two. Is it too late to grab a few pamphlets from the office?"

"Heck no—come on down, I'll unlock the door."

Alison took her room key, locking the door behind her. Hurrying down the sidewalk to the office, she found Betty waiting at the office door.

"I hope I didn't disturb you," Alison said.

"No, no, not at all. I keep the office locked at night

because I live here. Never know about people these days."

"How well I know," Alison said as she viewed a display of pamphlets. She took a few, then turned to leave. "Thanks. I'll just get back to my room now."

"I was about to make myself a cup of tea. It's been a while since I've had a guest in my place." She tilted her head in the direction of a door behind the front desk. "Would you like to join an old lady for a cup of tea?"

Surprised at the invitation, yet flattered Betty felt comfortable enough to invite her, Alison said, "I'd love to." It was unlike her to act so spontaneously, but she felt sorry for the old woman. There was no harm in spending time with her. She had nothing better to do; plus, her kitties were content.

"Follow me," Betty said, opening the door behind her. "It's not much, but it's all mine. Paid in full."

Alison smiled. "This is nice." What she assumed was the main living area consisted of an avocado green sofa with an orange and green knitted afghan neatly folded across the back. Two matching tables on either side, a cream-colored doily on both, one with a lamp and the other holding a stack of books. Two chairs opposite the sofa in the same ugly green appeared new, or possibly no one ever sat in them. She followed Betty to the kitchen.

"I like a lot of sugar in my tea—you okay with that?"

"Sure, that's just the way I like it." A lie, but she didn't want to hurt her feelings. "Smells good in here."

"I had a craving for peanut butter cookies and made

a couple dozen this afternoon. That's what I was doing when you arrived." She patted her waist. "Doesn't do a thing for a gal's figure, though. Still, at my age, it's not a problem. I eat what I want, so when it's my time, I'll die happy. The heck with all those fad diets."

Alison laughed. "I never thought of that, but if it's what makes you happy, go for it." She wasn't the greatest conversationalist, but Betty made her feel comfortable enough to relax a bit.

The kettle whistled. Betty filled two brown mugs with water, then dropped a tea bag in each. With Betty's back to her, Alison watched as she filled their mugs with heaping spoons of sugar, enough to have a sugar high for a week, plus two plates piled high with the cookies.

"Sit," Betty instructed. In the corner was a small table covered with a plastic tablecloth, its pattern worn, barely detectable.

"This is so kind of you," Alison told her, then sat down.

"Kid, it's my pleasure, I don't have company anymore. Just a few guests now and then, as the season's over. Summer is slow. You from Florida?"

Alison expected this question, but for some reason, she felt compelled to keep her past private. "Uh, no, I grew up in Arizona." She needed an excuse to explain her tanned skin, but then she remembered the Jeep had Florida license plates. "I've been in Florida a couple months now. For work."

Betty sat in the chair opposite her. "That so?"

She nodded. "Yes, I freelance."

"What kind of freelancing do you do? If you don't mind my asking."

She summoned a fake smile. "I write for an animal magazine."

"And you don't need the Internet for your work?" Betty shook her head side to side.

"I do, but I'm giving myself the night off." She hadn't told Betty she didn't have a computer, only that she didn't need Wi-Fi. She took a sip of her tea. "This is so sweet of you," she said, taking another sip of tea.

"As I said, I don't get a lot of company these days, and you're a decent girl. I can tell. No tattoos, weird piercings in places that ain't normal."

"No tattoos or piercings for me. I'm afraid of needles. I do my best to stay on the upside of the grass." She had never been arrested, no traffic violations. Her life on the streets hadn't always been horrible; she'd never been in trouble with the police, other than the times she'd taken off when she'd been forced to live in one foster home after another.

"You get to that age where you know yourself, your likes, and dislikes. No shame in admitting that." Betty pushed the plate of cookies across the table. "My feelings will be hurt if you don't eat a couple of these. My waistline, too."

She took two cookies, sinking her teeth into the sweetness. "These are scrumptious." She finished one cookie, then another. "Just one more," Alison said. The cookies were mouthwatering. "Best cookies I've ever had. I didn't eat a lot of sweets as a kid." A wave of dizziness swept over her, and she gripped the edge of the table to steady herself.

"Are you all right?" Betty asked.

Alison closed her eyes, waiting for the dizziness to subside. "I think so. I, uh, need to lie down. I'll find my way out." She stood up, the kitchen spinning around her. "Sorry."

"Let me help you back to your room, kiddo. You don't look so good." Betty walked to her side and took her hand. "I'll get you settled in for the night."

Alison let Betty lead her out of the kitchen, through the living area, then to the reception desk. She leaned on Betty. Her body limp, she could barely manage to put one foot in front of the other. "Sorry," she muttered again. "I don't know what's wrong." Her words were muffled.

"Don't you worry, I'll take care of you."

Inside her room, Alison went limp when Betty helped her to bed. "Let's get you under the covers. Your skin is hot as a coal. You got a fever, I'm sure."

"Uh," was all she could manage.

"I'll get some aspirin. You relax; I'll be right back." Betty scurried out of the room. For the first time in a very, very long time, she was doing what she hadn't done. A young woman, alone and ill, who just so happened to be a guest at her motel, needed her. This was what she'd been wanting, waiting for. She'd forgive her lie for now, telling her she only had one cat. Her vision was pretty good—she was sure there were three cats on her pillow. Briefly, she thought of the deposit money. Betty planned to keep it and would remind the girl of her lie later.

She hurried to the office, making sure to lock the door. As she said to the girl, you never knew what kind of crazies were out there in the world. Not exactly her words, but close enough. She went to the kitchen, found a bottle of aspirin and a thermometer. She searched the bathroom medicine cabinet for a vapor cream in case the girl had a cold. Betty remembered when she was a little girl, her mother would rub the smelly stuff on her chest and lay a warm towel on her. It never failed to help. Back in the kitchen, she took a paper bag, stuffed the items inside, then returned to room number two.

Chapter Two

Alison opened her eyes to unfamiliar surroundings. Rolling onto her side, she saw the clock on the bedside table. It was almost noon.

"What the heck?" she said out loud. It took her a few moments to remember where she was. In a motel, from the looks of it, though she couldn't recall the name. As she sat up in bed, the room whirled around like a roller coaster. She closed her eyes when a sudden wave of nausea sent her bolting out of the bed to the bathroom, where she emptied the contents of her stomach.

Alison raked a shaky hand through her hair, her memory of the previous evening sketchy. She stood up, the bathroom mirror giving the impression of one of those fun house mirrors she'd seen years ago when she'd gone to a circus. Couldn't remember what city, but she remembered that it'd made her sick as she struggled to find an exit. That's what she felt like now. Turning on the shower, she stepped inside, letting the cool water slide down her back. She tilted her head; the icy blast of water felt good on her face. When she felt steady enough, she opened her eyes, the room no longer out of focus. With extra care, she toweled off. Alison felt like she had the hangover from hell. Every heartbeat sent a searing pain behind her eyes. She had a sour taste in her mouth and brushed her teeth twice. She needed caffeine, but the thought of drinking coffee made her gag.

Dragging herself back to the bed, she saw a bottle of aspirin, a thermometer, and a container of vapor rub. Clueless as to how they got there, Alison forced herself to recall the day before. The pillow where she'd let the cats sleep was gone, along with the cats and the supplies.

Trying her best to recall the previous evening, she remembered stopping in Fort Charlotte, where she'd found this motel, though she still couldn't bring up the name. She'd unpacked; the only reason she knew this was that her toiletries were on the bathroom counter, yet she didn't remember putting them there. Had she gone out? Yes, she'd bought stuff for the cats. With no way of knowing exactly what had happened to her, she closed her eyes, tried to relax. She dozed off for a bit, then opened her eyes, only this time without the dizziness.

Glancing at the clock again, she saw it was after one. Edging to the end of the bed, she saw her shoes on the floor. Her luggage was open, her clothing hung over the sides. Alison always packed the few clothes she owned very neatly. Why were they scattered about now? She rifled through the messy pile, finding underclothes, her favorite pair of jeans, and a Tampa Bay Buccaneers T-shirt she'd found in a consignment shop when she'd first moved to Tampa. After she dressed, she repacked her clothes. In the bathroom, she gathered her toiletries, plus the extras provided by the motel. Picking up the shorts and T-shirt she'd worn, she scanned the room to see if she was forgetting anything,

She recalled eating a hamburger last night. A hazy memory surfaced of driving to that island, Palm something-or-other; then she spied the pamphlets on the bedside table.

The motel lady, Betty—they'd drunk tea in her residence in the motel. In bits and pieces, she summoned up minute details from her visit. They drank hot tea and ate peanut butter cookies. Try as she might, Alison didn't have a clear memory of the rest of the evening. She zipped her luggage shut, spotted her purse on a hanger in the tiny closet. Now she knew something was off, as she never put her purse in a closet; plus, she didn't remember doing this. She always kept it next to her, wherever she slept. She gave one more glance around the room, but she didn't find anything else. Not much of a drinker, she was positive she hadn't consumed any alcohol. She decided she had a sugar hangover, because she'd had too many of those cookies that were so sweet. The thought of them now made her nauseous.

Ready to get the hell out, Alison opened her purse to get the keys to her Jeep. Feeling around, she couldn't find them, so she dumped the contents out on the bed. No keys.

"Shit," she said to herself. Had she locked them inside the Jeep? If so, she didn't have an extra set, and no room key in sight. Without insurance that covered this type of screwup, if she needed a locksmith, she was up a creek without the damn paddle. She propped her luggage against the door to keep it open.

It was hot and humid, so she used her hand as a visor to keep the sun out of her eyes. She tried opening the car door; it was locked. Peering in the window, she saw the ignition. No keys there, either.

Returning to the room, she ripped the sheets off the bed, lifted up the mattress, looked beneath the bed. No keys. A small drawer in the nightstand was empty. Not even a copy of the Bible placed there by the Gideons.

She had no other option but to return to the office to see if she'd left them in Betty's residence. She took her luggage with her, afraid to leave it by the Jeep.

Alison found the office door locked with a note that read, "BE BACK SOON." She wondered what "soon" meant to an old lady. It was possible she'd stepped out for groceries, though she didn't recall seeing a car parked in the area next to the office. It didn't take a genius to figure out that the parking area was exclusively for whoever worked in the office. Maybe she'd had a family emergency—but hadn't she told her she didn't have company very often? Slowly, the events of the previous evening were coming back to her. And where were her cats? She planned to keep all of them. It might be difficult to drive with them, but she'd buy them a large bed and put it in the back of the Jeep, along with the other items she had a fuzzy memory of purchasing.

John, the jerk from Palmetto Island, she remembered. He'd followed her from the beach back to Matlacha Pass. They'd argued, but she didn't remember what they'd argued about. She went back to room number two, but since she had no key to let herself in, she plonked down on the iron chair outside.

"Damn it!" The chair was hot as coals. Ready to explode, she tipped her luggage on its side, then sat on top. Who knew how long it would take for Betty to return? She shook her head in disgust. She'd made a stupid mistake accepting Betty's invitation. This is why she didn't make friends, didn't need them. Trouble had followed her most of her life for whatever reason, and now it had returned once again, leaving her stuck with nothing to do but wait.

Maybe she should rethink her decision and purchase a cell phone. She could use one now, though she had no one to call other than a locksmith, and that would cost a pretty penny. But Alison had plenty of money. She'd worked her ass off all these years, saving every cent she could. Henry Adler had invested her money wisely. One day she planned to settle down, maybe buy a little house somewhere, but not now. She wasn't ready, though knowing her money was safe gave her a sense of security. When the time was right, she would know. For now, all she needed were the keys to her Jeep so she could get the hell out of here and head for the Keys. Once there, if the islands' magic was to be believed, she would think about her future, possibly making Key West her forever home. Maybe she'd add a dog to her newly found menagerie. She loved animals. Their love was unconditional. After working part-time at a pet shop during her last two years of high school, she'd fallen in love with every animal in the place, even the fish, the snakes, and the birds. Yes, she would definitely look into getting a dog when she settled down. Living in crappy motels and even crappier tiny efficiency apartments would've been cruel for a pet. They needed sunshine, fresh air, a place to run.

For now, all she wanted were the keys to her frigging Jeep. Wishing she'd dressed in shorts and a tank top, she opened the suitcase and took out a pair of khaki shorts and a navy top. Checking to make sure there were no weirdos lurking around, she made fast work changing into the cooler clothes. She folded her jeans and T-shirt, then closed the luggage again. This was ridiculous. How in the hell did one own and operate a business without being there to run the damned place? Hadn't Betty told her checkout time was at noon? Yes, she remembered that, telling her she would be long gone by that time. Unable to account for a big part of last night was beginning to frighten her. She was a woman alone with only her wits and her gun for protection.

Her gun. *Where in the hell was her gun?*

It was not in the room. Not in her luggage, and it wasn't in her purse. Something very strange was going on, and she intended to find out exactly what it was. Resigned, she had no other choice except to wait for Betty to return.

Had the old woman ripped her off? Taken her keys, her gun? Her purse still had the cash inside. Wouldn't a thief want that, too? She was beyond angry at her own stupidity. Alison knew better. She'd keep to herself as she'd done for the past fifteen years. If Betty had done something to her cats, she would have hell to pay.

Alison had spent her entire life with people who were supposed to care for her and failed to do so. She had no idea who her parents were, if they were dead or alive. She didn't give them much thought until she was old enough to understand that the only parents she had known were actually her first set of foster parents Craig and Martha Sterling, and they weren't exactly like a normal family. She'd been nine years old, in third grade, when her world shattered. Her class had to make a family tree. They were studying ancestry, so they had to ask their parents to help with the assignment.

She'd been so excited; she couldn't wait to go home, so her parents could help her. Alison had three older brothers, Tommy, Steven, and Philip, and a baby sister, Mandy. She would fill up the leaves on the tree really fast. That evening at the dinner table, when she told her parents about the class assignment, they laughed at her. She remembered the words as clearly now as she did then: *"We aren't your biological parents, Alison. You're nothing but a foster child. You have no real family. I'll contact your teacher and explain why you can't complete your assignment."*

The next day, when she woke up to get ready for school, her eyes had been all red and puffy from crying all night. She went through all the motions of her normal morning routine: a bowl of oatmeal, a half slice of dry toast; sometimes they had orange juice, but most of the time she drank water. But she didn't care today. At the bus stop, her three brothers teased her for being stupid. *"That bitch ain't your mom, or ours either, Alison. The only reason they take care of us is for money from the government."* They'd all laughed at her then. Later that day, when it was time for the class to show their homework project, she was so scared, but her mom had said she would call her teacher to explain why she didn't have her project completed. When it was her turn to share her family tree, she realized her mother hadn't made the phone call she'd promised, so she'd stood up, her legs shaking like a dried-up leaf in autumn, and said, "That bitch ain't my mom. She just takes care of me because of the government." She hadn't a clue what this meant, but she'd been yanked out of the classroom and taken to the principal's office.

Alison spent the rest of that day waiting for her mom to pick her up. When she didn't show up at the end of the school day, the principal, Mr. Cleveland, had walked her to the bus. All the kids laughed at her, pointing at her. One of them, a girl from her class, said, "She called her mom a bitch in class!" All the kids on the bus laughed at her. If that hadn't been enough, she'd tried her best to hold her bladder all day, afraid to ask Mr. Cleveland for permission to go to the restroom. Tears streamed down her face as she searched for a seat on the bus. None of the kids wanted to sit next to her, so she started to cry, and as she'd stood in the center aisle of the bus, she'd peed all over herself. For the rest of the year, the kids who rode the bus and those in her classroom called her a "piss-pot-peckerhead."

That was the start of her running away. She smartened up a bit that summer. No one was ever going to be mean to her again. In August that year, a week before she started fourth grade, she'd packed what little clothes she had in the old book bag handed down to her, crawled out the bedroom window, and never looked back. The police picked her up the next day but didn't return her to the only real family she'd known. Instead, the state of Ohio sent her to a new foster home, in a new town where no one could make fun of her. Mr. Beamer insisted she call him by his formal name rather than Dad or Father, and Mrs. Beamer said she should call her Sheila rather than Mom. She didn't have to share a bedroom, because the Beamers didn't have other kids. She'd learned enough by this time to keep her life at home a secret from her new classmates. Refusing to make friends, she spent most of her time studying, and when she could, she'd go to the school library and bring books home.

Alison excelled in class, and for the first time in her young life, she'd had a sense of pride and accomplishment. She recalled being so excited to tell her new family she'd made the honor roll. They said all the right words to her; they were proud of her, all that she expected. Later that night, alone in her bedroom, Alison read about fairies and bears that talked, and a little girl who'd been scared by a wolf. When she read, she escaped into the lives of the characters, pretended they were her family, and sometimes she wished she could jump into the actual pages and disappear. That night, she'd started reading *Alice's Adventures in Wonderland*, wishing she could fall through a rabbit hole like Alice. She'd make friends with the queen, that silly cat, and the hatter. She couldn't wait to finish this story so she could read the second book, *Through the Look-ing-Glass*. With these thoughts, she fell into a restful sleep, dreaming about the zany characters in the novel. Unsure how long she'd been asleep, she suddenly woke up to see Mr. Beamer sitting on the edge of her bed. Uncertain why, she remembered inching her way toward the wall, scooting as far away from him as possible. He'd reached beneath the covers, touching her in places that little girls shouldn't be touched. Beyond afraid, she'd cried, because she knew she'd have to sneak out the window again. Just when she'd settled into her new home.

Once again, the authorities found her, though this time, they returned her to the Beamers. Nothing was said about the incident with Mr. Beamer that had sent her running. Life returned to normal. Happy to be back in school, she forgot about Mr. Beamer's nighttime visit.

Christmas break had been so much fun. She helped Sheila decorate a giant tree. They strung lights on all the outside windows, even though it was freezing outside. She'd been so cold her fingers were numb. Back inside, Sheila made both of them cups of hot chocolate with big spoonfuls of whipped cream. Alison thought life with the Beamer family close to perfect. They bought her nice clothes, she could eat whenever she was hungry, and no one told her to get her ass away from the refrigerator if she wanted a snack. It was the night before Christmas Eve. She helped Sheila wrap presents for Mr. Beamer, they shared a bowl of popcorn, and Sheila let her have two root beer floats with scoops of vanilla ice cream.

When they finished, she returned to her room to find Mr. Beamer lying on her bed. The covers were pulled down, the nightlight turned off. The moon shining in through the window gave off just enough light for her to see that Mr. Beamer was not wearing any clothes. Knowing this was not what a father or foster parent should do, she had screamed loudly. Sheila came running down the hall to her room. She turned the light on, saw Mr. Beamer hastily putting his clothes on, and started to scream so loud, Alison put her hands over her ears. Every cuss word Alison had ever heard of, and some she hadn't, spewed from Sheila's mouth as Mr. Beamer finished dressing.

Sheila then walked toward Alison very slowly, her eyes filled with rage. Sheila slapped her across the cheek so hard, she fell to the floor. As she tried to get up, Sheila kicked her in the back, Alison's head slamming into the edge of the bedframe. Crying, she'd tried to crawl under the bed, hoping Sheila would leave. Alison scrambled as far away from her as she could when Sheila yanked her out from under the bed, slapping her several times.

"You little tramp, you're just like all the rest! A trashy seductress!"

Alison hadn't known what a tramp or a seductress was at the time, but she would learn soon enough. They'd spent Christmas Day pretending they were just like any other family, but that evening, when Alison went to bed, she knew there was no way she was going to spend another night in the Beamer house. She'd snuck the dictionary from Mr. Beamer's office. She learned the definitions of *tramp* and *seductress*. She'd already been through the *trashy* stage when she'd lived with the Sterlings.

Since it was bitterly cold outside, she'd packed all the warm clothes that could fit inside her backpack. She dressed in two pairs of jeans, two pairs of socks, and the new winter coat she'd received for Christmas, along with a matching set of gloves, a scarf, and a beanie hat. Sheila had bought her a pair of Ugg boots at the start of winter so her feet would stay warm. On Christmas morning, she knew this would be her last day in this house, so every chance she got, she took food to her room. Mr. Beamer always kept his wallet on the nightstand beside his bed. During one of her trips to her room to hide food, she'd taken all of the cash from the wallet. She'd counted 326 dollars. Plenty of money to get by on. After midnight, when Sheila and Mr. Beamer had gone to bed, she opened her bedroom door. She heard both of them snoring loudly, as they'd both been drinking all day. She made her exit through the window, soon forgetting about her second foster family.

Alison pushed the memories to the back of her mind where they belonged. Rarely did she allow herself to indulge in remembering the horrors of her childhood. Sitting here in this miserable heat, she'd had nothing better to do while she waited for Betty to return. Alison would find a pay phone and call a locksmith if the old lady wasn't back in half an hour. She had no clue where she'd find a pay phone, as they were rarely used these days. If she didn't locate a phone, she would return to the dollar store in the shopping plaza, where she'd purchased her cat supplies. If they had cell phones, she'd break her own rule and purchase one, in case she ever caught herself in another situation like this. This was frigging bull. Dying for a drink of water and a cup of coffee, she decided to walk to the dollar store now. She wouldn't dare leave her luggage behind. Dragging the old beat-up suitcase behind her, Alison had walked almost a mile when a yellow cab slowed down beside her.

"Hey there, missy," said Betty from the front passenger seat of the cab. "Climb on in."

Alison slid into the back seat, her luggage beside her. Her heart raced; she was beyond angry. "What the hell happened to my gun? My cats? They were in my room last night. Someone rifled through my luggage. Is this the kind of shit that goes on at your place? Did you steal my car keys, too?" Alison was enraged by the sheer audacity of this woman, picking her up in a taxi, acting as though this was all normal.

"Now, now, Alison, calm down."

The taxi pulled into the parking spot reserved for the office. "Need help bringing in your groceries?" the taxi driver asked Betty.

"No, Tank, Alison can help me, but thanks. I'll see you next week," said Betty as she hustled her bulk out of the passenger seat.

"You stay in touch," he said to her.

Alison watched the old woman take three paper bags from the trunk.

"You gonna help or what?"

"I shouldn't," Alison said, yanking one of the bags

from her. No way in hell would she let her luggage out of her sight.

Betty managed both paper sacks, then fiddled in her pocket for the keys, opening the door to the office. Alison stepped inside and dropped the bag on the counter. "Where are my cats? The keys and my gun? No one else had access to my room but you. I'll give you five seconds to tell me, or I'm calling the police."

"Okay, don't be so impatient. Follow me." Betty opened the door to the residence area.

"No, let me have my keys, gun, and my animals." No way would she follow this old woman again. She'd ingested something that made her feel like she'd drunk a gallon of whiskey; she wasn't going to make a second mistake.

Betty didn't say a word. Three minutes later, she emerged from the back room and handed Alison the keys to her Jeep and the gun. Alison popped the clip to make sure it was still loaded. "Out of curiosity, what gave you the right to remove these from my room?"

"You were so sick—I'm not sure what it was, but you had a fever. I gave you aspirin and took your temperature. I was concerned about you being in such a fevered state and didn't want you driving. I saw the gun and your *three* cats. I thought it best to let you sleep off whatever you had, and I'd return them later. People do crazy things when they're burning up with a fever. I assumed you'd still be asleep, so I went to the store for some eggs and bacon. I wanted to send you off with a good breakfast, that's all. No need to get angry," Betty told her.

"Who ransacked my luggage?" Alison tucked the

gun in the waistband of her shorts and then checked her keys. She had four keys with a keychain in the shape of a bright green taco from Besito's. They were all there. Briefly, she had the thought that Betty could've made copies of her keys. But maybe she'd overreacted. She'd always been wary of strangers.

"I searched for a nightgown but didn't find one, so I just left you in your shorts. You were terribly sweaty."

This old woman had an answer for everything. "I guess I should thank you for taking care of me and my animals last night, though I don't ever get sick. It must've been too much sugar in those cookies."

Betty shook her head. "I suppose it could've been, but I ate my share of them, too. I think you just had a twenty-four-hour bug."

"And where are my cats?"

"Sleeping in the back room," Betty said, gesturing behind her. "I figured you were too sick to look after them last night."

"Then thanks, for everything," she said. "I'll be on my way as soon as I load up my animals."

As Alison turned away from the counter, Betty shouted at her.

"Wait!"

She turned around. "What?"

"You stayed past noon. You owe me another thirty dollars; plus, you lied about having only one cat. I'll have to keep your deposit for the pillow."

"Are you frigging serious?" She didn't give a hoot about the deposit, just that the old woman was brazen enough to say all this.

"Checkout time is at noon. I'm sure I told you that."

Not wanting to stay another minute, Alison took a twenty and two tens out of her wallet and tossed them on the counter. As soon as she had the animals and the items she'd bought for them in the back of the Jeep, she returned to the office with the pillow. "Have a nice freaking day," she said, then tossed the pillow over the counter, as well.

Chapter Three

A lison couldn't believe the audacity of the old woman, but it was well worth the forty bucks to get out of there. Right now, she needed caffeine, water, something to eat, beds for the cats, and more cat food. They were meowing. Momma cat crawled to the front of the Jeep, settling in Alison's lap while her babies rested on the sleeping bag.

"You're such a good girl. We need to give you fluffy felines names." Alison scratched the cat between her ears.

A few miles past the motel, as she drove along Highway 41, she saw Mel's Diner, the sign flashing "Breakfast served twenty-four hours a day." She parked the Jeep close to the entrance, where she'd have a bird's-eye view in case Betty and her buddy Tank had made copies of her keys. They might try to steal the car and the cats. And who in the hell named their kid Tank? It wasn't like he was big, as in the size of a tank. The guy was as scrawny as a broomstick.

Hating to burn up the gas, but knowing she didn't have a choice, Alison left the Jeep running so she could keep the air on. Those poor souls would burn up in this heat; plus, leaving an animal in a car was against the law, unless it was cool or the air was left on.

Inside the diner, a young girl with short black hair, wearing black pants, a matching apron, and a white blouse, said, "Welcome to Mel's."

"Can I get a booth close to a window?" Alison asked. There were only a few tables occupied.

"Sure you can," the girl said. "Follow me."

Alison sat in a booth large enough for at least six, but she didn't care, because it wasn't like there was a line of folks waiting to be seated. Her Jeep was just a few feet away.

"Can I get you a drink?" the girl asked as soon as Alison was seated.

"Yes, please—a water and a coffee."

When the waitress returned with her drinks, Alison gulped down the water before looking at the menu. Scanning the selections, she decided on the biggest breakfast offered. She didn't plan on stopping for food, just for gas, until she reached Key West. Though now that she had three passengers, her plans were apt to change. "I'll have the Fisherman's Feast, eggs over easy, with crisp bacon. Wheat toast."

"Gotcha." The girl scribbled on a notepad, then returned a few minutes later with a pitcher of water.

"Thanks." Alison drank the water, then took a sip of black coffee. She spied a newspaper on the counter by the cash register. When the waitress refilled her coffee, she asked if she could have a look at the paper.

"Of course, that's what it's for." The girl placed the paper on the table. Alison would wait until she finished breakfast, then she'd scan the paper. Even though most news sources were online, she still preferred an actual newspaper.

Her breakfast arrived. Her mouth watered as she took a bite of crispy bacon. She made fast work of finishing her meal, drinking a third cup of coffee while she perused the ads in the *Fort Charlotte Sentinel*.

Scanning the real estate page just for the heck of it, she saw a few houses that sounded promising, but they weren't in Key West. One was a small beach house on Palmetto Island. "Miss, can I borrow a pen and paper?" she asked the waitress.

"Of course. Here you go." She tore a sheet of paper from her pad and took a pen from her apron. "Keep the pen. I've got more where that came from."

"Thanks," Alison said. The pen had WELCOME TO MEL'S in hot pink cursive writing, along with the address and phone number. She jotted down the real estate agency's phone number. Not that she had any firm intention of going there, but she'd keep her options open.

When the waitress brought her bill, Alison laid a twenty on the table and told her to keep the change, knowing how hard it was to earn tips off-season. As she was about to push the door open, someone on the other side pushed forward. Losing her balance, Alison grabbed onto the first hand she found. It was Tank, the taxi driver.

"Better watch where you're goin', lady," he said.

"Kiss off," she said, stepping away from him with

her hand firmly on the door. He reeked of body odor and dead fish. Maybe he worked on a shrimp boat when he wasn't driving a taxi.

He turned around and gazed at her, his eyes settling on her chest. He snickered, "You ain't got nothin' to kiss."

"And if I did, your nasty ass would have to beg before I'd let you within sniffing distance. You're disgusting." She opened the door, in a hurry to get away from his unpleasant odor and attitude. Men like him reminded her of the many foster dads she'd had. Perverted and filthy, with nothing on their minds but sex. No wonder she'd never had a long-term relationship.

Inside the Jeep, she put the car into reverse, then turned the air down, as the car was now too cold, if there was such a thing in Florida. The cats were on the sleeping bag. Momma cat was grooming her kittens, so they were occupied. Alison's thoughts were all over the place. Her experience on the island had been strange. The motel stay was unlike any she'd experienced, and now this restaurant, where Tank the taxi driver seemed to think he had the right to treat her like trash.

Instead of heading south on Highway 41, she headed back toward the shopping center she'd been walking to before Betty found her. She was going to purchase a cell phone. Alison had never needed one before. She got by using a pay phone when she found one, or she'd borrow a stranger's cell, and most folks were happy to let her make a call. Pulling into the parking lot, she went inside the Dollar General store, surprised at the variety of merchandise they carried. Last night, she didn't recall paying much attention to anything except cat stuff.

There was everything from groceries to arts and crafts supplies. Clothes, makeup, toys, anything one could purchase in Walmart or Target, though she'd guess the dollar store items were deeply discounted.

"Anything I can help ya with, just let me know," said a woman with a gruff voice from somewhere unseen. Alison would bet a hundred bucks this gal smoked at least two packs of cigarettes a day. The woman coughed, cleared her throat, then spat.

What kind of person does that? In public?

"I'm looking for a cellular phone," Alison said, when she noticed a MISSING sign posted behind the register. "Do you know who put this sign up?"

More coughing, hacking, then came the gruff voice. Alison stood in front of the register and saw the woman emerge from a back room. She was probably in her forties, her skin so tanned it looked dry, like old leather. Her bleached blonde hair was short and thin, teased into the shape of a football helmet. Her hair was as stiff as a board, lacquered with hair spray. She wore thick black eyeliner and too much blush.

"Me. My kitties got out of the car two days ago when I was at the filling station, and I ain't seen 'em since. They're all I got," she said, tears welling up in her overly made-up eyes.

"I'll be right back," Alison said. When she returned with the three missing kitties, the clerk's eyes sparkled with delight. "Where in the name of Pete did you find my babies?" she asked.

Alison told her. As much as she hated to, she had to return the cats to their owner. The lady cuddled all three of them, then took the MISSING sign down from the wall behind her. "I wasn't sure I'd ever see them again."

"I stopped for gas at the exit before Tucker's Grade and heard them crying by the gas pumps. Little momma was scrounging for food in the garbage can, and so I took them with me. I have food and bowls in my car. They're super sweet," Alison said.

"Ma'am, I swear you've made me the happiest woman alive. I've had Peaches, the mommy, for eight years, and these two stinkers, Lyla and Lili, are just about two months old. I haven't slept a wink since they went missing."

Alison felt sad at the thought of giving them up, but they weren't hers to keep. Peaches rubbed against the clerk's legs. Alison knew the animals were well-loved. "Just keep an eye on them next time," she said, feeling protective of her rescues.

"I'm Tammy," the clerk said and came around the counter to give her a hug. "Thank you for being honest. Not much of that around here anymore, and I promise I won't let them out of my sight next time I'm pumping gas. I shouldn't bring 'em out like that at night, anyway. I was lonesome," Tammy explained.

"I'm Alison, and I would never intentionally steal a pet. They were lost, and now they're not. I guess this goes down as my good deed for the day. So, I'll leave their things with you, then you can help me choose a cell phone." Alison ran out to the car, took the bowls and food inside. "They liked this food, and I gave them regular milk."

Tammy placed the little fur babies in a box inside a shopping cart. "That's fine, kid; Peaches loves just about anything you give her. I bring 'em to work with me sometimes. Now, we got a few different phones here. Whatcha lookin' for?"

"Just a basic cell phone."

"Yeah, but what kind? You want one of the throwaway phones, or you want one where you gotta set up a service with the phone company?"

"What is a throwaway phone?" She should know these things, but she didn't.

"Girl, you ain't never heard of a throwaway cell?"

Alison shook her head. "No, I never cared to negotiate the technical world."

"Then let me hook you up."

For the next ten minutes, Tammy walked her through the directions on how to use the phone, how to use the card to purchase minutes as she needed them. After the lesson, Alison purchased the flip phone and bought two hours of phone time with the knowledge she could purchase more through the actual phone if and when she needed to.

"Appreciate your help," Alison said as she gave Tammy three twenties.

"No worries, it's part of my job. You don't need to thank me, kid, you made my day. I wish there was something I could do to repay you."

"You have—you took the time to show me how to use this." She held the bag with the cell phone in the air. "And for a while, I had three of the best companions I've ever had." She smiled at her.

"You ain't from these parts, are you?" Tammy asked.

"No, I'm just passing through," Alison told her.

"We get a lot of folks like you," Tammy said, then

gave her change to her. "If you ever decide to come back to shop, call me." She scribbled her name and number on the back of an old receipt. "I'll bring the girls in so you can see them."

"Thanks, though I doubt it, as I'm headed for the Keys. And thanks again for your help with the phone. I guess it was time for me to get a phone, and time for you to get the kitties back. Kind of a karma thing," Alison said.

"Yep, it is for sure. I do believe that one good deed deserves another, or whatever it is."

"Me too, Tammy," Alison said. "If I'm back this way, I'll call you and come visit the girls."

She left the store feeling there was something about Tammy that made her feel sorry for her. Maybe she was on her own, like she'd been most of her life, though she had her animals, and Alison could tell they were well-loved. Whatever it was, she felt a little sad when she backed out of the parking lot. Was she becoming a pushover in her old age? In a couple of months, she would turn thirty. Maybe you did mellow with old age, but Alison still had a lot of life to live. Besides, these days, thirty was practically a teenager.

Leaving the store, she had the choice to drive south to Key West or west toward Palmetto Island. The place called to her, which was odd, given her experience there hadn't been the least bit positive. She'd had nothing but crap happen to her since she'd stopped at the motel, other than reuniting Peaches and her kittens with Tammy. She still couldn't recall all the events of the night before too clearly, but she did remember the beach, the soft white sand, and bubbly waves tickling her feet as she'd stared out at the gulf. It was the quiet, she decided. Nothing like some of the other beaches in Florida. No spring breakers, no families with groups of screaming kids playing and laughing. No drunks whistling or propositioning her; no one to bother her. And that is what she'd been searching for.

Maybe she'd wait another day before she headed to Key West. It wasn't like she had a schedule to adhere to. Footloose and fancy-free, just the way she liked it. If she did stay another day, she wouldn't return to the motel. Though it was clean and the rates beyond reasonable, she would rather spend more of her hard-earned cash on another motel than go through what she'd gone through last night. She truly didn't believe she'd instantly gotten sick in Betty's kitchen. Alison was pretty sure the burger she'd eaten was what had made her so sick, even though she'd insinuated otherwise to Betty. Food poisoning: she'd had it once before. She'd been eating out of a garbage dumpster behind a steak house in Atlanta, kind of like Peaches. Within hours of eating the meat she'd scrounged up, she became so violently ill, she'd spent the night in the emergency room. When it came time for her to check out, they'd asked her for an insurance card. She'd laughed, telling the staff at the hospital since she was eating out of dumpsters, health insurance hadn't been a top priority. They'd sent her to the business office, where she'd been advised to claim that she was indigent, and her bill was forgiven. Humiliated, yet grateful she wouldn't be leaving behind a medical bill, from that point on, she was very careful to really pick through the garbage when she was in need of a meal.

Alison had vowed to herself she would never live that way again. When she could, she cleaned up at a shelter, had a hot meal and a bed. After two days, she began searching for a job where she could make fast cash. There were days between jobs where she went without food or shelter, but she never gave up. Waitressing had been hard work, but she'd learned the ropes. A few years later, when she felt she'd had enough experience under her belt, she started applying for jobs at the finer restaurants, where tips were big and plentiful. Her desire to better herself promoted a strict work ethic, and she'd saved enough and made excellent investments so she could live comfortably, meaning no more eating from dumpsters or sleeping in parks and crappy hotels. If she chose to, she could live off her investments.

She decided to revisit Palmetto Island. Today was Saturday, when the beaches were usually packed with tourists. She wanted to see if the place really was as tranquil as she remembered. Before she could change her mind, she headed west on Pine Tree Road. She'd drive around, see if she could find the public parking area for the beach that idiot John had told her about. Most likely, he'd lied to her, using that as an excuse to stalk her. At least she still had her weapon, except this time, she'd take it with her. No more leaving her gun beneath the driver's seat, where it was absolutely useless if she were to need it for protection. She continued driving until she reached Matlacha Pass. The bridge was just as crowded as the day before. Anglers were out in full force, rods and reels positioned over the sides of the bridge, barriers separating them and their bright yellow bait buckets from the traffic. From the looks of it, most of the fisherman were locals, wearing the white fishing boots that professional fishermen wore, long-sleeved shirts, and wide-brimmed hats to protect them from the sun. No fluorescent T-shirts, no "Welcome to Florida" logos. At least none that she could see.

The bridge was open, the traffic flowing at a steady pace. She did not like driving across the wooden bridge, even though the distance was less than a hundred yards. As soon as the tires were safely on solid ground, she let out the breath she'd been holding. The speed limit was thirty-five, allowing her to glance at some of the businesses she hadn't noticed the day before. Several unique shops, cottages to rent by the week, a coffee shop called The Daily Grind. Grinning at the name, she thought it appropriate in so many ways. She drove the rest of the way, remembering to turn onto Dolphin Drive, then Loblolly Way, where John said she would find the public parking area. She turned down the small path that was barely visible due to all of the plant life overgrowth and not really what she'd call a road. Branches hit the sides of the doors and windshield. Due to the dips in the road, the Jeep jostled from side to side before Alison saw the clearing, a slab of blacktop. This must be the parking area, with maybe enough space for ten or twelve cars.

She saw one vehicle parked in the handicap spot, a gray sedan with Florida license plates. Taking her small bag, she put the gun inside, put her sunglasses on, then locked the Jeep. Alison smelled the briny salt air; seagulls cawed in the distance. She walked along the water's edge. The tide was out. Spying a few shells she found interesting, she used the hem of her shirt to dry them before putting them in her pocket. The large, white puffy clouds above reminded her of tufts of cotton candy; the sky was the color of a robin's egg. The temperature was hot, the breeze from the gulf enough to keep her from sweating.

Walking along the beach, she dared a glance as she strolled past the large homes facing the beach. They appeared empty, devoid of life. No one sitting on deck chairs, no grills wafting scents of barbecue, no loud music blaring. All the things one would expect on the weekend, but Alison guessed most of these home-owners were snowbirds, leaving their winter homes empty in the heat of summer. She continued to walk, stopping to take her shoes off. Lacing them together, she tossed them around her neck, then walked into the gulf, the sand soft against the bottoms of her feet. In the distance, she spotted another beachcomber, unsure if they were male or female, as she was too far away to see. She proceeded to stroll in the direction of the person, thinking if it was John, she would whip out her pistol to threaten him if he tried to harm her. She could see the figure now. It was a woman. As she moved closer, she saw she was barefoot, her long legs tan and shapely in the denim shorts she wore. She didn't dare call out to her, but the closer she got, the woman still didn't sense her presence, or if she did, Alison guessed she was purposely ignoring her. Not wanting to frighten her, she decided she'd best head back to the Jeep.

"Hey, you don't have to leave," called the young woman.

Alison stopped. She turned around to face the woman. She couldn't be more than eighteen. Her eyes were the most stunning shade of blue she'd ever seen; maybe she wore contacts. Her blonde hair was long and thick.

"I didn't mean to disturb you," Alison said.

"You didn't. I was just finishing up my yoga. It's quiet this time of year, so I love doing yoga on the beach. Actually, it's pretty quiet most of the year." The woman smiled, her teeth as white as the puffy clouds above. "Are you here to visit or what?"

Alison wondered that herself. "I'm just passing through."

"I'm Renée Dubois."

"Alison." She wasn't going to give her last name, as it wasn't necessary.

"Pretty name," Renée said. "My dad was French, or at least that's what my mom tells me. Hence my name."

"Your name does sound very French, very *Parisian*." Alison emphasized the last word, trying to emulate the proper French pronunciation.

"And I've never been out of Florida. Lived here with Mom my entire life."

She wanted to ask if they lived in one of the beach houses, but she didn't want to appear too nosy. "That's nice, to have roots and all."

"So you move around a lot?" Renée asked.

Alison gave her credit—she was very perceptive for her age.

"I do, but it's what I like. Never really wanted to stay in one place too long. So many places to explore," she said, hoping she sounded like a free spirit, not a woman who'd spent her entire life searching for a place to belong.

"Wow, you're lucky. I wish I could travel. When I finish high school, I am outta here. I can't wait to see the world."

So she was much younger than Alison first guessed.

"How long before you graduate?"

"I'm starting my junior year in the fall. I like school most of the time; other times, it totally sucks. Especially math, I hate it," she said, smiling and showing off her perfect teeth.

Up close, Alison saw Renée's features were that of a much younger girl, a beautiful girl who would morph into a knockout in a couple years. "I'm not a math whiz, either," she said, even though she'd made excellent grades when she attended school, and shockingly she'd graduated with honors. Little good it did her, as she'd never pursued a college education. There were times when she'd thought about taking a few classes, but felt she was too old, and she knew what she needed to get by in this world. A college education wasn't in her future.

Renée sat down on the sand, patting the spot beside her. "Have a seat. I'm staying for the sunset, but I told Mom I'd be home right after."

Alison thought she'd spend a few hours waiting, as it was early afternoon. "So you stay on the beach all day?" She didn't want to sit on the damp sand, so she stood beside Renée, digging her bare feet in the sand.

"It's my day off from the shop. Mom lets me hang out till sunset. Only in the summer, though. During the school year, she's so strict I want to pull my hair out."

Alison laughed. "Your mom loves you, that's why she's strict."

"Do you know my mom? Has she ever read for you?" Renée asked.

Puzzled by her question, she shook her head. "I'm just passing through, so no, I don't know your mom."

"Well, you should see her before you leave the island. She's the real deal. 'Gifted' is what she calls it."

Curious, Alison asked, "What is she gifted in?" This was unknown territory, so maybe she shouldn't have asked.

"She's psychic," Renée said.

Expecting anything but that, Alison knew her surprise showed on her face.

"It's okay, we know it's odd to strangers who don't live around here. Mom reads the Tarot, all kinds of cool stuff. I never tell her I think it's cool, but it is."

"So how does one make an appointment with your mom?"

"Just walk in the store or call. She does her cards and readings in the back of the shop most of the time. I work most weekends, but not today. Mom said I needed sunshine and fresh air so she gave me the day off."

"I see."

"It's the souvenir shop across the street. That's Mom's main business, but the other stuff she does is way cooler than selling T-shirts with alligators on them."

Last night, Alison remembered she'd parked there. "Does she close early?"

"No, though Friday nights, she goes to Naples. Tampa

sometimes; wherever she's paid to go, she gives group readings."

Renée's mother sounded like someone Alison would like to know better. "So, if I wanted to see her, what's the process?" It might be interesting to see if what Renée told her was actually true. Though she doubted Renée would tell an outright lie, it could be that she just believed what her mother told her. Alison had never really believed in such nonsense, though she did believe in karma.

"Just go to the shop and see when she's available."

"Sounds easy enough." Before she left the island, she would visit the shop and see what vibes it gave her, given the services offered.

"Summers are pretty slow. If you want, I'll send her a text to see if she's busy now."

"No, that's okay. I might stop by her shop on my way out."

"She could be booked up by then, but it's up to you," Renée said.

"Thanks for the offer," said Alison. "I want to walk the beach a while, then I'll see."

"Mind if I tag along?"

"Not at all." Alison found the teen's company quite amusing. Never having a real friend in high school, she was curious to see what a teen girl's thoughts were now that she was no longer one of them.

They walked alongside one another past the last house, then veered left. "This isn't the best part of the beach. The marina is always noisy with all the boats stopping there. They gas up, then cross over to the bait shop, which is a totally gross shithole."

"The one owned by John?" Alison had to ask.

"You know him?" Renée asked, her tone of voice odd, almost *angry*.

Not in the way she was asking. "No, he saw me on the beach, introduced himself, that's all." She wouldn't fill in the gory details, as they weren't necessary.

"Mom thinks he's weird, won't allow him in her store," Renée told her. "He's in and out of trouble all the time."

"Thanks for warning me. I thought he might be a rotten egg." Which was putting it nicely.

"You're spot-on, Ali. Is it okay if I call you Ali?"

"It's fine." Pedro had called her "Ali" the day she'd started working at Besito's, but no one had used the nickname recently. "So tell me more about this little island." She said it as a way to avoid more personal questions.

"Let's turn back, and then I'll tell you. I don't want John to see me."

Alison agreed and followed Renée.

"So, the rumor is that John is weird. With girls," Renée explained. "Not girls my age, or yours. Little girls, like eight or nine. It's sickening. Mom says he's been arrested a lot, but that's as far as it goes. His family is like really, really rich. Mom says they pay his way out of trouble. I don't know if this stuff is true, or just island gossip. I think it's all made up, but I wouldn't ever tell this to Mom. She'd croak."

Alison felt sick, given the unwanted attention from a few of her foster fathers. "Isn't this type of crime an automatic prison sentence, when a child is involved?"

"I don't know much about that stuff, but I do know

he's in and out of trouble a lot, though he's always here, so it must not be as bad as Mom tells me. If he did all the stuff she said, I think he'd be in jail."

"I would listen to your mom, as they know best. Stay away from sickos like that."

They continued down the beachfront, stopping when they reached the parking lot.

"If you want, I can meet you back here at sunset. Like I said, Mom lets me hang out till then," Renée said.

"Thanks. I can't promise anything, but if I change my mind, I'll see you at sunset."

"Great," Renée said. "Nice meeting you."

"Same here," Alison said, sliding into the driver's seat, then backing out of her parking spot. The sedan that was there earlier was gone. Odd, she thought, as she hadn't seen anyone besides Renée while she was on the beach. Probably nothing, as she really didn't know anyone on the island except Renée and John the idiot. She'd add Betty and Tank, but they didn't live on the island.

So Saturday was quiet on the beach. She liked it this way—no tourists scattered about like ants at a picnic. Heading east on Dolphin Drive, she drove slowly, taking in the island, trying to locate the real estate office. She had the number from the ad in the paper, but that didn't necessarily mean the number was from an office here on the island. Unsure of the prefix to use with the number, she pulled off the road, parking on the side before she reached the bridge. Using her newly purchased cell phone, she dialed the number from the paper.

"Diamond Realty; this is Kimberly. May I help you or direct your call to a particular agent?"

"Uh, no. I found your number in the *Sentinel*; I'm calling about the house—at least I believe it is—on the beach. Palmetto Island. Does your office have that listing?" Alison knew the listing had stated "beach house," but she also knew that people tended to exaggerate when they were trying to sell something. At least this had been her experience on more than one occasion, though this was the first time she'd actually called a real estate agent to see a house for sale. She always rented, but maybe this was the start of a new beginning.

"Yes, ma'am, it's only been on the market a few days. Beautiful home, if you don't mind doing a few updates."

"What do you mean, 'updates'?" Was she talking new roof, windows, or anything major?

"The place is actually in decent shape. I believe the previous owners installed a new central air system. The inside hasn't been updated in a while, though it's very quaint. If you'd like, I can show you the house today."

She was eager, Alison thought. That could mean a few things: Either the woman was desperate to make a sale, or there was more wrong with the house than she was telling her, or both.

"Yes, I'd like to see the place." Decision made; it couldn't hurt to look. It wasn't as though she had a schedule to stick to, though Alison realized she kept making excuses for postponing her drive to Key West.

But maybe she wouldn't have to drive that far south to find a forever home. Palmetto Island called to her, for some unexplainable reason. The quietness, the beach, and the sunsets, according to Renée, were extraordinary.

"Is three o'clock this afternoon convenient for you?" Kimberly asked.

"That's fine, though I'll need an address."

"Are you familiar with the island?"

"Not much," was all she said, which was true enough.

"Well, then do you have a GPS?" Kimberly asked.

"No, I don't, but if you give me an address, I'm quite confident I'll be able to find the place." Did she think she was stupid?

"It's a bit out of the way," Kimberly told her. "Take Dolphin Drive to the beach, then turn left on Loblolly Way. There is a public parking area; it's somewhat obscure, but keep driving until you see a small parking area. I can meet you at three. The house is just a short walk from there."

"I'm familiar with the area. I'll be there at three this afternoon."

"Miss, before you hang up, I need your name and a contact number, just in case."

In case of what? Alison thought, but gave her the information, because she knew this was expected. Real estate agents probably always needed this information, in case their clients decided not to show.

"Then it's a date! Again, I'm Kimberly Everette. I'll be in a white Range Rover. See you there."

"Sure thing," Alison said, ending the call. She didn't want to waste her minutes on idle chitchat with a complete stranger. She had a little bit of time to kill before she had to meet Kimberly. She headed toward Matlacha Pass, remembering there was a coffee shop there, The Daily Grind. She could use another dose of caffeine. She spied the coffee shop and pulled into the empty parking lot. Thinking they were closed, she was about to turn around when she saw a couple go inside. Directing the Jeep to a parking spot, she shut off the engine and grabbed her purse with her weapon still inside. She locked the Jeep, then entered the coffee shop.

The scent of burnt coffee and grease hit her as soon as she opened the door. If the smell was indicative of their coffee, she couldn't imagine how the place stayed in business. Starbucks didn't have to worry, that much was clear. She idled up to the area where a sign read ORDER HERE. Standing there, she read the menu on the white board behind the counter. They offered every kind of coffee drink the big guys offered, but the prices were way less. An older man appeared from the back of the shop. He had steel-gray hair and brown eyes. His glasses were so thick, his eyes reminded her of a dead fish, only twice the size. "What can I get you today?"

"I'll just have a coffee, black," she said.

"Don't let the smell scare you. We had a newbie leave a pot of coffee on the burner too long. This place smells hideous." He smiled at her.

Alison smiled back. "Just black coffee. And sorry about your newbie."

"They're a dime a dozen these days, coming and going like the tides."

Alison didn't know how to respond, so she took a ten from her wallet, placing it on the counter. "Just keep the change," she said before leaving.

"No, you take this back. Coffee is only a buck," the owner with the fisheyes said.

Okay, so nine dollars was a ridiculous tip. He held a five and four ones up in the air. She took the five, then waved before returning to her car. She looked at her clock on the dash. She still had half an hour to kill before it was time to meet Kimberly. She contemplated making a stop at the souvenir shop, but she didn't think half an hour would allow time for a reading. Maybe after she saw the beach house. A shiver of excitement rivered through her; owning a home seemed impossible. She didn't want to get her hopes up, as more than likely, the place was a dump, like all the other apartments and hotels she'd lived in. Still, she couldn't help being excited by the prospect of a home of her own, even if she was just looking.

With nothing but time on her hands, she drove back to the beach and parked in the same spot as before. No gray sedan or white Range Rover, but it was early. She didn't really expect the real estate agent to already be waiting here. She rolled down the windows, turned the radio on, and found a local station here on the island, WPMO. According to the radio, low tide was apparently at 5:28 this evening, the sunset at 7:49, and the moon phase was in the waning crescent. She knew the tides were dictated by the moon, but that was it. Maybe if this place turned out to be her forever home, she'd learn about the tides, the moon, and its many phases. She remembered learning about the cosmos when she was in fifth grade, though she didn't think her teacher referred to them as the cosmos, just the solar system. She learned the phases of the moon, and knew the sun lit up the half-moon except during a solar eclipse. That was the extent of her knowledge. The disc jockey went on to other local topics, such as fishing and who was having a special on bait. None of that interested her, so she turned the radio off.

She took a brush from her purse and ran it through her hair, pulling it back in a ponytail. She wiped sand from the hem of her shirt before getting out of the Jeep. She leaned against the rear bumper. The sounds of the island were so different from Tallahassee and Tampa. This was more tropical, a true island. Private. She saw a blue heron swoop down into the water, flying away with a small fish in its grip. Three brown pelicans flew low across the gulf, their wings flapping loudly as they emitted hoarse sounds she was familiar with. You couldn't live in Florida without seeing a pelican. Animal Kingdom in Orlando had pink flamingos. Alison remembered the first time she saw one. She thought someone had actually colored them, thinking how cruel to do this to an innocent animal, until she learned the reason for their color was their diet of pink shrimp. She smiled at the memory of her first jaunt to one of Florida's main attractions.

The white Range Rover pulled into the lot, parking beside her vehicle. A woman who looked in her early thirties got out of the vehicle. She had blonde hair, brown eyes, and a killer tan. She wore a pink sleeveless shift dress and pink heels to match, and a small designer handbag hung from her wrist. Alison suddenly felt dowdy. But who in their right mind wore heels to the beach?

"You must be Alison," she said. "I'm Kimberly." She held out her hand. Alison shook hands with her, then noticed her discreetly wiping her hands on the back of her dress. This was a bad idea. This woman was a first-class snob. She could practically smell it on her.

"I'm Alison, yes." She wasn't going to make this easy for her, especially after seeing her wipe her hands off on the back of an expensive dress. At least it looked expensive to her; everything tended to.

"So you realize the house is for sale? Not a weekly rental?" Kimberly asked, her tone implying Alison didn't truly know why she was here.

"I do."

Kimberly seemed flustered. "Then let's go have a look."

Alison nodded. "I'll follow you."

"Of course, it's just a short walk."

Alison trailed behind Kimberly, in awe of her expertise navigating the sand in heels. Must have a lot of practice, she thought as she followed her. She was surprised when Kimberly stopped in front of a pale-yellow cottage with an actual white picket fence, hidden slightly behind one of the larger beach houses. She hadn't ventured into this area, had no idea there was even a house here.

"This is it." Kimberly punched a code in the key box on the doorknob, then stepped aside. "Come and see if this is what you're looking for. As I said on the phone, it's a bit dated inside, though it's structurally sound and the air conditioner is new. I went through the original specs—someone replaced the roof five years ago. This was before my time, but that's good. You could get another ten to fifteen years out of the roof, provided we don't have a major hurricane."

Alison stepped inside the cottage. The knotty pine walls had to be original. "This was built when?" she asked Kimberly.

"Early nineteen-sixties," she said. "The knotty pine is original; the oak floors, too. Some white paint would do wonders for these ugly walls. Maybe the floors could be restored. As I said, it's old, but in decent shape."

Alison felt the same trickle of excitement she felt when she'd made the call earlier. She saw the potential this adorable cottage had due to its location, just a few yards from the beach, but not too close. The house to the right of her looked empty. "Does someone live in the large house?" she asked.

"It's a vacation rental. The owners bought it about three years ago and rented it out after only a month. So, not much life here until the winter season. It's actually very quiet here, even with the snowbirds coming and going."

"Why?"

"Palmetto Island is a hidden gem. It hasn't been discovered by the big developers yet. It's charming, close to everything one needs. If you cross the bridge to Matlacha Pass, you'll find grocery stores, and further down Pine Tree Road will take you to Fort Charlotte.

You won't be isolated in the sense that you can't take a thirty-minute drive to the nearest Walmart."

Was that a dig or was she being too sensitive? Probably the latter, as she was overly sensitive at times. "That's a bonus, since that's the only place I shop." She couldn't help herself.

"Then you'll feel right at home. Go on, have a look through, see the place, then we can discuss the financing. See if you're able to qualify for a mortgage. You do have a job, correct?"

"No, I'm unemployed."

Kimberly sighed. "Then you're wasting my time. No bank will lend money if a borrower isn't gainfully employed. I'm sorry."

"I don't need financing from a bank." Alison took great delight in the look on Kimberly's face.

"Oh, well, I just assumed. Most people do."

"I'm not most people," she said, then ventured through the rooms. There were two bedrooms, with a full bathroom between them, which she thought was kind of nice. The kitchen was a true relic, with an old gas stove, the white ceramic worn down to the cast iron in some places. The refrigerator was newer, but not by much.

"There is an ice maker," Kimberly said as she opened the freezer, then jumped back. "It needs a good cleaning, for sure. I don't know what was in here last. Obviously, the previous owners didn't bother cleaning. You'll want to scrub this, if you're buying."

"I can clean." A white porcelain sink flanked by two more sets of the knotty pine cupboards offered plenty of storage. The window above the sink looked out onto a large path, possibly a driveway at one time. The shrubbery was definitely in need of care. The overgrowth looked more junglelike—bamboo skirted the sides of the drive, and small shoots devoured the land, taking over the grounds. She knew bamboo was a fast-growing plant but wasn't sure of its purpose.

Kimberly rambled on. "There is no dishwasher, but there is a hookup for a washer and dryer, off the side of the porch. It's separate, a utility room, though the place doesn't come with a washer or a dryer. Something else you might want to consider."

"Is there a laundromat nearby?" She wanted to ask if one could be found near the Walmart, but she refrained from being a total smartass.

"Yes, it's near the coffee shop."

"Then I won't need to consider purchasing a washer and dryer." She actually would, but this woman irked her. Miss Snob probably had her laundry washed by a maid.

"Of course not," Kimberly said. "The laundromat is . . . clean."

Alison checked the main living area. Large windows offered a magnificent view of the strip of beach and the gulf. She ran her hand along the windowsill, checked the locks to make sure they worked properly. She returned to the bedrooms, repeating the process. In the bathroom, she checked the plumbing beneath a small cabinet for signs of a leak, checked the faucet to make sure it worked. She lifted the tank off the toilet, checking to see if the chain was rusted. Not that she cared, as these things were easily repaired. She just wanted to annoy Kimberly. The main attraction of the bathroom was an old cast-iron bathtub with claw footing, the back much higher than its front. The faucet was rusted. Alison tried the knob, and it turned easily. Drips of water tinged with brown trickled from the spigot.

"This needs a bit of work," Alison stated. "I'm sure you'll consider that in the price." She liked the old tub. Surprisingly, it was in good shape, other than the faucet.

"I'm sure the owners are willing to negotiate the price," Kimberly replied.

"Even though it's only been on the market for a few days?" Alison asked. Wasn't it usually just the opposite? "Looks like no one has lived here in a while."

Kimberly picked at her pale pink fingernail. "You don't have to live in a house to own it. They're simply in a rush to sell."

"How long has it been since someone actually *lived* in this house?"

"Maybe five or six years. I'm not sure."

"Odd," Alison muttered.

"May I ask why you find this odd?"

This woman was a real snob. "A house on the beach doesn't usually remain empty for that long," she said.

"As I said, I'm not sure. Does this matter to you?"

Now the woman was downright bitchy. Alison really didn't care, but she did find it strange the place remained empty. "Actually, it does," she said, lying through her teeth. "I would like to know the name of the seller, too. I'm sure you have this information somewhere in your office?" Seeing the snob in defense mode was entertaining.

"Of course, but I was asked to keep their identity private. Diamond Realtors is the seller to you. Or someone else," she added, catching on to her sarcasm.

Kimberly hit a nerve.

"Okay, I get that. If I decide to buy, I'll find out myself."

"Do what you must. This is a good investment for anyone willing to live here and make the necessary repairs."

"I'm sure it is," Alison said. "Do you mind if I walk through the house alone?" She needed to imagine herself in this space. She wanted to walk through the rooms again, unobserved, without the pink snob's smart-aleck attitude.

"Well, I've never been asked that before, but I suppose there is a first time for everything. I'll be on the front porch." She rolled her eyes as she walked out of the bathroom.

Alone, Alison walked through the rooms. She opened the closets in both bedrooms and the closet in the front living area. There was a small pantry in the kitchen, not very big, but she wanted to see the inside of that, as well. When she finished, she went to the porch, locating the small utility room. A concrete floor, with block walls, a power outlet, and a small window. Satisfied, she found Kimberly waiting.

"It's what I've been looking for," Alison told her, "but I need to think about this a little longer. Can you hold off on any other offers?"

"No, I can't, but I'm fairly sure your offer will be the only one today."

"Good enough," Alison said. "What time does your office close?"

"We're open until six on weekends, but you can call my cell number if it's later." She reached in her designer handbag to retrieve a business card. "Though being Saturday, I won't be able to actually sell you the house. Well, at least as far as the banking end of things go."

"I appreciate you showing me the place. I'll get back to you one way or another." Alison was confident in her decision, but she wasn't going to jump the gun.

As soon as Kimberly left, Alison lingered behind for a few minutes, as she didn't want her nosy ass to see where she was going. Five minutes later, she was on Dolphin Drive, headed to the souvenir store. Two cars were in the lot. She parked as far away from the door as she could. She backed into a space so she could pull onto the road quickly. If she were to encounter John Wilson again after she finished her business, she wanted to put as much distance between them as possible.

She wished she'd asked Renée for her mother's name, then decided it didn't matter. For now, she'd simply browse the store; then she'd decide if she dared to ask for a reading. Inside the Souvenir Store, which was actually the name of the place, she was greeted by cool air and the scent of gardenia, one she recognized, as it was her favorite flower. Soft music played in the background, which sounded Celtic. Calming, she thought, as she stood beside a display of postcards. She removed a few from the rack because she liked the pictures. Plus, they were only a quarter each. Across from the postcards was a display of mirrors with a variety of seashells glued onto the frames. Not her style, but to each his own. There were ashtrays in the shape of alligators and miniature orange crates with orange gumballs inside, which mimicked an orange, just downsized. Different sizes of starfish filled a wicker basket. A handwritten sign said they were fifty cents each. Couldn't you find these for free on the beach? She knew these gimmicky items screamed "buy me" to tourists. Alison had seen many such items in the shops in Tampa Bay.

She lingered over the rack of T-shirts, searching for one she liked. If she was going to make this place her forever home, then she'd need a T-shirt. She found a gray shirt with a palm tree on the upper left pocket that read PALMETTO ISLAND, the letters in dark green. Basic, she thought as she took the shirt off the hanger. Seeing no one else in the store, Alison figured the two cars she saw belonged to whoever was having a reading. It would be easy to walk out the door without paying for her merchandise. Maybe this so-called psychic knew when someone was about to rip her off. Not that she had any intention of doing so. She wanted to make a purchase; then she'd decide on a reading. Her gut had always been reliable, yet it couldn't hurt to see if this psychic picked up on her decision.

A bell chimed, and Alison looked up to see a stunning woman emerge from a room in the back of the store. This must be Renée's mother.

"Hello, I'm Valentina Dubois. You must be new to the area."

Alison gasped, then took a deep breath before she spoke. "How do you know that?"

"I've never seen you before, plus you've got a handful of postcards. The locals usually don't come in for postcards." She smiled, her words teasing, but in no way were they condescending.

"True. I'm not from Florida."

"But you've lived in Florida for a while," the woman, Valentina, said with confidence.

"I met your daughter at the beach earlier today. She told me about you," Alison said, adding, "Said you could read cards, minds, or both, something to that effect."

Valentina laughed out loud. "That girl amazes me. In one breath she tells me she's embarrassed by my ability, then in the second breath, she's telling anyone who'll listen that her mother has a gift."

"Do you?" Alison blurted out. "I'm sorry, but I am curious."

"Would you like a reading? Maybe the Tarot cards?"

Now that Alison was here, and the opportunity was presented to her, she wasn't sure. "I don't know," she answered honestly.

"You're a skeptic," Valentina said. "Most people are. It's not unusual to be a little nervous if you've never had a reading before. So, what do you say? It's on the house, but just this once." She winked at her.

Alison placed her shirt and postcards on the counter. Doubtful, but since she was offering a free reading, why not? "I'll give it a try."

"Fantastic! Now, do you want my special gift, or would you rather go with a Tarot reading?"

"Your gift," she said. She wanted to see what this woman did, how she managed to convince people she was psychic or gifted.

"I thought so," she said. "Leave your things here—I need to lock the door and put my OUT TO LUNCH sign on the door. Be right back." She reached under the counter for her sign, walked around the lengthy counter to the door. She hung the sign up, then said, "I know I'm not what you expected."

Ten points for that, Alison thought. The second she'd stepped away from the counter, she thought Valentina looked like a young girl. She wore a pair of white Bermuda shorts and a bright yellow blouse with matching sandals. Her hair was the same color as her daughter's, her smile just as bright.

Alison smiled. "So how did you know that? Can you read minds?"

"No one expects a medium or psychic to look normal. Follow me," Valentina said. "It's more comfortable in the back."

Alison followed her down a short hallway, stopping in front of a door with a sign that read: SILENCE, I'M READING.

"That was Renée's idea, not mine."

"Catchy," Alison remarked, still amazed at her ability to home in on her thoughts almost instantaneously.

"And to answer your question, I can't read minds. Come inside, let's get comfortable."

Expecting a round crystal ball, candles, and incense, Alison was pleasantly surprised when the room looked just like any other room in the back of a shop. Small, with two cushy chairs, a small table between them with the latest novel from James Patterson on top.

"Can I get you a soft drink or water? Or I think I still have iced tea." Behind the chairs in the corner stood a small refrigerator with paper cups on top. Valentina searched through the bottles.

"A water is fine, thanks."

"Good! I was hoping you'd say that. I'm out of tea, and the sodas are all diet. I'm due for a trip into town." She gave her the water. "Have a seat." She motioned to the chair closest to the door.

Alison sat down. The chair's soft cushion against her bare skin felt luxurious, soft. "This is nice," she said, for lack of anything better. What did one say to a person who may or may not be able to guess her thoughts?

"So, how long are you planning on staying on the island?" Valentina asked.

"I was hoping you could tell me." Alison chuckled. "Truly, I don't know. I went to the—"

"Don't tell me anything about yourself. I don't want you to feel you've influenced what I tell you in any way. Are you good with this?"

"Sure," she said.

"We're simply going to have a conversation, and if I say anything that is or isn't true, try not to respond. Verbally or visually, as it will distract me. Lots of fakes out there, and this is part of their method. They'll get you to open up with a few basic questions, then before you know it, you've told them something about yourself that you'll think they just whipped out of thin air later. These types give people like myself a bad name."

As instructed, Alison didn't comment or show any physical response. No eyebrow lifting or chewing on her lips. She'd learned way too early in life how to blend in with the background. Now was no different.

She waited for Valentina to close her eyes, put her fingers on her temples, anything to indicate she was receiving a message. Instead, she remained calm, as though she were waiting for a bolt of lightning to jar her into a semiconscious state. She spoke just like she did before, as though this were a normal conversation.

"You have concerns about many issues in your life. Pretty basic for most folks, but yours are intense. Life isn't easy all the time, but you're an achiever, maybe an overachiever, though you don't acknowledge these things about yourself. Hard work is your strength. You like being alone. Now you're considering a change. A first for you, possibly what brought you here. Whatever you decide will change you, in ways you've never thought of, but you will walk through this change with much success, though not right away. Struggles will cause you to question yourself, your ability to make decisions. You will work through the struggles. It's in your core—you never give up." Valentina took a sip of water before continuing.

"You value your intuition, your instinct. Go with your instinct. Never doubt yourself. You have strong values." She stopped speaking again, took another drink of water.

She was quiet for a moment, then said, "This is all I'm able to say now. I believe in my heart this decision you will make when you leave here today will be the right one." She smiled. "Not sure if any of what I said hit home with you, and I don't want to know. I'm not getting much else right now. But there will be other times."

"Very impressive," Alison said, though she wouldn't dare tell her how spot-on she was. "Renée is right to brag about you. Speaking of, she asked me to meet her at the beach at sunset. Does she usually cozy up to strangers so easily? Not that I'd ever harm her; she's a sweet girl, but you know how the world is today."

"Renée never meets a stranger. However, she has excellent instincts, so I trust her to trust in them."

"Good. She told me about John. I had an encounter with the guy last night; not a pleasant one, either. I told her to be careful."

"He is an evil man. I won't allow him, or anyone related to him, inside the store. He's rotten with young girls. The family has connections with the governor and the local police. Renée knows to stay away from him. He's bad news." Valentina's face turned several shades of red. "He disgusts me."

"I sensed bad vibes about him the moment I saw him. I didn't know the beach was public. I hoofed down a path next to his house, and he followed me to my car. We had a few words, and then again later at the mango festival."

"Which was a total bust this year," Valentina concluded.

"Yeah, I thought so, though I'd never been before. I didn't see a lot of mango anything, just a few boats anchored around that old bridge."

Valentina shook her head side to side. "They have a boating club on the island. It was probably them, though they rarely converge at the bridge. Must've been there for the festival that wasn't."

Alison stood. "I appreciate the reading. I'll just pay for my stuff, then get out of your hair."

"Sure thing, though you're not in my hair at all. It's been nice meeting you. If you decide to stay on the island, don't be a stranger. Come in for a soda or something. I get bored in the off-season."

"I saw you're reading the latest bestseller," Alison commented, searching for something to say as she followed Valentina back to the front of the store. She'd never had a real friendship with another female.

"I read all the time. Matlacha Pass has a decent library, if you're interested. They offer all sorts of activities. I've been thinking about taking their computer class. I'm not up to date in this technical world," she said as she added up Alison's items on an old-style adding machine. "Though as you can see, this old thing gets the job done."

Alison gave her a twenty-dollar bill. "I understand. I only bought my first cell phone today. I had a quick lesson on how to use it at the store, but I've messed around with the computers a time or two." She wouldn't tell her she'd lived in Tampa and frequented the library when she needed to use their computer. Just in case she ever wanted another reading, she didn't want Valentina to know this.

"I need to update to the twenty-first century, but I do have a cell phone, and Renée taught me how to send text messages."

"She's a great girl," Alison said. "If I see her later, I'll tell her I met you, and thanks for the reading."

She went to the door to leave but stopped dead in her tracks when Valentina spoke.

"Buy the cottage. It's the best deal you'll find on the island."

Chapter Four

Alison sat in the Jeep for a few minutes without cranking the engine. Valentina's parting words had shocked her. Had she known about her visit to the beach house with Kimberly? Maybe, but she couldn't be one hundred percent sure. Kimberly struck her as the kind who'd run her mouth about anything at the first opportunity, yet Valentina didn't seem to be the kind of person who listened to gossip. Her gut told her this, and she listened, just as she'd been instructed to.

Sweating, she cranked the engine over, then switched the air-conditioning to the highest setting. It was humid, and she felt sticky. She couldn't wait to get a shower and wash off the sand still clinging to her. She directed the Jeep back to the beach, parking in the public lot. It was after five. She needed to make a decision about the beach house, one way or another. Half of her craved stability, yet the other half didn't want to give up her freedom, the ability to pick up and go anytime she felt the urge for new surroundings. Owning a home would tie her down, and buying the house would take a chunk out of her bank account. Wanting to see the house one more time, she locked the Jeep, taking her purse and cell phone with her.

The yellow cottage, though old and in need of a few basic repairs—at least that's what Kimberly led her to believe—was what she'd always envisioned. Small, with a glorious view of the beach. She knew she'd be a fool to pass up this opportunity. The price was so below market value that it concerned her. Maybe the well was on the blink. Many of the homes she'd seen in Florida had wells and water softeners. She'd stayed in a few places without city water. It wasn't a make-or-break issue for her. Valentina said she was making the right decision. Should she make a life-changing decision based on a psychic's prediction? Was it even a prediction? Maybe it was just good advice coming from someone who'd spent her life on the island. Either way, she needed another look. She followed the path she'd taken with Kimberly, just a short jaunt from the parking lot.

The cottage was just as it was a couple hours ago. She circled the perimeter, saw the workings of the well. The aerator appeared to be in decent condition outwardly, but she wouldn't know for sure until the utilities were on. Most of the larger homes were on pilings, but she saw the cottage had a decent foundation. Old, but sturdy, which was usually better, she thought as she continued her walk. Unsure how to access the house other than the way she came, she walked to the edge of the property that faced Dolphin Drive. A narrow gravel driveway, not much in the way of parking, but that could be fixed. Now she understood why Kimberly asked to meet in the beach's parking lot. The turn from the main road was overgrown with vegetation; if you didn't know there was a so-called driveway, you'd drive right past the place. That, too, would need work.

Still undecided, Alison returned to her car. She considered the pros and cons; both were justifiable. Good or bad, she decided for once in her life, she'd take the plunge, and if she regretted her decision later, then so be it.

She dialed Kimberly's number.

"Diamond Realty; this is Kimberly."

"I'll take the cottage," she said, as fast as she could, before she changed her mind.

"Well, I must say I wasn't expecting you to buy the place, but now that you have, I'll get the paperwork in order. Can you meet me at my office Monday, say around nine?"

"Yes," Alison said. "I'll need an address."

"Of course." She recited the address, and Alison wrote it down with the pen from Mel's Diner. "Then it's a deal. I'll see you Monday. Don't forget to bring a check," she added, then hung up.

Alison wondered how much of a commission Kimberly would make. It couldn't be too much, given the price of the place. This nagged her, but she wasn't one to kick a gift horse in the mouth. Decision made, and excited at the prospect of making a forever home here on this quaint little island, she wanted to share her good news. Remembering Renée was staying on the beach until sunset, she would meet her and tell her about her new house, though a teenager probably didn't care one way or the other about such things.

For the umpteenth time that day, she locked the Jeep, taking her purse with her phone and weapon with her. She wouldn't take any chances with John or anyone else who might be a threat.

On the beach, she spied Renée lying on a towel, immersed in a book. Once again, she felt as though she were interrupting her.

"Hey there," Renée said, closing her book. "I knew you'd come back."

Alison laughed. "Maybe you're as gifted as your mom."

"No way, she's out of this world."

"I met your mom earlier. She's super nice," Alison said. "I had a reading, too." She sat on the sand next to the girl.

This got Renée's full attention. "Isn't she everything I said and more?"

"She certainly seems to know a lot about a person." She didn't want to reveal any details of her reading, as Renée might tell her mom. She still wanted an unbiased opinion in case she decided on a second reading in the future.

"I know Mom tells you not to talk about the things she tells you, but if you want to tell me, you can."

Alison laughed. "No, I'll keep this to myself, only because it's my way." She waited for her to digest her words. "Nothing personal."

"It's okay. Most people don't want to talk about that stuff, anyway. So, forget that. I'm all good with what you do. I'm nosy, just so you know. At least Mom says I am."

Another laugh. "Are you?" Alison couldn't help asking.

She grinned. "Yep, I am. In the summer, it's so boring here, I have to be nosy when I meet someone new, though I would never ask you to reveal personal stuff, like if you have a boyfriend, girlfriend, or both."

"I'll be happy to let you know; at this point, I don't have a boyfriend, and I'm not into girls."

"I didn't think you were, but you never know. I have a major crush on Blake Hamilton. He'll be a senior this year, and he is so hot. I'm hoping we'll hook up once school starts."

"So does Blake know you're crushing on him?"

"No, he has no idea I even exist. He's a football player, and they only go for the cheerleaders, so really there is no hope."

Alison nodded. "Times haven't changed. Same thing when I was your age."

"You crushed on a football player, too?"

She didn't want to lie to the girl, so she said, "A little, maybe. I was more into studying than boys at your age." She was more into surviving, finding her next meal.

"So how old are you?" Renée asked. "Nosy me, huh?" She smiled, and her perfectly white teeth sparkled.

"I'm twenty-nine. Thirty in September," she told her. "Old."

"No way! I thought you were like twenty-one. You look really young."

Alison didn't believe this for a minute. She'd aged badly, from living a rough life, but she appreciated her kindness.

"You're too sweet, thank you." Not wanting to spoil the girl's opinion of her, she would let this one slide.

"So you want to stay with me, see the sunset? We still have a couple hours."

She really wanted to, but she had to search for a place to stay for the weekend. "I have to go. I need to find a hotel for a couple nights, though I may take you up on your offer as soon as I get settled in that little yellow cottage behind us," she said, a smile as wide as the beach on her face.

"Really? You're moving here?" Her blue eyes brightened. "Cool."

Alison nodded. "I can't believe it either. I meet with the real estate agent Monday; then it's all mine." Saying the words out loud cemented her decision, at least in her head.

"Mom will love this. We're right over here." She pointed to one of the grand homes behind them. "It's two doors down, a little bit behind us."

No wonder she spent the days on the beach. If she needed a drink or a bathroom break, all she had to do was walk a short distance.

"Do you know who lived in my house before?"

Renée clammed up, looking away. "You'd have to ask Mom."

"I will do that as soon as I get settled in. So, I'm going to call it a day, kiddo. Find a place to stay for the night. I'll be seeing you around for sure," she said, standing and brushing the sand off the back of her legs.

"Wait! You don't need to stay in a hotel. We have five bedrooms. You can stay with us."

"No, I can't do that. You hardly know me, and besides, I wouldn't want to impose. I could be a weirdo, for all you know."

"If you were, I would know. I have good instincts about people. You're good to the core."

Alison was surprised, as this was basically what Valentina had also told her. It wouldn't be too much to assume Renée had her mother's gift, as well.

"I'm going to call Mom now, so stay here for just a sec," Renée said, taking her cell phone out of her pocket.

Because the girl was as sweet as sugar, Alison waited while she called her mom, but no way was she going to impose on strangers.

Renée spoke so fast, Alison could barely keep up with the one-sided conversation. Once finished, Renée stashed her cell phone in her pocket. "Mom says you *have* to stay with us. There's nothing decent on the island as far as hotels go. Closest motel is the Courtesy Court, but no one in their right mind stays there."

"Why?" Alison had to ask.

"The lady that owns the place is wacko. Her son, too," Renée explained. "They've been involved in shady stuff, though I'm not sure exactly what kind of stuff. I've heard Mom talk about them, and it's not like her to talk about people behind their back, but those two are the exception."

Should she tell Renée about her experience? Didn't Betty tell her she had no family? She wouldn't stay at that place again if hell froze over. She knew something happened to her other than a twenty-four-hour bug. She didn't believe the hamburger she'd eaten gave her food poisoning, either.

"I did see weekly cottages for rent as I crossed the bridge," Alison said.

"They're okay, I guess. I don't know much about them, but I suppose it's an option."

Renée was wise beyond her years. "Tell your mom thank you, but I'll find a place tonight. I'll be back tomorrow. I want to start cutting back the overgrowth so I can use the driveway."

"If you want company, I can help."

"That would be great," Alison said. "Not much fun, though."

"Anything is fun if you have the right attitude."

This kid is too smart for her own good. "You're spot-on. I'll see you sometime tomorrow."

"I'll be right here catching some rays," Renée said. "If you change your mind, come back anytime. Mom and I are night owls on the weekends."

Alison wished the girls she'd met in school had been as sweet and kind as Renée. *The past is prologue.* Bad times were over. With a renewed sense of purpose, she waved goodbye as she headed back to her Jeep. She'd drive into town if she couldn't find a place to stay.

She drove to Matlacha Pass, where she'd seen the cottages for rent. Matlacha Mariner's Cottages looked decent. Deciding this was as good a place as any, she parked her car. The office was a small cottage painted aqua blue. Inside was just as cute. A pale blue desk held a lamp, the base of which was a blue marlin. Fish-themed. She smiled to herself. Cute, but not her style. Unsure what her style was, she cleared her throat, hoping whoever worked here had heard her.

"Be right there," a woman's voice called.

Reminiscent of Betty—she hoped this woman wasn't also an oddball.

"Hi, sorry to make you wait. The twins are throwing their evening tantrum." The woman looked to be around her own age. Wholesome, with short brown hair and brown eyes, she looked tired, but in a good way. She wore cut-off jean shorts and an orange T-shirt with a gator on the front. Like Kimberly, she had a golden tan, shapely legs, and Alison noticed she wore a gold toe ring. Weren't those out of style? As in, the 1980s out of style?

"No problem; I didn't hear your kids," Alison said. "I just wanted to see if you had a place for tonight, maybe tomorrow night, too."

"I'm Lacey. We've got a few vacancies. Just you?" she asked as she took a seat behind the blue desk. Clicking the keyboard, she swirled the monitor around so Alison could view the rooms.

"This is the Pink Flamingo. It's available this week. This"—she scrolled down to another cottage—"this is Suzi Sails Seashells and Pelican Landing, both of which have two bedrooms."

Alison smiled. "Very appropriate names," she said, seeing the décor in each cottage replicated the name. "They're all adorable, so whatever you have for a couple nights, I'll take."

"Normally we only rent by the week, but it's off-season, so a couple nights is fine. You need to stay longer, no worries," Lacey said. "I just need an ID and a credit or debit card."

Alison was a cash-only person. She had checks from her investment account, but no credit or debit card. "I have cash," she told Lacey.

"That'll work, too. Nowadays, everyone seems to forget we still take cash. Just an ID, and I'll set you up in the pink cottage."

"That would be great." She took her driver's license from her purse and three one-hundred-dollar bills.

"That's too much . . ." Lacey glanced at her ID, then gave it back to her. "Alison. We're fifty bucks a night, and since you have cash, you'll get the Florida six-percent discount."

"You're sure?" she asked, thinking the price too low, given that each room was more like a mini apartment with a full kitchen, bathroom, and living area; plus, the area where the bed was placed appeared as though it were a separate room.

"Yep, I'm sure," Lacey said. "Here is the key; you can park in the front of the cottage. The password for the Internet is Mariner-one-one-two-one."

"No need, but thanks." Maybe once she settled into her new home, she would think about getting a computer.

Lacey chuckled. "That's usually the first question our guests ask. People come here to get away from it all, and as soon as they get here, they want to get back to Facebook and Instagram. Can't leave their social media behind."

"I'm a little behind in the tech world," Alison said, gripping the key. She debated whether she should share her news with Lacey, then decided to, since she was soon to be a permanent resident. "I just bought the yellow cottage on the island, so we'll probably bump into one another at the store or some place," she said awkwardly.

Lacey's expression went from pleasant to surprised. "I see."

First Renée, now Lacey. Odd that Valentina didn't seem to think her purchasing the cottage was a bad idea. "Is there something I should know about? The real estate agent said the place is in decent shape."

Lacey shook her head. "I think you need to ask your agent. Was Brian McMann your agent?"

"No. Kimberly." She took the girl's card from her purse. "Everette."

"She must be new," Lacey said. "Brian is my brother-in-law. He owns Diamond Realty, though he isn't around much these days."

"Now I feel like I've been ripped off," Alison said.

"Have you taken a mortgage out? I know it's none of my business," Lacey said.

"No, I was going to pay cash, I *am* going to pay cash. It needs a bit of work, but I didn't see anything unusual when I was there."

"You misunderstand me. It's not the cottage itself. Though I've never been inside, I assume it's structurally sound; otherwise, Brian wouldn't have taken the listing."

"Then what?" Alison said. Before she plunked down a hundred grand, she wanted to make sure she wasn't throwing her money down the drain. She'd worked too hard to earn enough to live the life she'd always wanted; she wasn't going to let some half-assed real estate agent rip her off.

"This Kimberly, she didn't tell you anything?"

"If you mean did she tell me something horrible, no. She seemed quite comfortable, brought the specs from the architect that originally built the cottage. A first-class snob is the only complaint I have about her."

"Look, I may be wrong, I've only lived here for six years. Right after we bought this place, I heard there was an accident there. A bad one." Lacey paused. "A little girl's body was found buried there, or at least what was left of it. Bones."

"What? No one mentioned this to me. Are you sure?" The island was isolated. If this was true, surely Valentina would've told her this. Alison knew small towns, and the gossips were always the same. A tragedy in a small town would be repeated until it was totally out of proportion. Valentina had said it was the best deal on the island. She would struggle, she'd told her, but whatever she struggled with, she'd get through it with no problems. Had she only heard what she wanted to hear? No, she was positive Valentina said to buy the place. She'd had good vibes, the house was just that, a house.

Lacey twisted a bracelet made out of seashells on her wrist. "I could be wrong, so please don't base your decision on what I heard. It might be just gossip. I've never spoken about this to anyone, though I'm sure if you really wanted the facts, Brian would know. I can call him, see if it's true."

It couldn't be that simple. If a body had been found on the property, it would be the talk of the island. Even that jerk John would know about it. She recalled what Renée and her mother said about him. He hurt little girls. Maybe he'd done more than that. Maybe he was involved somehow. "Did you ever hear how old this child was?"

"No, though I assume she was very young, maybe seven or eight, the way folks talked."

"I'll call Kimberly first thing tomorrow. If there is anything she isn't telling me, she'll be really sorry she lied to me, tried to rip me off."

"As I said, I'm not positive, but I'll call my brother-in-law. I can ask him."

"No, I won't involve you in this. I'll find out if this is true one way or another."

If it was, could she live there?

"If you change your mind, I'll call Brian. As I said, he wouldn't have listed the place if he thought it wasn't up to par."

"It's fine, really. I'll call Kimberly in the morning, so no worries," she told Lacey. Concerned, but smart enough to know that gossip could spread like wildfires, until Alison had actual confirmation, she wasn't going to allow Lacey's bad news to spoil her good news.

"If you're sure," she said.

"I am," Alison told her. "I appreciate the room and the rate."

Lacey nodded. "You're most welcome. As I said, it's slow in the summer months."

Heading for the door, Alison stopped and turned to

face Lacey. "Do you know anything about the Courtesy Court Motel in town?"

"Not much, though again, there are rumors, gossip, whatever you want to call it, that the owner is a bit looney, has a son who has issues. Not sure if it's true. Lots of gossip goes on here, folks in and out of the cottages. Some of them are local. I guess it keeps them occupied when they're not working."

"I guess if you don't have anything better to do," Alison said.

Lacey hesitated, then spoke. "Did you stay there?"

Alison nodded. "Just one night." She wasn't going to go into detail about the insane night she'd experienced. In due time, she'd make a point to learn what she could about Betty.

"I guess that was enough," Lacey stated.

A loud scream, followed by another scream, then crying, captured Lacey's attention. "The twins," she said, then, "We're here twenty-four-seven if you need anything."

Alison nodded before returning to her car. Poor Lacey—the lady was sweet, but Alison guessed her to be one of the gossips she spoke of. She parked in front of the carnation pink cottage and couldn't help but grin. Someone either had a sense of humor, or they were truly into flamingos. Inside, the room reminded her of a real live dollhouse. A pelican border encircled the entire space. The bright white chairs had pink pillows with white flamingos; the bed coverings were bright pink with white pillows in the shape of the bird. Alison walked through the small space, seeing most of the décor was the same throughout. The shower curtain sported pelicans, and the pink towels, with more white pelicans, continued the theme. Cute, Alison thought, but after a while, you'd go crazy with all the pink. Tonight, she didn't care. All she wanted was a hot shower, a cool drink, and a soft bed. Tomorrow would be here soon enough. She would deal with life one day at a time, as usual.

Chapter Five

A lison rolled over in bed, sighing as she delved deeper into the plush bedding. She'd never slept in a bed so comfortable, one she wanted to spend the day in. She lay there, thinking about her plans for the day, what she hoped to accomplish, remembering what Lacey told her. Surely there had to be a mistake; she'd simply attribute it to island gossip. She decided to make a quick stop in the Souvenir Store if there was time and ask Valentina if it was true. She soaked up the luxurious comfort for another half hour before dragging herself out of the bed to take another long, hot shower.

She dressed in cut-offs, a purple T-shirt, and a pair of sneakers. Alison planned on spending most of the day working on the overgrowth on the property. Even though it didn't officially belong to her, she was ninety-nine percent sure she would go through with the purchase. She locked up after hiding her old, battered suitcase in the closet. There was a coffee maker in the tiny kitchen, but no coffee. With caffeine on her mind, she cranked up the Jeep's engine, heading over to The Daily Grind.

The parking lot was packed. She found a tight spot, maneuvering the Jeep between a red Ford truck and a white Nissan Sentra. Careful not to ding the door on the Nissan parked on the driver's side, she slid out of the Jeep, cautiously closing the door.

Inside, the coffee shop buzzed. It made sense that it would be crowded like this on a Sunday morning. Alison scanned the tables for a familiar face. Seeing no one she'd encountered, she waited her turn, then ordered two large black coffees to go. She gave the barista a five, then returned to her car wondering where the fish-eyed owner was on such a busy morning.

The traffic was unusually light, she thought. Church, maybe? Alison hadn't seen a church, but that didn't mean there wasn't one. Churches didn't necessarily have to be in a structured building. She'd attended a few services inside garages, a basement, and once in a park.

She drove along Pine Tree Road. She needed to stop at the hardware store by the marina. Not relishing the idea of potentially bumping into John the jerk, she needed tools in order to clear out the driveway. She couldn't see herself parking in a public parking lot, trudging in and out with shopping bags and such; not to mention she wanted a clear view of her Jeep just in case she needed to run.

No, she had to change her way of thinking. There would be no need to run again. She would have a home of her own, maybe friends, a life. Years of running wouldn't be easy to shelve, but she knew she could do this. She had to. At almost thirty, she knew it was past time to settle down, leave behind what she'd been running from. Years of living frugally had paid off. Trusting Henry Alder to invest for her had been another smart move on her part. Owning a home had been her ultimate goal; in a matter of hours, she would check this off her bucket list. Excitement swelled in her heart, her head, as she thought of all the dreams she'd had, this being the biggest.

Gibbons Hardware was located next to Terri's Diner, which was directly across from John's bait shop. Parking the Jeep, she went inside the store, the odor of paint strong, along with fresh cut lumber, and something else . . . grease, maybe.

"Somethin' I can help you with, Miss?"

The man had to be in his seventies. He walked slowly, his back stooped a bit, though he met her with friendly eyes when he spoke. In faded blue coveralls with a rag hanging out of his pocket, a wrench in the other, he spoke in a hoarse voice. "I ain't see you around these parts."

"No, I'm new to the area. I wanted to get some tools—not sure exactly what I need. I'm clearing out some overgrowth, a couple of small trees, tons of bamboo shoots."

"You wanna rent or buy?"

"I didn't know you could rent tools," she answered.

"Follow me," he said.

Alison followed him to the back of the store. There was a counter with three sides, one with a cash register, the two others piled with an assortment of tools. He took a catalogue, thumbed through a few earmarked pages, then slid it across the counter. "This look like what ya gotta clear out?"

It was a gardening manual. "It's close, but I have more wild vegetation, some bamboo. A couple of shovels, maybe some pruning shears?"

"That'll break your back, but you look like a strong gal. I can give ya a list of tools to make your work easy. Can you operate a riding lawn mower?"

"Never tried, though I'm a fast learner."

"I can rent ya one with a brush grubber. I'm guessing you'll need a weed hacker and a chain saw, too."

Alison nodded. "And you'll instruct me on how to use them?"

"I can't, but I've got someone who can."

Thinking she might be jumping the gun, she told the old man, "I'm going to buy a few tools for now. Basic stuff. If I can't clear out the rest, I'll rent your mower. I need two sets of shears, a couple saws, and shovels. To start," she added.

"You want two of everything?"

"I have help," she said. At least she hoped Renée would help, or at least hang out with her, because Alison enjoyed the young girl's company.

"I'll get your tools, then," he said.

"Thanks."

She waited while the old man gathered the tools in the back. Wondering how much they'd cost, she figured that owning a home, she would need all sorts of tools. And a lawn mower for the large strips of grass flanking the drive. Or she would hire a service.

"Here ya go." The old man placed the tools on the

counter. "I know these are kinda old-looking cause the handles are worn, a bit rusty in places that don't matter. No need wasting your money on new ones—these will get the job done, and you're only out twenty bucks."

"No way, twenty dollars isn't nearly enough," she said as she took some cash from her wallet.

"Now listen here, I've owned this old shop for almost forty years. We buy used tools and sell 'em. No harm in that, don't ya agree? If I told ya what I paid for these"—he nodded at the tools—"you'd think I's ripping you off charging twenty bucks. Now, let's get these bagged up. If you need to rent the mower, you know where to find me. I'm Gib," he said. "Least that's what folks been calling me most a my life." He chuckled.

"Gib, I'll remember that," she said, giving the old man a smile. "I'm Alison."

"Nice to meet ya, Alison. Where ya gonna live? In the Pass or the island?" he asked while he put her tools in a box.

"You mean Matlacha Pass?"

"The one and only. Best fishing spot in Florida."

"No, I'm in the process of buying a place on the beach," she told him, wondering if he knew which house, and if he had a story to tell, too.

"Lucky gal, the beach is quiet most of the time. Purdy sunsets, too," he added.

She was relieved when he didn't have a negative comment. "I haven't watched a sunset, but I plan to this evening. I'm sure it's stunning."

"Ain't nothing like it, Miss Ali," he said. "One of

the best in the entire state a Florida. Colors you ain't never seen before."

She couldn't help but laugh at him calling her "Miss" Ali, though she didn't mind it in his grandfatherly way. And since she was starting a new life, she decided then and there to call herself Ali from now on.

"I'll find out this evening, Gib. I'm good with the secondhand tools. When they wear out, I'll just sell them back to you." Grinning as she said this, she was fairly sure she wouldn't need to sell them back. If all went according to plan with Kimberly on Monday morning, when the time came, she'd purchase more supplies from him.

"You're a smart gal," he said. "Now remember, if ya need to rent the mower, you just give me a call, and I'll have Hal deliver it to your place. He'll show you how to operate the mower and the scrubber too. You got an address, just in case?"

She was almost afraid to give it to him, fearing he would start spouting off horror stories as Lacey had. "The little yellow beach house."

"I know where the place is," said Gib, his expression hardened.

She was prepared for another tall tale, and when he didn't add a story about the old house, she sighed in relief.

"When or if I need that equipment, I'll give you a call," she said. "Do you have a card?"

"Yep," he said, taking a card from a holder in the shape of a wrench and giving it to her. This old guy was the nicest person she'd encountered, other than Renée and Valentina. Lacey and Fish-Eyes from the coffee shop weren't going to ruin this for her. Though Fish-Eyes hadn't really offended her, just wouldn't accept her tip.

"I'll be seeing you soon."

"Hey now, no need to rush out of here so fast," Gib told her, turning around and shouting to someone named Hal. "Hal, I need ya up front." To her, he said, "No need for you to carry this; it's on the heavy side. Hal's a strapping fella. Got more muscle than he does brains."

Hal came out of the back room. He was over six feet tall with muscles that Arnold Schwarzenegger would envy. He sported a shaved head, military style, and a patchy beard. He had dark brown eyes and smiled when he saw her. Ali guessed him to be in his late thirties, maybe early forties.

"Morning, ma'am," Hal said in a friendly voice. "I can lift heavy stuff. One time I lifted Mr. Gib over my head. I don't think he liked it very much. I can drive too, right, Mr. Gib?"

Gib winked at her. "As I said, he's a strappin' fella. Lifts just about anything you could imagine."

"Thank you, Hal. I appreciate your help." She realized he had the mentality of a young child, maybe ten or twelve.

"It's my job, ma'am. But I would carry anything Mr. Gib asked me to. I carry lots of stuff for Mr. Gib all the time."

"I'm sure you would. You look like a strong man," she said.

He grinned at her, then flexed his right bicep. "See my muscle?"

Childlike, but kind. She guessed her first impression of him was accurate. She had more respect for developmentally disabled folks than most.

"I do believe that's the biggest muscle I've ever seen," said Ali, and it was true.

"Really?" Hal asked, his eyes opening wide when she told him.

"Yes, really."

"Hal, Miss Ali has work to do. You take this box to her car, then you come right back, you hear?"

"I will," Hal said.

Ali said, "My Jeep is in the parking lot." She took the keys from her purse. "Follow me. Gib, I can't thank you enough for your help, and the best deal I've had in a very long time."

"It's all right, Miss Ali," he said. "Now go on—you got lots a work to do."

As instructed, Hal brought her box of new old tools to her Jeep. She unlocked the back, showing him where to put the box.

"Okay, Miss Ali."

Unsure whether she should tip him, she reached in her purse and took out a ten-dollar bill, giving it to him.

"What is this for? Mr. Gib pays me," he said, a perplexed expression on his face.

"That is a tip. It's for good work."

"Oh. Then I will tell Mr. Gib to make all of his customers do this too," he said. " 'Cause they don't."

"Okay, Hal. That's between you and Mr. Gib. I'll see you soon." They spoke for a couple minutes more before she left.

Once inside the Jeep, after several assurances that

Hal would do an excellent job if she needed to hire him for anything, she drove to the beach's public parking lot. No way would she park here when she moved into her new home. Whatever she needed to do to clear out all the growth, she was determined to have a private drive like the grander homes. Instead of dragging the box with all the heavy tools, she took just the ones she'd need to get started. They weren't heavy, just awkward.

Her purse and weapon strapped across her chest, she held her big shovel in one hand, the shears in the other. If Renée showed and still wanted to spend her day ripping the roots out of the ground from the more manageable shrubbery, they'd go get the rest of the tools. At least that's what Ali called all this green overgrowth. Later, she would learn to identity the plant names; for now, it didn't matter.

She clipped the overgrowth that reached her shoulders down to a more practical level, just below her knees. Gib had been right about the tools—they were old, not shiny, but they were extremely sharp. Rather than wait for her little helper to show up, she wanted to go deeper into her mini jungle to check for snakes or anything that might frighten Renée—or herself if she were being truthful. She realized the brush grubber would work better than her shears. She'd need heavier equipment to complete the removal of the overgrowth, including all the bamboo shoots. She didn't know how late the hardware store was open, though Gib had given her his card. Fumbling through her purse, she located the business card. *Six o'clock in the morning to six o'clock in the evening.* She'd make another trip to the hardware store, as there would be plenty of time later this afternoon.

For the next hour, Ali clipped away the wild growth, then used the shovel to get to the roots of some of the smaller plant life. She took the shovel and began to dig beneath the trunks of small trees she couldn't identify, figuring it didn't matter, because they were history. Laughing at her thoughts, she directed her shovel's tip deeper into the soil, which was surprisingly hard. With both feet, she stood on either side of the shovel, using her weight to wedge the shovel deeper into the soil. She did this for a few minutes, then decided she might have to rent a backhoe, or some kind of heavy machinery. Not ready to give up on old-fashioned labor just yet, with the tip of the shovel she managed to loosen the soil.

She inspected her work. So far, she'd only dug about a foot deep. She definitely needed more tools, just as Gib had predicted. The old guy knew what he was talking about. Ali was stubborn, so she repositioned the shovel, practically jumping on either side, then felt it dig deeper into the packed soil. It took her several more times doing this until she was roughly two feet down. Surely this was enough to enable her to yank all the wild roots she saw. She repeated the process a few more times, then stopped when she hit something hard. A rock or an old piece of coral; she wasn't sure. On her knees, she bent over, using the blades on the shears as a spade. Like a dog digging for a bone, she reached into the deep hole in the earth. Grabbing hold of the obstruction, she yanked hard, stunned when she realized what she held in her hand.

A bone.

Not the kind a dog gnaws on. No bully stick here. If Ali had learned anything from years of beatings and a few broken bones herself, she knew the bone she held in her hand was human. The femur was easily identifiable, as it was the largest bone in the human body.

Her hands shaking, she removed her cell from her purse and dialed 9-1-1.

Chapter Six

It took over an hour for the police to arrive. Ali returned the bone to the hole as she was instructed to do by the 911 operator. Pretty sure this was not normal procedure when one located a bone at a crime scene, she did what she was told, even though she thought it very strange.

Renée arrived a few minutes after she found the bone. Ali asked her to leave, as she didn't want the young girl to view what she'd dug up.

"It's that bad?" Renée stated when she arrived to help.

She nodded. "Just stay back, okay?" Ali instructed. "Better yet, go see your mom. Like now," she added, raising her voice. "You do not need to see this, go!"

The girl nodded, apparently knowing Ali wouldn't use such forceful words if they weren't necessary.

Ali stood next to the vile discovery when a Fort Charlotte cruiser's siren alerted her to the police's arrival. She watched as the deputy parked on the edge of the road in what should've been the entrance to the drive.

He came toward her, giving her a few seconds to size him up. Average height and build, with the beginnings of a potbelly. Probably too many donuts, she thought as she scanned him.

"You the lady that found the bone?" The sheriff's deputy wore a forest green shirt with a gold star on each sleeve. He also wore mirrored sunglasses and was chewing gum, his thumbs encircling his belt loops on either side. A gold-plated badge read: DEPUTY RICKY SANDERS.

Immediately, she was turned off by him. He reeked of know-it-all-cop, and if one dared to defy him, they would have hell to pay.

"I did." She refused to say more than needed to him. She knew a forensics team would take charge of the scene, and then she would tell them whatever they needed to know. Ali would bet a hundred bucks this guy was one of the cops Valentina spoke of. He seemed the type who would cover up a crime.

"You got any reason to be on this property?" he asked, his Southern accent heavy.

"Yes," she said. And if she had to, she could prove it.

He spat out his gum, the pink wad landing near the hole where she found the bone. "Isn't that contaminating a crime scene?" She'd watched enough television to know this wasn't standard in any way.

He laughed, then kicked at the dirt to cover up his gum. "You need to answer my question. Now, let's try again. You got a reason for being on this property?"

Again, she answered, "Yes."

She could do this all day if that's what it took for this guy to leave her alone.

Pent up with testosterone, his chest puffed out. "You gonna give me trouble over this, then I'll have to bring you down to the station."

"Whatever," she replied, knowing she wasn't breaking the law. At least she didn't think she was. Tomorrow morning, this land would officially belong to her. If need be, she'd call Kimberly and have her draw up the papers today. She'd write a check and be done with the process.

A white van with FORENSICS spelled out in dark green letters on the side parked on the shoulder on Dolphin Drive. The only other way to get to the property was to park in the public lot.

Ali didn't say anything when three people got out of the van. They wore full body suits with hoods, face masks, booties, and gloves. Each carried a large case, and one had a camera dangling around their neck. As soon as they saw the deputy, they converged on her.

"You the lady who called?" said a man with creepy pale blue eyes, and a recent shave, as Ali could smell an overload of too much Old Spice, a cologne one of her foster dads had used.

"Yes, I am."

"Good," said Old Spice. "Are you searching for something on the property?"

Ali thought it very odd they weren't asking more pertinent questions, such as asking for her identification and all. Maybe this entire force was dirty. The two others from forensics took out equipment, placing numbered signs around the hole where the femur lay like a fallen tree branch. The deputy strung crime scene tape along the perimeter of the drive, while another deputy appeared, dressed in the same forest green shirt. He spoke on a cell phone, his head bobbing up and down, as though the person on the receiving end could see him.

"Ma'am?" Old Spice said.

All she'd wanted was a normal life, a new start, to leave the past behind. Finding a human bone and having deputies scattered all across the property wasn't exactly her idea of a fresh start, the quiet life the beach promised. "Yes, I'm trying to clear out all of this." She gestured with both hands, pointing to the vegetation around her. "I'm buying this property. Kimberly Everette showed the house to me. I decided to buy, as it's a good deal. I wanted to start clearing this land so I could actually use the drive."

He nodded, wrote something down in a small notebook. Didn't they use iPads these days? "You have the agent's info?"

She'd stuffed the card in her pocket instead of returning it to her purse that lay next to the shears. "I do." Ali handed him the card. He wrote down the information, then returned the card.

"I expect we're going to be here most of the day, maybe tomorrow. Too early to say. You have a number where we can reach you if we have more questions?"

She gave him her new cell number, almost regretting the purchase.

"The detectives will call you. Most likely they'll want to see you at the station in Fort Charlotte, so you're free to go," he told her.

"That's it?" she asked. "They can't speak to me now while I'm here?"

"Ricky," Old Spice shouted, "over here."

The deputy who had arrived first sauntered over like he had all the time in the world. "Yep. What's up, Sharp?"

"Can we get a full interview of the witness now? She isn't keen on going to headquarters."

He looked at Ali. "You hiding something? You got a reason for not complying with Dr. Bruce?"

Ali could've sworn he'd called him Sharp. "No, I have nothing to hide. I'd like to get this over with, that's all."

He leaned back on his heels with his hands in his pockets. "I bet you do," he smirked. "I'm not so sure you're telling the truth."

Enough was enough. She didn't give a rat's ass if he believed her. "Look, I am simply trying to make this property accessible, as I intend to live here. Do whatever you need to do, but don't accuse me of a crime. Call Diamond Real Estate. Kimberly will vouch for me, and Lacey at Mariner's Cottages. I rented a place from her last night." Even though she had absolutely no reason to be defensive, she felt like she'd taken a hundred steps back into her former life as a kid not looking for trouble, yet somehow it had always seemed to find her.

The doctor closed his notebook. "Rick, don't make this into something it's not." He turned to Alison.

"I'm Dr. Ray Bruce, though people call me Sharp because I am."

No modesty here, Ali thought. "Okay, Dr. Bruce, ask me what you need to know, and I'll be more than happy to answer your questions, though I haven't been formally questioned by whoever is supposed to be in authority here."

"Ricky, can you help Juan?" Dr. Bruce asked, though from the tone of his voice, Ali was sure this wasn't a simple request.

"I suppose. He ain't too bright, if you want my opinion. Probably needs a pro like myself to show him the ropes."

Ali didn't comment, as she was sure Ricky's opinion was completely opposite of the truth, and Dr. Bruce knew this, as well. As soon as the overzealous deputy was out of earshot, Dr. Bruce spoke. "Ricky is not representative of the department." The doctor cleared his throat. "He's related to the sheriff, which he believes entitles him to say or do whatever he pleases. Sorry about him, though I do have a couple of questions. Is there a reason you started digging in this particular area? Possibly you've heard rumors about the place?" His blue eyes never wavered from hers.

"I've only been in the area a couple days, so to answer your first question, I started clearing this area because it's the most obvious place to start if you want to be able to turn off the main road and park a vehicle in what's supposed to be a driveway. I did hear a couple rumors, but I just assumed that's all they were. Rumors. Small towns, there's always some kind of gossip being spread. Does this actually matter? Is there a connection I'm missing here?" She wanted to hear what the doctor had to say.

"Rumors only matter if they're not," he said. "You should probably hire someone to clear this out for you, or rent the equipment, though it will have to wait until we've completed our work."

Ali thought about this. "Wouldn't it make sense to clear the place out now, see if there are more bones?"

"Are you an officer of the law? Perhaps you have a legal background?"

"Neither. Just common sense, Doctor."

"This bone"—he directed his gaze to the hole where the bone still lay—"has not been formally identified. It could be from a large animal. We won't know this until we've done our jobs."

"Look, I'm not a doctor and I don't have any legal experience, but I excelled in science, and I know what a femur bone looks like. This isn't from an animal. I know this, and I'm sure since you're quite sharp, you know this as well. You have no right to insult my intelligence."

"We have your information, Ms. Marshall. If we need to question you further, someone from the department will contact you."

She stood there watching him. While she didn't know the exact procedures this little island followed, she was pretty sure it wasn't the norm for the forensics specialist to control the scene and ask questions. Before she left, she couldn't help but say, "That rumor I heard—you never asked me what it was."

He looked away from her. "As I said, rumors are

only rumors unless they're proven to be true. Then you have an actual fact."

"Then you would know if the rumor I heard is true, right? I take it you've been around here for a while."

"As I explained to you, Ms. Marshall, I only deal in facts."

This so-called professional just became an obnoxious idiot.

"I get that, but just so you know, someone told me a little girl's remains were found on this property. Maybe this bone belongs to her." She picked up the shovel, along with the shears, turning her back on the doctor. She had questions, and she was going to get answers. Ali headed back to the Jeep, tossed the tools in the back, then headed to Fort Charlotte.

She did not like being treated like she was stupid. So much of her life was spent in defense mode, and she wasn't going take anyone's crap. Those days were gone. With this new start, as insane as it was, she'd never felt more alive in her life. Clueless where this bone discovery would lead, she wouldn't alter her plans. Tomorrow, she'd give Kimberly a check; then she would return to her new house and start working to make it a home.

She reached the bridge at Matlacha Pass. A large fishing boat puttered its way through the water, heading into the gulf. As soon as the stern cleared, the old swing bridge closed. Ali waited a couple seconds just to make sure the bridge was secure when the car behind her honked. Startled, she pressed the accelerator too hard and swerved to the right of the bridge. Regaining control of the Jeep, she punched the accelerator down to the floor as soon as she felt her tires hit the pavement. Checking her rearview mirror, she saw the vehicle behind her was the same gray sedan she'd seen earlier in the parking lot at the beach.

She didn't believe in coincidences. Slowing to the thirty-five miles per hour speed limit, she glanced in her mirror again to see if she recognized the person driving the sedan. Unable to identify the driver at this distance, she returned her attention to the road ahead, focusing on why she was making this trip to Fort Charlotte. Without knowing where the sheriff's office was located, she'd have to stop and ask for an address. Or, she reminded herself, she could call with her cell and get the address that way.

In Fort Charlotte, she spotted a Raceway station, stopping since she needed to fill her gas tank, make the call, then head to the sheriff's department. Inside, she paid cash for the gasoline and bought a soda before returning to the Jeep. Tammy had told her she could call information on the cell just like she would on a landline, so she did and asked for the sheriff department's number and address. A couple seconds later, an automated voice gave her the information and also sent her a text. "Nice," she said to herself, glad she'd bought the cell phone, her earlier regrets gone.

She gathered her thoughts, as she wanted to make sure she didn't come off as some psycho when she called. She dialed the number, then hit send. Her call was answered on the second ring.

"Palm County Sheriff's Department; how may I direct your call?" said a friendly voice.

"I need to speak to someone about a body that was

found," she said. "A long time ago," she added, knowing the operator might assume she was reporting a new body.

"Do you have the victim's name?"

Surprised by the question, she said she did not.

"You'll have to visit the clerk's office when they're open, as I don't have another way to search their records. Sorry," the operator said.

"Palmetto Island. A young girl's remains were found there. I think it's been a few years."

The operator's response wasn't as immediate as before. "Yes, I seem to recall this. Can you hold for a moment?"

"Yes," Ali said, thankful the woman was willing to find the information for her.

A few minutes passed. Ali was starting to think she'd somehow disconnected the call when the operator returned. "Ma'am, are you a member of the victim's family?"

"No."

"Then I can't give you this information on the phone. You'll need to go down to the clerk's office on Monday, as I said. They'll direct you on what steps you need to take."

"Thanks, but can I ask why? Why did you want to know if I was a family member?"

She heard the operator sigh. "I shouldn't tell you this, but this particular case, no one has claimed . . . the victim's remains."

It took a few seconds for Ali to absorb her words. "I see," she finally said, though she didn't. "I appreciate your help." She hit the end button before the operator became suspicious or asked her why she wanted to know or exactly how she was connected to something that Ali, only a short while ago, thought was nothing but a rumor. What she wanted to know now was did "the rumor" have a name?

Chapter Seven

Ali sat in the parking lot for a few minutes before heading back to Palmetto Island. Lacey hadn't been spreading rumors after all. Wishing she'd asked the operator for her name, Ali would make a trip to the clerk's office as soon as she got settled.

The drive back to the island was uneventful. No gray sedans following her. The island was small—seeing the car at the beach, then behind her while waiting for the bridge to close, was nothing more than unwarranted paranoia. Having spent most of her life looking over her shoulder, she knew it would take time before she completely rid herself of the habit.

As she approached Matlacha Pass, a few fishermen were on the bridge, their buckets, rods and reels with red-and-white bobbers on the tips just waiting to be cast into the deep waters below. Maybe she'd try fishing. She had no clue how to get started, but if and when the time came, she would prepare herself by reading up on the subject. She was self-taught in many things—why not add fishing to the list?

Thankful the wooden swing bridge was closed, she punched the gas, going too fast, but she didn't care. She didn't like driving across the bridge, as it didn't feel secure. Given her luck, it would collapse when she drove across the antiquated structure. Admittedly, there was an old charm about it, but she'd much rather have her wheels on solid ground.

Ali wanted to return to the beach but decided against it, as she did not want to encounter Dr. Bruce or Deputy Sanders. She pulled in front of her rented cottage, heading inside and wishing she'd asked Renée for her cell number. Then she remembered the Souvenir Shop would have a phone. She again called directory assistance for the number. A follow-up text let her know the address, too. Modern marvels—how had she managed to go without them for so long?

Dialing the number to the store, she realized it was Sunday and was unsure if they were open.

Valentina picked up. "Hello," she said in a cheery voice, "Souvenir Shop."

"This is Alison—Ali. I hope I'm not bothering you. I wasn't sure if you were open," she said, feeling foolish all of a sudden. There was no reason for her to call, and if she asked for Renée's number, her mother would think her immature.

"We're always open on weekends, even in the summer," Valentina said. "I hear the police are at the beach house. Are you still planning on purchasing the place?"

"I think it's too good an offer to pass up, so yes, I'm meeting the sales agent in the morning to complete the paperwork. Is there some history I should know about the house? When I told Renée I might buy the place, she clammed up." She didn't tell her what Lacey said, though Ali felt sure Valentina already knew this.

"Just about everyone here on the island knows about the little girl's remains they discovered. It's been a few years. I honestly haven't thought about it in a while. No one ever came forward when they were found. Poor girl was left in the morgue."

Knowing it might be out of line, but doing it anyway, Ali asked, "When I mentioned I was going to buy the place, you didn't think to tell me?" She doubted Valentina would outright lie to her, but wouldn't someone with her gift share their knowledge of this tragedy?

"Actually, I did. I didn't want to scare you off. As I told you, it's a great deal, and I saw no reason to share the story, knowing you'd find out on your own."

Ali thought that made sense . . . but still. "How did they know the bones belonged to a young girl?"

"If memory serves me correctly, they found a little dress, shoes, and a bracelet. The bones were analyzed in Tampa, and the DNA was sent to a missing children's website where they keep records of unsolved cases. No one has claimed her remains, so it's still a mystery. No one reported a missing child," Valentina explained. "At the time, Renée was young, so I tried to keep her away from the news. I didn't want her to be afraid."

"I can understand that, though I'd be more worried since they haven't found the person or persons who did this. It's odd that I dug up that bone. Don't you agree?"

"It's very odd," Valentina agreed. "Not the best impression of our little slice of paradise. After a while, you just forget the bad things, and do your best to live in the moment."

"I understand." Ali got the feeling Valentina did not want to discuss what happened. She'd forget about it, too. For now. But Ali had a hard time letting sleeping dogs lie. Wanting to ask more questions about the little girl, she held back. She would search the local records, but another time. Beyond curious, she didn't want anyone, especially Valentina, to know of her intense interest in the girl's remains, so she changed the subject. "I wanted to thank Renée for offering to help clear out the drive this morning. And apologize, as I was a bit harsh when I told her to leave."

"I'm glad you did, and she is, too. I wouldn't want her to see what you found, so thanks."

Not the response she expected, but it rang true. No mother in her right mind wants her child to see the horrors of the world. They would soon enough.

"You're welcome," Ali said. "Does she know what was found?" She had to ask.

"Around here, news like this spreads quickly, so yes, she does, but I'm not allowing her near the beach until the authorities clear out."

"Do you have an idea how long they'll be there?" Ali wanted them out now but knew that wasn't being realistic.

"I wish I did," Valentina told her. "They aren't the brightest bunch, other than Dr. Bruce, who is so full of himself it's hard to imagine him focusing on his job. He spends most of his time checking himself out in a mirror."

Ali wondered if Valentina and Dr. Bruce had been

involved at some point. Not her business; if Valentina wanted her to know, she would tell her. "Deputy Sanders is an ass. I found that out real quick. He practically accused me of a crime."

"I'm sorry. He gives all law enforcement a bad name. His uncle is the sheriff in Palm County, and honestly, that's the only reason he has his job. No one on the island likes him, at least that's been my impression. As I told you, most of them are crooked in one way or another."

"I think Sanders is for sure, and the doctor, he is a strange one," she said, not wanting to give Valentina the idea she liked to gossip.

"Listen, I was about to run to the house to make lunch for myself and Renée. Why don't you join us?"

Alison had never been invited to anyone's home for lunch. New life, new choices, she reminded herself. "Sure, that would be great. Can I bring anything?"

"Just yourself. Renée said she told you where we live. We'll be neighbors once you're settled in."

"Yes, she pointed out your place when we were at the beach. What time should I arrive?" She sounded stupid—at least she thought so, as she truly wasn't sure of the island's etiquette or Valentina's.

"Come on over as soon as you can. I just need to close up, then I'll meet you at the house."

"I'm on my way," she said. Before leaving, she changed into a pair of khaki shorts and a pale blue tank top. Brushing her hair, she wore it down, but added a hair tie to her wrist, a habit she'd had since living in Florida. She switched her sneakers for her second-hand Birkenstocks. She was in dire need of a new pair of sneakers, but for now, they'd have to wait. Ali also needed to call Henry, something she'd been putting off. He would need her authorization in order to release funds for the house. She'd memorized his number years ago. Using her new cell, she dialed his number.

"Henry Adler," he said, his usual brisk greeting.

"Hey, Henry, it's me."

"Well, I'll be damned! The long-lost investor. What's up with you, kid? I was starting to worry."

Ali usually went weeks without speaking to Henry, so why should he be worried?

"I'm buying a house on the beach. I just wanted to make sure you know it's me, and not some scammer. I'm paying cash, rather than a check from the investment account. Just wanted to give you a heads-up."

"Appreciate it, kid. You found a deal?"

He knew her well—knew she wouldn't let go of one red cent foolishly.

"A hundred grand for a house on the beach on Palmetto Island," she told him, unable to keep the excitement from her voice.

"Darn, you hit the jackpot, and your dream. I knew you'd do it," Henry said encouragingly.

"Not without you, Henry. You're the financial wizard."

"Yeah, I guess I know a thing or two," he teased. "I'll make sure there are no bumps on the road and make this easy for you."

She didn't see how it could get any easier. She would write a check, and she'd have a home of her own. She knew purchasing a home was more than just writing a check, but Henry liked to baby her, and she let him. He was kind, and in his own way, he'd always looked out for her. "I appreciate it."

"It's what I do, kid."

She finished her call, then took off for the beach. She was excited at the prospect of seeing the inside of a fancy beach house, plus having lunch with her new friends. If it weren't for that damn bone she'd dug up, she would say today was her best day in a very, very long time.

As she drove past Dolphin Drive, she spied several official vehicles still parked on the side of the road. She maneuvered the Jeep down the path, because it wasn't what she would call a road, then parked next to a vehicle she hadn't seen before. She was certain it had to be someone associated with the investigation. Though she didn't have a clear view of her future cottage, she could hear voices—someone shouting orders, the clank of metal, the sound of an engine revving. Unsure if they'd brought in the heavy equipment as she'd suggested, she crossed her fingers that they would be finished today. She wanted them off the property before she formally moved in. For now, she tried to focus on the moment, on meeting her new friends. In time, she'd have to deal with her discovery, but for a couple hours, she wanted to be normal. A woman on a lunch date with friends.

Not a hundred percent sure how to get to the large house, she opted for the beach, remembering where Renée practiced her yoga. Once there, she backtracked through a narrow area, a large fence on either side, until she could see the house Renée had pointed out.

"Hey," Renée shouted from a balcony. "Up here."

Alison went up three flights of stairs before reaching the top deck. "Wow," was all she could say. The view from the deck was out of this world.

"It's an awesome view, right?" Renée stated. "I'm used to it, but it's so cool to see it through another set of eyes, like now."

Ali laughed. She knew exactly what she meant. "It's beautiful." Simple words, but fitting. "I bet the sunsets are . . . mind-boggling." She laughed at herself, but felt her description was adequate.

"Spot-on! Mom and I have dinner out here sometimes so we can watch the sunset. It's pretty amazeballs," Renée told her. "Come in. Mom's still making lunch, so I'll show you around."

When Alison stepped inside, surprise didn't describe what she saw. The kitchen was bright white with marble counters, stainless appliances as large as those in a restaurant, a dining table made from birchwood, with aqua-colored cushions in the chairs. She counted sixteen chairs. Damn. There was a giant living area, with white plush sofas and matching chairs facing the gulf. A large flat-screen television hovered above a gorgeous fireplace.

"It's a lot to take in," Valentina called out as she prepared lunch in the kitchen.

Alison hadn't noticed her when she first entered their house. "I've never seen anything like this," she said, and it was the truth.

"Let Renée finish giving you the full tour, then we'll have lunch on the deck."

She nodded and followed Renée upstairs, the winding staircase leading to a large landing that overlooked the downstairs. "The bedrooms are all up here, all with a view of the beach."

Renée showed Ali her bedroom, that of a typical teenager, other than the fact she had an awesome view of the beach, a bathroom fit for a queen, and closets filled with more clothes than Ali had ever seen in one closet. "It's a lot if you're not used to it."

Ali thought this an understatement, but just nodded.

She saw the other bedrooms, each grander than she expected. They were all white, with shades of aqua blue throughout. Alison imagined this place could easily cost a few million bucks, though she'd never be so crude as to ask. Even unsophisticated folks like her had some class.

"This is the most gorgeous place I've ever seen," Alison told Renée as they headed back downstairs.

Valentina carried a large aqua dish to the table on the deck. "I hope you like crab salad," she said. "I can make you something else if not. Rummy—he owns the seafood house right before the Pass—brought these in yesterday, and I like them when they're fresh."

Crab was one of Ali's favorites. Could this day get any more perfect? she thought. "I love crab, shrimp, oysters. All seafood, it's the best."

"Good, then come on out, and let's eat."

There were large chunks of shrimp with big bites of chilled blue crab piled high on a bed of butter lettuce drizzled with a delicious citrus dressing, the lettuce so tender one barely had to chew. Fresh tomatoes and cucumbers topped with flakes of freshly grated parmesan and white pepper. Ali closed her eyes, relishing every single bite. The crab was sweet, the shrimp tender.

When she opened her eyes, Valentina and Renée were smiling.

"Sorry, but this is the best crab salad I've ever eaten. In my entire life," she added for extra emphasis. "Thank you for inviting me."

She wanted to tell Valentina how impressed she was with her home, the view, the table settings, which were thick white bowls with tiny aqua blue seahorses etched around the rim. She was almost afraid to use the aqua blue cloth napkins, encircled with white rings and the same seahorse design. A basket of warm garlic rolls was the icing on the cake.

"I made these last week, had a few in the freezer, so I figured all of us girls needed a few carbs with our salad." Valentina winked at Renée.

"Mom, don't lie to Ali—you and I both eat carbs all the time. Almost every meal."

"We do, but it sounds nice to pretend we don't," Valentina told her daughter.

"Whatever you two are eating, it certainly looks good. On both of you. If I didn't know better, I would guess you were sisters," Ali said.

"Thanks, but I'm just the mom. With an amazing daughter," Valentina stated, giving Renée a smile.

For the next few minutes, no one spoke while they consumed the fresh crab salad, washing it down with tall glasses of sweet tea with sprigs of mint and lemon slices.

Alison wondered if Valentina's dinners could top lunch. Part of her couldn't wait to find out, and another part of her felt kind of cheesy for even having the thought. If they turned out to be good friends, she was sure she would be invited for another meal, but in due time. This new life was wild, all over the place in so many ways. Ways she never expected. Some were bad; obviously, digging up that bone being the worst. Then there was that weirdo John, but meeting Renée and Valentina made up for all the negativity she'd encountered. So far.

"She is amazing," Ali agreed. "Both of you are. I can't tell you how kind it was of you to do all this." She waved her hand across the table. "It's the fanciest lunch I've had."

Valentina smiled. "Thanks, but it's a simple meal. I did use the good dishes though, just so you know we don't always set the table this way, except on special occasions. I thought a new friend and neighbor was a special occasion."

"Yeah, Ali, next time you'll get paper plates and leftover napkins saved from McDonald's."

She couldn't help but laugh. "Then I'll make sure not to toss any extra napkins from McDonald's."

"Waste not, want not," Valentina said.

"Absolutely," Alison agreed, as she'd spent most of her adult life scrimping and saving. When she had enough to start investing, she found Henry.

"Mom, please don't start with your sayings." Renée rolled her eyes, though she had a grin as wide as the strip of beach below them on her pretty young face. "She does this to me all the time. 'A dime a dozen,' 'biting off more than you can chew,' plus a zillion others."

"I guess you're not up for a *piece of cake,*" Valentina said, using another idiom.

"Mom, you know I'll bite off more than I can chew!"

Ali laughed at them. They were unlike any mother

and daughter she'd seen. Love radiated from both. Ali could see this in their eyes, their actions. Never having experienced such a relationship, she was in awe of this mother-daughter duo.

"It just so happens I have a scrumptious key lime pie from Terri's," Valentina said to Renée and Ali.

"Mom! You know that's my favorite. I told you I was off dessert for the rest of the summer. I don't want to look like a whale when I go back to school."

Ali and Valentina laughed.

"I bet you could eat a pie every day, and you'd look just as perfect as you do now," Ali offered, and believed it to be true. The young girl was totally unaware of how stunning she'd appeared when Ali first saw her on the beach, with her long, shapely legs, a tiny waist, and sandy blonde hair that most girls would envy. Ali couldn't imagine Renée having any worries about her looks. Though she knew girls could be so cruel to one another, and there was always a chance of young girls suffering from unrealistic versions of how much they should weigh. She remembered a girl from eighth grade who'd suffered from anorexia. She'd been so thin, malnourished to the point where she'd had to leave school. Ali wondered whatever happened to the girl, as she'd never returned to school. She hoped Renée didn't have a negative body image that got out of control.

"I know I'm not overweight, it's just a thing Mom and I fuss over sometimes. She knows I'll probably eat half of the pie, too." Renée grinned.

"Now that's settled, Alison—Ali—would you like a slice of pie? Maybe a cup of coffee or tea?"

"I would love a slice of pie, and coffee, but you have to allow me to help out," she said, following Valentina to the kitchen with her plate and flatware.

"Thanks, but another time. Today you're a guest, tomorrow you're a neighbor and friend. Enjoy this while it lasts," she teased.

"Yep, first time over, Mom treats guests like royalty. After that, you're part of the family, then you have to help out," Renée said.

"Okay," Ali said as she cleared the rest of the dishes from the table, bringing them inside. Renée trailed behind her with her own plate.

"Really, Mom likes to play hostess sometimes. I think selling souvenirs and telling fortunes gets boring. Right, Mom?" Renée asked while rinsing her plate, then adding it to the dishwasher.

"Yes, I suppose so, but I enjoy it most of the time. Now, get the dessert plates, and I'll bring the pie."

"Yes ma'am!" Renée saluted her mother.

"Teenagers," she said. "Can't live with them, can't live without them."

"Like men," Ali said, then realized she probably shouldn't have said that.

"Exactly," Valentina agreed. "Most of them are asses. If not, they're either gay or married." She took the pie from the refrigerator, and Ali followed her out to the deck.

"Yes, most of them are jerks. Maybe there a few good ones out there, but who has the time to search? I've been on a couple of dates that turned into nightmares, but I'll save that story for another time." Ali didn't want to discuss her horrid dates in front of Renée.

"Come on, I love dating disasters," Renée encouraged her. "Right, Mom?"

Valentina sighed. "Yes, you've watched too many episodes of that *Bachelor* show. Real life isn't quite the same. Besides, Alison's personal business is none of ours."

Valentina sliced the pie, each portion enough for two. She placed the matching dessert plate in front of Ali. "This looks delicious. I can't remember the last time I had pie." She did remember wishing for pie when she was a little girl. More than once, the Sterling family would have dessert in front of her and her foster brothers, but never offered them any. At the time, she thought pies and cakes were only for grown-ups. After her episode with the family tree assignment, she'd realized Craig and Martha Sterling were not an example of normal parents.

"Ali, are you okay?" Valentina asked, her voice laced with concern.

"I'm sorry, I was lost in my thoughts," she explained, forcing the images of the Sterlings from her brain.

"So, what were they?" Renée asked as she dug into her pie.

"Renée! Stop being so nosy."

"It's okay. Honestly, I was thinking about my foster parents."

"Oh wow, were they mean?" Renée asked, not caring that her mother had just scolded her for asking too many personal questions.

Ali cleared her throat. "That is a loaded question." Unsure how or if she should answer, she explained, "Some were, and others had financial motives."

"Well, crap, how many foster parents do you have?"

"Renée, that's enough! Ali's past is none of our business. Your nosiness is going to get you in trouble soon," Valentina admonished.

"It's fine, really. I don't mind telling my story," she said, knowing she wasn't being completely honest.

"So what happened? Did they like lock you in the basement, or did they try to starve you?"

Ali couldn't help but laugh. "No, I never starved, though I did stay in a basement once when I was being punished. Caring for children, whether they're your own flesh and blood or a foster child, is the ultimate responsibility. Folks who start out with good intentions often find kids from broken homes, or those who've had dealings with law enforcement, are too much for them to handle, yet they're afraid to admit this. To themselves and those in authority who place the children in their care, it puts them in a bad light, so they continue to take in kids who find themselves in situations where the parent can't care for them. They collect money from a government agency, and often the kids suffer because the foster parents don't want to give up the money."

"Mom, do we know any foster families?"

Valentina shook her head. "None that I know of."

"So, how did you end up, you know . . . living?"

Alison said, "I was fine, really. I had a few issues with some of my foster parents, but in the end, it worked out for me. It was a long time ago. I'm content with my life now." This was a total bullshit story, but sometimes revealing the truth, at least *her* truth, scared those who hadn't lived as she'd had to. There was no point in upsetting her new friends. Maybe in time, if they really got to know each other, she would tell them more about her past, though she would leave out the part that had sent her running when she graduated from high school. That alone would be enough to lose any hope of remaining friends with them. Again, the past is prologue. Maybe that idiom—if it even *was* an idiom— popped into her head when she needed to be reminded of what she had to lose if that particular part of her life were to be uncovered.

"I, for one, am glad I saw you on the beach. We don't have any neighbors that stay here year-round, except for . . . John."

Something about the way Renée said his name struck Ali as off.

"Is he that bad?" Ali asked, her thoughts returning to the bone she'd dug up earlier.

"I don't like to talk about him," Valentina said. "I get so pissed off, but you should know, it's best to stay away from him. His family continues to pay those in power, hoping people will forget all that he's been accused of, but most of the islanders know better."

Ali wanted to ask Valentina what she thought about the bone she'd discovered. Did she believe John had any connection to it, and possibly the other bones that were discovered years ago?

"As I said, I had a brief encounter with him at the mango festival. He didn't impress me," Ali told Valentina. "His kind are usually bad news." That was putting it mildly.

"Mom, tell her all the crap he's accused of," Renée said, her voice pumped up a level. "She should know, just in case."

"I know he's been accused of messing around with little girls." Just saying the words made Alison sick. How did a man like this have the audacity to ruin the life of an innocent child?

"This isn't a conversation to have with new friends," Valentina told Renée, then spoke to Alison. "Another time, maybe, but be careful around him. He's dangerous. Has been for as long as I can remember."

"You've known him a long time?" Ali had to ask.

Valentina picked at the graham cracker crust left on her plate. "Since we were kids. Even then, his behavior was off the charts. His parents sent him to a private Catholic high school in town, hoping the strict environment would have a positive effect on him. I think he's just a bad seed. He hangs around the bait shop owned by his family, acts like he's just another beach bum, but when you're around him for a while, he'll show his true colors."

Alison knew men like him were evil. She would do her best to avoid him, but if he initiated trouble of any kind, she wouldn't hesitate to use her weapon to intimidate him. Could she actually shoot him if it came down to that? She never wanted to be in that position.

"I saw a bit of his true colors, and that was enough for me. Not my kind of guy," Ali added.

"Just beware if you see him lurking around. He's been known to peep into windows more than once," Valentina told her.

"Sounds like he's covered all the basics of a predator," Ali said. "I can handle men like him if I have to."

She didn't want Valentina or Renée to think she was unable to defend herself if need be, though she wouldn't tell them she carried a gun. Many people were frightened by guns, and some rightfully so. She'd been trained by an ex-military captain. While in Tampa, she would visit the shooting range as often as she could to keep the skills she'd mastered up to par. After years of living on her own in places that weren't fit for a rat, as soon as she'd been able to afford lessons, she'd jumped at the chance.

"He's that and more," Valentina said, then stood. "I could sit here all day, but I need to get back to the store. I've a reading scheduled later this afternoon."

"So, Ali, are you gonna go to your new house? I could come and help clean or paint or whatever."

"Renée, that's enough," her mother ordered in a no-nonsense tone. "Alison has enough on her plate."

Unsure why Valentina's mood had changed toward her daughter, Ali wondered again if Valentina or Renée had personal experience with John.

"I can't thank you enough for the best lunch I've ever had, and the tour of your home. Top of the line," she said. "I'll see you both as soon as I get settled in the cottage. I'll have you both over for dinner, too." She was a decent enough cook but wasn't sure she could match Valentina's skill.

"I'll look forward to it," Valentina told her. "Really, it's going be so refreshing having you as our neighbor."

"Thanks. I'll show myself out." She returned the way she came, via the beach. As soon as she returned to her Jeep, she drove down Dolphin Drive to see if the sheriff and his gang were finished. Only one deputy car remained; the white forensics van was gone. She took this as a good sign.

Once back in her rented cottage, Ali paced, trying to decide if she should call Kimberly to see if she had the paperwork ready. The sooner she had possession of her property, the sooner she'd be able to relax. It was such a life-changing decision, one she felt good about, though she couldn't help those creeping doubts that always ruled over any decision she made.

Wishing she had someone to talk to about her choice, during times like these, she longed for a mother, a sibling, a family member that knew her, and one she could trust. Many times she thought about trying to find her birth parents, knew there were many ways to do this, but something always held her back. She feared her mother's lack of love, given that she'd been placed in foster care the day she was born. At least that's what the Sterlings led her to believe. Maybe her mother was just a kid like she'd been, with no means to care for a child. If that was the case, then she probably did what she thought was best for her.

What about her father? Men should be just as responsible as women when a child was involved. Over the years, she'd had a couple of decent foster dads and a few bad eggs, too. One that beat the daylights out of her and another who did things to her that she didn't want to think about.

And then there was *him*. She would not allow herself to even think of his name. What he tried to do. What he did. Often she was reminded that, had she not bolted when she did, the walls she saw now would only be in her dreams.

"Enough," she said out loud. Letting her thoughts lead her down this road always caused her to feel shame, anger, and regret.

She took her luggage from the closet and found a nightshirt, deciding she'd spend the evening enjoying the comfort of the bed while she indulged in watching a movie. Tomorrow would be here soon enough. Tomorrow, she would officially become a homeowner.

Chapter Eight

Alison was showered and dressed before six. She loaded her things in the Jeep, left the key to the cottage in the room as instructed, then headed over to The Daily Grind, where she would hang out until her appointment with Kimberly.

As it was Monday morning, the place was booming with customers. All the tables were full, the line long, but she had nothing better to do, so she waited her turn. When she saw Fish-Eyes had a large cup of black coffee ready for her as soon as it was her turn to order, she smiled. "Thanks for remembering."

"A pretty girl that drinks black coffee is easy to remember."

Was this old dude another pervert? If so, she'd find a new coffee shop. As she reached into her purse for some cash, Fish-Eyes stopped her.

"On the house," he said.

"Why?" Was he trying to hit on her?

"Sign says so." He pointed to the whiteboard behind

him, where it read: *Thirty-first customer on Monday gets free coffee.*

Relieved, she asked, "Why such an odd number?"

"We draw a number out of a hat on Mondays, though it never goes past fifty."

"Then I guess today is my lucky day. Thanks," she said. Spying an empty table, she hurried to sit down before someone else saw it. She would read the paper, killing time before she had to meet Kimberly.

The Matlacha Weekly was a respectable publication. Surprised the place even had a newspaper, Ali flipped through the pages. She read the tides for the upcoming week, saw John's bait store had a sale on minnows. How the heck did one put a price on a minnow when anyone could get them for free if they took the time? It would take a while for her to get used to island life. All she wanted was a peaceful existence. In time, she would find a job. She'd let Henry work his magic on her finances, but she wasn't lazy. Once she got the cottage in shipshape, she couldn't see herself spending all of her free time doing nothing. She saw the want ads, and that Terri's Diner was hiring. Was this the same diner that Valentina got the pie from? If so, maybe she'd apply for the job if it was still available when she was settled in. She wasn't going to make any commitments until she was satisfied with the repairs she would need to make on the cottage.

Suddenly, the door flew open, a man pushing it so hard it slammed against the wall. Shocked when she saw Tank, the taxi driver, Ali quickly shoved the paper as close to her face as she could without looking like a character in a spy movie.

Was it her imagination, or had the buzz of conversations paused for a couple seconds when Tank entered? She continued to hold the paper as close to her face as possible without garnering attention. The last person she wanted to deal with was another idiotic male, pumped up with too much testosterone, though in Tank's case, it was in name only. Alison doubted the man weighed more than a hundred pounds. Drugs, she guessed, as weight loss was an indicator. Bad teeth, sores; it all made her sick. In Tampa, she'd seen more than her share of addicts. Her heart went out to them. Though she didn't truly understand addiction, she knew it had to be horrendous for it to dominate one's life to the point that the addict's only goal was finding more of whatever drug they were hooked on. She'd been offered a variety of drugs when she lived on the streets. At the time, food and shelter had been her main priorities. Having a will of iron, Ali had refused to go down that path of destruction.

"I ain't got all day!" Tank the taxi driver yelled at Fish-Eyes. "Hurry up."

All eyes focused on Tank, some folks shaking their heads and some deciding it was time to leave. Ali stayed in her seat, waiting to see what he would do next.

Fish-Eyes gave Tank a to-go cup of coffee. Tank tossed a few coins on the counter, then took the lid off the cup. "Put some more cream in here. Damn. You cain't get nothing right these days, old man."

The owner added more cream, returning the cup to the counter. Tank took his coffee, then turned his attention to the dining area. Ali kept her head down, wishing for a pair of sunglasses, a cap, anything to serve as a disguise, though in this small space, it would only draw more attention to her.

She literally felt his gaze on her but refused to acknowledge him. Ali didn't need to look up in order to see him inching his way to her table. Her heart rate accelerated, knowing he'd recognized her. She'd hung her purse over the back of her chair, feeling secure knowing her weapon was within reach should she need to use it.

Tank pulled out the chair across from her and sat down. "Thought you'd skipped town," he said before slurping his coffee.

"Leave me alone," she said. She knew from his reaction from when she'd bumped into him at Mel's Diner that it would give him immense pleasure if she were to start an argument.

"I ain't botherin' you, girl," he said.

She smelled cigarette smoke and sweat. "Actually, you are." Her blue eyes fixated on his. "So leave. Now."

"Do as the lady says," came a male voice from behind her.

"Who the hell are you, tellin' me what I cain and cain't do?" Tank asked the man.

"I'm asking you to leave the lady alone."

Tank laughed, sending spit flying across the small table to land on Ali's chin.

"Get out of here—you're sickening." She gritted her teeth, stood, and reached for her purse. With her hand inside her purse, she gripped the gun's handle, her index finger on the trigger. She could shoot through her purse if she had to.

"You're a bitch, ya know that?" Tank stood up, shoving the chair so hard it tipped over. "You ain't heard the last from me!" He grabbed his cup, gave her an evil grin, then used his thumb and index finger to point at her, the same movement John used when he'd threatened her. "Be careful." Laughing, he left the coffee shop, slamming the door behind him.

Humiliated, Ali prepared to leave, but then thought better of it and waited. She sat down again, as she sure as hell didn't want another confrontation with that idiot in the parking lot.

"Ma'am, are you all right?" asked the man who'd come to her defense.

She would be as soon as she left but didn't say it. "Yes, I'm fine. Thank you for . . . you know," she added, not wanting to say, "thank you for defending me," as it made her feel weak and fearful.

"No problem, I see guys like him all the time."

Alison wanted to ask where he saw these types of men but didn't. "Well, thanks. I have to go," she said, standing and then walking as fast as she could to the exit.

As soon as she was outside, she took out her keys and then unlocked the door to the Jeep. Once she was inside, she was surprised when she saw how badly her hands were shaking. The man from the coffee shop tapped on her window, startling her enough to cause her to drop her keys on the floorboard. Feeling around for her keys, she found them, somehow managing to fit the key in the ignition, even though her hands trembled.

There was another knock on the window. She turned the key but didn't crank the engine. She hit the automatic button, lowering her window a few inches but not enough for a man's hand to reach inside and grab her.

"I don't mean to frighten you. I'm Kit Moore. I don't live around here—just doing some fishing. Did I overstep my boundaries? That guy seemed shady."

No kidding, Alison thought. She hit the control for the window, opening it a few more inches. "I don't know him either, so thanks again. Good luck fishing, *Kit*," she said, emphasizing his odd name. He didn't look like a Kit. Then she hit the switch to close her window. As soon as she cranked the engine over, she hit the gas pedal so hard, her tires squealed on the pavement. She didn't care. No more trips to this coffee shop, she thought as she pulled onto Pine Tree Road. Maybe her decision to make Palmetto Island her forever home was a bad one. She'd had so many negative encounters here in such a short span of time. If she stayed, would this continue, or would she simply blend in with the rest of this hodgepodge community? It seemed the men in Matlacha Pass were rough, dim-witted rednecks. Ali guessed that most of them were shrimpers, maybe fishermen. A tough job only the bravest—or maybe the stupidest—would take on. She feared this kind of man, having experience with their type. Not romantic, but more along the lines of barbaric.

No longer confident with her decision as she headed

toward Diamond Realty, she thought it wasn't too late to change her mind. No contracts were signed, no money exchanged. Because it was the decent thing to do, she glanced at the business card Kimberly gave her. No need for an explanation; she'd just decided this place was bad news. Her original decision to head south to Key West was reignited. To back out or not? Damn, the beach house was a steal; she wouldn't find another place on the beach, especially in Key West, for the price.

"No!" she shouted, then banged her fist on the dashboard, remembering what sent her running all those years ago. "I will not allow another man to ruin my life!" Shaking, yet determined to avoid a continual repeat of her past, she figured: screw it. She wanted the beach house, she had cash, and she also had her weapon.

Alison Marshall was not going to give up her dream for some idiotic, rotten, smelly taxi-driving druggie. Too many times she'd given in; too many times she'd been too frightened to stand up for herself. She was no longer that seventeen-year-old girl who'd struggled her entire life in the hopes of having a home of her own, a life, and maybe, one day she'd meet a nice fellow and have a family. Were her dreams over the top? No, she thought. They were simply what every decent human being desired. It wasn't as though she expected life to run smoothly all of the time. Thoughts and hopes like these weren't unreasonable.

Back and forth, she debated with herself. When she glanced at the clock on the dash, she realized her appointment with Kimberly was in thirty minutes.

Men like Tank and John were a dime a dozen. Beach houses were hundreds of thousands, even millions, of dollars. She could handle men like those two idiots. She'd done it before.

Alison would regret having an opportunity like this and passing it up it for the rest of her life. She directed the Jeep to Diamond Realty, where she would seal the deal on her dream.

Chapter Nine

Three hours later, Ali had purchased her first home. The necessary paperwork was completed, minus the deed that would be filed with the county clerk. Ali's eyes filled with tears when Kimberly gave her a bill of sale for the cottage. Having no idea what to expect, she'd found the process was simple, especially when you had the financial means to simply write a check.

Even if the sheriff's department was still searching her property, Ali assumed she would still be able to go inside the cottage. She would need all sorts of furnishings. Excited at the prospect of decorating her place any way she pleased, she had a dozen ideas, but nothing set in stone.

She drove down Pine Tree Road, taking a right and then a left on Loblolly Way, which was now her new address. Odd, she thought, since the overgrown drive faced Dolphin Drive, where she saw a mailbox that'd seen better days. But Kimberly had informed her this was not the case, and that the house was technically on Loblolly Way. Alison didn't care one way or another. She had a beach house, and right now she wasn't going to allow anyone or anything to diminish the pride and accomplishment she was feeling.

Grateful the bridge was open so she didn't have to wait, she headed to her new home. There was hardly any traffic. Ali figured most people on the island were working, and tourists were minimal this time of year, so there was no one on the bridge fishing like when she'd arrived. Once she made the turn, she parked in the public lot, knowing she wouldn't have to do this much longer. She would call Gib, maybe ask him to show her how to use the equipment, or maybe she'd hire Hal to help out—though Ali had to remind herself not to spend her money needlessly. She would do as much of the work herself as she could in order to keep her expenses as low as possible.

She locked the paperwork in the glove compartment of the Jeep, then made the short walk to her new home. She was so excited that chills went up and down her spine. She wondered if the Beamers, or the Sterlings, or the other foster family whose name she couldn't even remember, had ever thought she would accomplish anything in her life, much less pay cash for her very first home. It didn't matter, she thought as she walked down the path to her house. Most likely, she was nothing but a distant memory to them, if even that, and this was fine with her.

With shaking hands, Ali used the code Kimberly had given her to unlock the key box so she could use the house keys. Kimberly had said she would pick up the key box later that evening. Pushing the door aside, Ali wished for a photo to document this milestone, but the cell she'd purchased didn't have a camera. She closed her eyes and took a deep breath, relishing the scent of the golden knotty pine, the salty air, even the stale odor of whatever had been in the freezer. This was all hers, and no one could ever force her to leave her home again.

Ali closed the door behind her, locking it, even though she felt pretty confident no one would barge in and attack her. Then she remembered the bones. How could she forget what she'd found yesterday? Who did the bones belong to? Ali would do her best to find out, but not now.

Focusing on the present, she walked through the rooms again, imagining how she would decorate them. She went to the kitchen and opened the refrigerator, the smell forcing her to take a step back. It occurred to her she hadn't bothered to have the power turned on.

"Crud," she said. Apparently, Kimberly thought she'd taken care of this, or purposely didn't tell her. She wasn't sure how one went about this on the island. Ali had the number to Valentina's store on her receipt, so she dialed, hoping she wouldn't interrupt her if she were giving a reading or with a customer.

Valentina answered on the first ring. "Souvenir Shop."

"Hi, it's Alison—Ali. I hope I'm not interrupting anything. I need to have the power turned on at the cottage, and I'm clueless."

"Congratulations! Of course you need power," Valentina said. "Palm County Cooperative is in Fort Charlotte. I can't believe your real estate agent didn't give you the info."

"Honestly, I think she assumed I knew. It's my fault, as I was so excited when I left her office," she admitted.

"We haven't had one single customer today. If you'd like some company, I could go with you," Valentina offered.

"No, I wouldn't want to screw up your day, but thanks," said Alison.

"You wouldn't be. As I said, the store is dead. Renée left me a note saying she was going to the mall with a friend. You'd be doing me a favor."

"Then I accept. I'm at the cottage now," she told her. "Do you want to meet me here or in the public parking area?"

"I'll meet you at your place. It's been a while since I've seen the inside. Give me ten minutes to close up shop."

"Thanks," Ali said, glad for the company. She really liked Valentina and Renée. They were both kind and helpful. She hoped to remain friends with both of them.

Ali made a mental list of the items she would need for the night. Starting from scratch, she needed a bed, but this late in the day, she'd simply use the sleeping bag, now covered in cat hair, that she'd had for years. Since she was going to town, she planned on stopping at the dollar store to get a lamp and a few basics for the night. Maybe she'd run into Tammy and see the kittens she'd rescued.

She heard a light knock on the front door. "Hang on," Ali called.

She unlocked the door, and Valentina came inside, walking with her to the kitchen. "Wow, I remember all this knotty pine. Looks like it's still in decent condition."

"I don't know a lot about the wood, but I'll learn. I'll polish it up, and hopefully, the walls will sparkle, though it's a bit dark. Not sure what I can do to give this place some light. Like at your place," Ali said.

"This is rustic, but charming. Don't knock it, seriously. I'll help you, if that's what you want. I'm pretty good at decorating. It looks like your windows have been covered with sun-protecting film. Remove that, and you'll get as much sun as my place does."

"I didn't notice, but I'll definitely remove the stuff. Your place is gorgeous," said Ali, not wanting to ask how Valentina was able to afford it when her souvenir shop wasn't that busy during the summer months.

"It's nice," Valentina said. "Too big for the two of us, though when we fight, it's great to have all that space between us."

Ali laughed. "I can't believe you two fight."

"Not often, but we have our moments. Renée is a good girl. A little nosy. No, I take that back—she is *extremely* nosy."

They both laughed.

"You're lucky you have her," Ali said. "At my age, I'm not sure if kids are in my future."

Valentina swiped her hair away from her eyes. "By choice, or you haven't met the right guy?"

"Maybe a little of both. I've been on my own for so long I don't know if I could share my life with a man, let alone a child. Though I like kids, don't get me wrong. If it's meant to be, I suppose it could happen, but I'm not looking for anyone."

"You're honest. I like that. Women often get pressured into marriage, then kids. I think society expects us to marry, have babies, and live happily ever after." Valentina spoke with a trace of sadness in her voice.

"Have you ever married?" Ali asked. Just because Valentina had a teenage daughter didn't necessarily mean she'd been married. "If that's too personal, it's okay."

"Renée is rubbing off on you," she teased. "It's fine, really. Yes, I was married once. A Frenchman, if you can imagine that."

"I can," Ali said. "You're refined, not like me."

Shaking her head, Valentina said, "No, I am not refined in the way you think. I was born into a wealthy family. An only child. My parents died in a fire when I was fifteen. I miss them still," she said. "I only wish they'd lived to meet my daughter."

Alison didn't know what to say in response to such revealing personal details from a woman she thought refined and classy, even though she said otherwise. She sensed her new friend didn't have such a high opinion of herself. She was unsure why, as Valentina seemed to have everything. But Ali knew better than most that appearances could be deceiving. Confidence and self-esteem weren't guaranteed regardless of one's family or wealth. She'd had a few experiences when she waitressed in some of Florida's finest establishments. Some of the female customers were competitive, childish, and downright mean. Ali had to bite her tongue more than once when she'd encountered the wealthy women who'd treated her like garbage. Always thinking of the tips, she learned to smile, agree, and do what was asked of her. In the long run, it didn't matter. She hadn't worked in fancy restaurants to make friends. It was all about the money. All about her future—and now that she'd achieved one of her main goals, she had the last laugh.

"I'm so sorry," Ali said, and meant it. "I never knew my parents."

"I figured as much. It's not always a bad thing, Alison. Some folks aren't meant to have children."

"I suppose. I'm not exactly sure what my mother or father's circumstances were, but it doesn't matter anymore. I'm an adult now, with my own life."

Valentina nodded. "You've a good attitude, and that's what matters. So," she said, "do you want to drive, or should I?"

"We can use the Jeep. I want to stop at the dollar store to pick up a few basics for tonight. You sure you don't mind tagging along?" she asked again.

"Not at all. As I said, the shop is quiet. Nothing to keep me there, and besides, I need a break."

Ali locked the back door, then used the code Kimberly gave her to lock the key box. "I'm all set," she said.

After the short walk to the public parking lot, Ali stopped dead in her tracks when she saw the gray car.

"Is something wrong?" Valentina asked.

Alison shook her head and resumed walking toward her Jeep. Once they were safely inside, she turned to Valentina. "I think whoever owns that gray sedan has been following me." She told her about the other times the car appeared out of nowhere.

Valentina raised her brow. "You're serious?"

"Either that, or maybe it's just a lot of coincidences—which I don't believe in. I'm pretty sure I saw a man driving when the car was behind me at the Pass, though I couldn't make out any details. His hair, build, that sort of thing."

Pulling onto Dolphin Drive, Ali kept looking in her rearview mirror, waiting for the gray car to appear. At the end of Pine Tree Road, she turned onto Highway 41, heading south with no sign of the gray vehicle.

"It's just a couple miles, then we'll take a left," Valentina directed her. "Slow times, so you should be able to get the guys out to your place before the end of the day. If not, why don't you spend the night at my place? You know I have a couple extra rooms."

Ali laughed. "Okay, if I don't have power, I'll take you up on your offer, but on one condition."

"What would that be?" Valentina asked.

"You'll let me take you and Renée out for dinner. Or let me make you dinner once I'm settled. I know my way around the kitchen a little bit. Your choice."

"We'll go out. There's a new restaurant that just opened in Fort Charlotte. I've been looking for an excuse to go, so this is perfect."

"Sounds good," Ali said.

"Turn here," Valentina said. "I'll wait here while you take care of business."

"I'll leave the keys. If it gets too hot, crank the air on."

Twenty minutes later, Alison Marshall had a bona fide utility account. When she returned to the Jeep to tell Valentina the good news that her power would be on by the end of the day, she was surprised to discover her friend wasn't waiting for her. She scanned the parking lot. No sign of her. Ali went inside to check to see if she'd gone to the ladies' room. Nothing.

Inside the Jeep, Ali's keys remained in the ignition, and it was hot, almost to the point of suffocation. She cranked the car over and adjusted the air conditioner as high as it would go. Ali felt she had no other choice but to sit and wait for her friend. A zillion possibilities ran through her head, and none of them made sense. Fearing Valentina might've been taken by some weirdo, she shoved the Jeep into reverse, then slammed on the brakes when she saw her speaking to someone. Someone in the gray car.

What the heck?

It was the guy from the coffee shop, the one who had come to Ali's defense.

Clueless, she eased across the lot, stopping when she was beside the gray car. "Is there something you aren't telling me?" she asked Valentina.

"Yes, but it's not what you think," Valentina said, then walked around the front of the Jeep to get in on the passenger side. "I saw this car as soon as you went inside. I thought he was following us, so I got out to ask him what he thought he was doing. Let him tell you." She motioned to the man behind the wheel of the gray car.

He opened the driver's side door, unfolding what had to be at least six foot five of total manliness. He had dark brown hair with streaks of white on both sides and wore a pair of aviator sunglasses so Ali wasn't able to see the color of his eyes. He also wore light denim jeans and a cream-colored shirt.

She rolled her window down as he walked over to the Jeep. "Why are you following me?" Not one to waste time on bullshit, she wanted an explanation now.

He held both hands up. "I'm not following you. I'm Kit Moore," he said, then took another step toward the Jeep. "Remember, we met this morning?"

"Of course, though you lied and told me you were here to fish. What do you want?" She asked. "I've seen your vehicle more than once, so don't try to tell me you aren't following me."

"Okay, so maybe I was fishing—not literally, but not for the reasons you're thinking," he defended himself.

"How would you even know what I'm thinking? Are you psychic?" As soon as the words flew out of her mouth, she regretted it. She faced Valentina. "Sorry," she said, then returned her attention to Kit Moore with the gray sedan.

"I'm an investigative reporter for the *Miami Journal*," he said, then removed a business card from his shirt pocket. "I've been on this story for more time than I care to admit. I'm close to tying the loose ends together. I'd like to speak with you, ask a few questions, if you don't mind." He stood there, sweat gathering on his forehead and the sides of his face.

"Go on," Ali said.

"You mean now?" he asked.

"No time like the present," she quipped.

He took off his sunglasses and wiped a hand across his forehead. His eyes were green. Jade mixed with emerald green, to be exact.

"It's hot out here. How about we meet some place where we can talk? Somewhere a little cooler?"

Ali looked to Valentina, who said, "Sure. I'm okay meeting him somewhere."

She trusted Valentina, in spite of how she'd found her in the parking lot with this man, *Kit*.

"Name the place," Ali said.

"Mel's?" he asked.

Familiar with the place, she agreed.

"Thank you," he said, then returned to his car.

Ali shifted into drive, heading toward the diner. "You sure about this?" she asked her new friend. "Does he seem like a weirdo?" She waited for Valentina to reply. Ali was hoping Valentina's psychic instincts would kick in. Maybe they already had.

"I think he's exactly who he says. I must admit, I'm more than curious about this story he's working on. I've lived on the island for a long time. I can't imagine what a reporter from Miami would be working on. Nothing exciting ever happens here, minus the bone thing. We've had the weekly paper for as long as I can remember, though I've never seen anything the least bit interesting that would draw a big shot reporter to Palmetto Island."

"What makes you think he's a big shot? Could be this is his first big story," Ali said.

"You didn't read what it said on his card?" Valentina asked.

Alison handed the card to her. "What does it say? I'm driving."

"Atticus Moore, *Miami Journal*, Pulitzer Prize–winning reporter, blah, blah, blah."

Ali focused her attention on her driving. When she spied the sign for the diner, she pulled into a parking spot next to the gray sedan. Apparently, Kit was already inside waiting for them.

"That's impressive," she finally said. "Odd name. No wonder he goes by Kit. Maybe his parents were fans of Harper Lee." Ali got out of the Jeep, locking the doors before they went inside.

It felt like she was stepping inside a freezer, but she wasn't going to complain, as the cool air was refreshing. Ali knew the hottest months were still ahead of them.

"There he is," Valentina said. "Do you want me to sit somewhere else?"

"Absolutely not! I want you with me, just in case he turns out to be a true stalker."

Valentina laughed. "Okay, though I doubt he's anything but what he says."

"You know what I mean," Ali added with a grin.

When they arrived at the table, he stood until they sat down. "I took the liberty of ordering iced tea—hope that's good for you two."

"Fine," Ali said. "I'm not here to debate what I drink. I want to know why you've been following me."

Kit grinned. "I like that. No need for niceties."

The same waitress Ali had before appeared with a tray of tall glasses of iced tea. "When y'all are ready to order, just give me a wave," she said before she left.

"I appreciate you taking a few minutes out of your day. Sorry if I frightened you. I wasn't sure who you were, though I know you," Kit said to Valentina. "I recognize your family name. I know you're a full-time resident, but just so we're clear, I want you both to know if you don't want to answer my questions, you don't have to."

"Just ask," Ali said.

"Are you familiar with Koreshan State Park? It's in Estero."

Valentina answered first. "Of course. Anyone living in Southwest Florida should be." Her voice raised a notch. "Who isn't?"

"Count me out," Ali said. "Palmetto Island is as far south as I've been. What's so special about the place?" she asked, then took a drink of tea.

"Depends on who you ask these days," Kit replied. "The park has a history of being dedicated to a cult around the turn of the century, when the leader believed the earth was hollow."

Ali laughed. "Okay, so what does this have to do with me?" She wasn't into cults or crazy beliefs; didn't even care whether the earth was round or flat. It had never been something she gave serious thought to, excluding elementary school, when they were learning about Christopher Columbus and his journey to America.

"I recall my parents taking me canoeing in the park when I was a kid, but I don't know anything about a cult. There were lots of gators; that I remember well," Valentina said to Kit.

"What does this have to do with me?" Ali said again. "I'm not involved in anything remotely cultlike." She had no clue why this reporter had homed in on her. "Are you sure I'm the person you want to speak to?"

"I believe so. Look . . ." He traced the condensation

on his glass. "I'm not in any way trying to suggest you are involved with this case. However, I've seen you talking to a couple locals I'm investigating."

Alison glanced over at Valentina. She appeared as clueless as she was.

"Who?" Ali asked. "I've only been on the island a few days. Valentina and her daughter are the only two people I know, and I just met them." Surely he wasn't implying they were involved with something.

"As I said, I know of your family. They've been on the island for a long time, but that isn't what I'm interested in. Ali, when you arrived in Fort Charlotte, you spent the night at the Courtesy Court, right?"

"If you weren't stalking me, then how do you know?"

"I'm a reporter—it's my job to know. I can't reveal my sources, so you'll have to trust me." His eyes met hers. "You're free to contact anyone at the paper in Miami. They'll vouch for me."

"What do you want to know about that place?" she relented, wanting to get this over with.

"While staying there, did you experience anything unusual?"

Taking a sip of tea, Ali nearly choked. Coughing, then clearing her throat, she nodded. "Yes," she managed to say.

"I had no idea you'd stayed there," Valentina said.

When she had control of her voice again, Ali spoke. "I didn't know it mattered, but now I understand why you'd want to know." She told Kit about her stay, how Betty invited her for tea and cookies, how sick she was after her visit. "The next morning is still a bit fuzzy. I thought I'd eaten too much sugar at first. I went to a local drive-thru for a burger that evening on my way back from the beach. I assumed I had food poisoning. I've had it before."

"It's not my business, but how does Ali's stay at that place connect to Koreshan Park?" Valentina asked Kit. "I don't understand. She's new to the island. How can you say she's involved? With your . . ." She paused. "Story, or whatever you're working on."

"I am not in a position to say," Kit said.

"Are you telling us you can't or that you won't?" Ali asked. This was getting weirder by the minute.

"I can't give you an answer, but if my investigation leads me in the direction I believe, then I'll have my answer soon. So will you, and all those involved and the public, as well."

"Is that all you wanted to ask me?" Ali said, thinking he'd gone to a lot of trouble for one question.

"No, there's more." Kit tapped on the table with his index finger. Ali noted that his hands were well-manicured, but not to the degree that they appeared feminine. "What is your connection to the yellow cottage on the beach?"

This captured her attention. "Why?"

"I need to know," he said. "It's part of my investigation."

"I just purchased the house this morning, but something tells me you already know this," she said. "You know about what I found when I was clearing out the overgrowth?"

"I wouldn't be much of a reporter if I didn't," he said. "That's what I wanted to ask you about—the house and the grounds."

Valentina held up a hand. "I doubt Ali knows anything about that bone or those that were found years ago. Is this what you want to know? I remember when . . ." She paused. "Never mind. It's your job to figure things out, not mine." She leaned back in her chair.

"This is about the bones, right?" Ali asked. "I can tell you this—the bone that I dug up was a femur. I couldn't tell you how long it'd been there, though it was tangled in the roots. It took a hard yank to remove it."

"What did you do when you realized what you'd found?" Kit asked.

"I called 9-1-1, and the operator told me to put the bone back where I found it. Which was unprofessional to say the least, but I did as she asked. An hour later, the sheriff's department arrived, then the forensics team. They asked me a few questions. End of story."

"But you're interested in the bones I'm thinking of, right?" Valentina asked Kit.

"Are there others you know about?" Kit asked Valentina. "Older bones, maybe twenty plus years ago?"

"Actually, about five or six years ago, bones were discovered close to Ali's new place, but as far as I know, they never identified who they belonged to. I never heard anyone mention another set of bones. Twenty years ago, I might've been traveling with my parents. Is there more going on that you can't discuss?"

Kit's expression went from questioning to intense. "Do you know who found these bones five years ago? I've been through dozens of records. I never came across anything that mentioned a second set of bones found on the property. I'm working on finding an older set of bones myself. Would you remember the investigator from five or six years ago? I'd like to speak with him."

"I don't know if there was ever a formal investigation. Renée was ten, and I refused to let her out of my sight until they made an arrest." Valentina's voice rose. "And as far as I know, there was never an arrest. No one around here likes to talk about this. After a while, everyone on the island seemed to forget. Myself included. From what I understand, the remains were never identified. Supposedly they're still being held at the county morgue."

"Lacey, the owner of Mariner's Cottages, where I spent the past two nights, knew about the bones. The ones found a few years ago," Ali offered.

Kit nodded. "Do you recall why this particular topic came up in your conversation?"

Ali finished the last of her tea. "I do, because it ticked me off. I told her I was planning to purchase the yellow cottage. That's what the locals call the place. She told me this practically as soon as we met. She said there was a rumor, that the remains of a young girl were found a few years back. Brian something-or-other, her brother-in-law, owns Diamond Realty. She told me she could call him, see if the rumor was true. Said she'd only lived in the area for a few years. I was excited about buying my first house and irritated at her for spreading gossip. Her bad news ruining my good news kinda thing," she explained. "Odd she would know all this, and you don't, being a reporter and all."

"Maybe she knows more than she's telling you," Valentina suggested.

"Is this just a thought, or something else?" Ali asked her.

Laughing, Valentina said, "A thought. I'm not always on, if you know what I mean."

"What does that mean? Am I missing something?" Kit asked.

No one spoke. Ali waved her hand in the air and the waitress returned to the table. "Can we get a refill?" Ali asked.

"Absolutely, sugar," she said.

She chewed on her lip, something she did when she was nervous. "You're the reporter—you tell me," Ali said.

Valentina sighed, then directed her attention to Kit. "You know about me, right?"

"I know lots of things about many people. Is there something in particular I should know about you?" Kit asked.

She let out the breath she'd been holding. "I give readings."

"You mean the psychic stuff?"

Valentina nodded.

"I'm a reporter, not a mind reader," he said, grinning. Ali noticed his smile reached his eyes, the corners crinkled from smiling. Or maybe he spent too much time in the sun, searching for bones that didn't exist. She found him very attractive in a preppy sort of way. She guessed he was a few years older than her, closer to Valentina's age, though she didn't know exactly how old her new friend was. It didn't matter.

"Good thing, because I'm not, either. Just because

I'm intuitive, doesn't mean I know what people are thinking," said Valentina. "I don't speak to dead people; I don't have a crystal ball. All the clichés one associates with a psychic. I connect with most, though not all the time."

"So, what vibes are you getting from me right now?" Kit asked.

Valentina laughed. "You're serious?"

Ali watched the two of them. Was there an attraction between them? Her stomach knotted at the thought. Valentina was acting different. Almost defiant, as though she had to defend her abilities.

"I am very serious," Kit said.

"I'm not getting any 'vibes,' or whatever you'd like to call them, coming from you. I assume if you want a reading, you'll find me and make an appointment like everyone does," she explained none too nicely.

"Sorry, but I had to ask. Back to the bones. You don't remember anything about an investigation then? Five or six years isn't that long ago."

"Just that bones were found, supposedly of a young girl. I did my best to keep Renée away from any news and folks that like to gossip. She was so young that I didn't want her knowing these things had happened. But she knew something was up. She's always been nosy."

The waitress brought them fresh glasses of iced tea and removed the empty ones. "Y'all want to order somethin' now? We've got baby back ribs on special this evening. Early bird starts at three."

"Give us a minute," Kit said, giving the waitress a smile.

"Sure thing, sweetie," she said, then winked at him before departing.

"Would you all like an early dinner? My treat," Kit offered.

"Maybe another time," Valentina told him. "I have plans."

"Ali, would you have dinner with me sometime in the future? Tonight? Not a business dinner," he added, his green eyes sparkling like emeralds.

Taken aback by his unexpected invitation, it took her a few seconds to form a sentence. "Maybe another time. I want to spend tonight prepping a few things at the cottage." She was tempted to ask if he wanted to help them out tonight and then come to dinner with her, Valentina, and Renée, but thought better of it.

"Sure, the new place and all, I get that. Maybe when you have it all fixed up, you'll invite me over."

Kit's words caused her heart to hammer so fast she was sure he could see the veins in her neck pulsing.

"Maybe." It was all she could commit to at this point. Reporter or not, she really didn't know him. He could be lying. Anyone could print out a business card these days. Maybe she would call the paper in Miami. Would a Pulitzer Prize–winning reporter be driving an ugly gray sedan?

"I'm staying in Naples with my brother. Do you think I could have a look around your property sometime? Maybe tomorrow? I promise not to get in the way."

"If the sheriff's deputies have finished up, I don't see why not," she told him, knowing as soon as she was out of his sight, she would be calling Miami. After what she'd learned in the past forty-eight hours about "the yellow cottage," she was not going to allow her home to become known as the place where bones were found and have onlookers gawking around. She'd made the decision to stay in Palmetto Island because the beach was quiet.

She planned to keep it that way.

Chapter Ten

"I think Mr. Moore has a crush on you," Valentina said to Ali as they headed to the dollar store.

Ali laughed. "He isn't too hard on the eyes, that's for sure." Maybe she liked him a little more than she should, given the fact they'd just met. It would be her luck to find out he really was a stalker. Telling her he was a reporter could be a ruse just so she would let her guard down.

"You're going to call the paper, aren't you?" Valentina asked.

Ali turned to look at her, accidentally jerking the car onto the shoulder, then veering a hard left to get the Jeep back onto the main road. "How did you know?"

"It's what any woman would do. You want to make the call, or should I?"

"You . . . no, never mind. I'll call myself." Ali trusted Valentina, but still, she needed to hear with her own ears that this guy was who he said he was. "I'll make the call when I'm not driving." Still new to

cell phones, she wasn't comfortable driving and using a phone—and besides, she thought there was a
law against it.

"Smart move," Valentina told her. "Lots of acci-
dents around here. Some folks can't put their phone
down when they're driving. Renée gets her learner's
permit this fall. I dread when she's able to drive on her
own."

Ali nodded. "Now that would drive me insane. I
guess it's a good thing I don't have children yet."

She parked beneath a Florida elm large enough to
cover a portion of the Jeep. Any shade one could get in
Florida to keep their vehicle from turning into a fur-
nace was a bonus, as there weren't too many shade
trees in this part of town that she'd seen.

"You want me to go inside with you?" Valentina
asked before she opened her door.

Ali laughed. "Of course I do. You've spent enough
time waiting for me today. Besides, it's way too hot to
sit in the car. I won't be long."

Once inside the store, Ali selected a cheap lamp and
a package of light bulbs, along with three bath towels
and washcloths. A bar of soap, and a new yellow tooth-
brush, just because it matched the cottage. She bought
every type of cleaning product she would need, as well
as a broom with an attached dustpan and a sponge
mop.

"Paper towels?" Valentina said, picking up a large
package. "These will go fast."

"Get two," Ali said. As crazy as the past few days
were, she was truly having a blast buying all this stuff.
Even though it was cheap, and she'd have to replace

some of it, she couldn't remember when she'd been this happy. Never in a million years did she think she'd go shopping with a girlfriend for cleaning supplies. Maybe Valentina would go with her when she was ready to furnish the house. It was obvious she had good taste. Her place looked like something out of a magazine.

"Looks like you've covered the basics. I've got old rags and other cleaning supplies if you need them," Valentina offered.

"Thanks. This is a good start." Expecting to find Tammy, Ali felt slightly let down when she saw a young girl working at the register. After she paid for her items, it took two shopping carts to get everything to the Jeep. Once she'd secured the bags, she and Valentina headed back to the island.

"That was fun. I never had a starter home, nothing I've ever truly earned. My mom and dad had so much money, plus life insurance, I feel like I missed this part of becoming an adult," Valentina said.

Ali chuckled. "This was fun, but it wasn't easy getting to the point where I could actually purchase a home." She wanted to tell her more, but it was too soon. When she got to know her better, maybe she would open up a bit, explain just how hard her life had been. It might make Valentina more appreciative of what her parents did for her. It was also sad. Losing a parent at such a young age must've been a nightmare. Ali had never experienced parents that actually loved and cared for their child, but she had no regrets. "Maybe you can tell me about them sometime. That is, if you want to."

"They were awesome parents. I only have good memories of them. They were older when they had me, and of course I was the apple of their eye, the child they'd tried to conceive for close to twenty years. Plus, with this gift of mine, I could do no wrong according to them, and that was pretty accurate. I was a people pleaser. They kept me very sheltered, and we traveled all over the world during the summer months. Dad would stay behind sometimes. His business would get in the way, but Mom and I always managed to have a blast when we were alone. Shopping in Paris, going to all the designer shops. By the time I was twelve, I had a Chanel bag, a Versace dress, and once attended fashion week in New York." She paused. "This sounds like I was a spoiled little brat, doesn't it?" She laughed.

"It sounds like a fairy tale to me. Tell me more."

"Dad was a dentist. He owned a chain of dental clinics—boring, but it was very lucrative for our family. And I've never had a cavity."

Ali looked at her, grinning. "You and Renée have beautiful smiles."

"Thanks. Being the daughter of a dentist makes you a bit obsessive about caring for your teeth. Silly, huh?"

"No, not at all, it's an important part of your health. Want to hear something funny?" Ali asked, knowing Valentina would find it hard to believe given her father's profession. "I've never been to a dentist."

They approached the bridge, which was opening for a large boat, so they had to sit for a few minutes to wait.

"You're kidding me, right?"

"Nope, I'm serious. Never was a priority growing up in foster care. Lucky for me, I have strong teeth."

"My father would get a kick out of that. Then he'd send you straight to one of his offices, where you'd get the works. I can set an appointment up for you. I still own all of the clinics."

So that was where all of Valentina's money came from. Some people had all the luck, but then Ali decided having everything one could possibly imagine hadn't prevented Valentina from losing a family she clearly loved.

"When I settle in, I'll take you up on your offer."

"Sounds good, though I hope you don't think I'm being critical," Valentina said.

"Not at all, nothing to criticize."

As soon as the bridge closed, Ali accelerated across the short distance to the paved road. In time, she'd get used to driving across the old wooden planks.

"I take it you're not too fond of the bridge?" Valentina asked.

Alison eased off the accelerator. "Obvious, huh? Not a big fan so far."

"I'm used to it, but I think it's time for the city council to consider building a modern bridge, one that allows the boats access to the gulf without stopping the traffic."

"That would be nice. Probably would take a while, don't you think?" Ali said as she turned onto Dolphin Drive.

"Oh, I'm sure they can build bridges pretty quickly, especially these days with all the modern equipment that's out there. But the local government around here moves about as slow as the turtles. You'll get used to living here—the slow pace, casual everything. I can't remember the last time I actually wore a nice dress. Not much of a social life," Valentina said, then laughed. "Listen to me, moaning and groaning. I sound like a two-year-old."

"This is what I've wanted for years. Quiet, living life on my own terms. I hope I made the right choice settling here on this little scrap of an island."

"You'll love it," Valentina assured her. "Of course, I've spent my entire life here, so it's what I'm used to. What about you? Are you from Florida? Not many people are."

Should she open up, tell Valentina her story? Deciding it couldn't hurt, she said, "I was born in Ohio. Spent most of my life there, then I moved to Georgia for a while. I was totally burnt out on winters, especially those in Ohio. I decided to head south, and here I am." Pretty generic, she thought.

"A true snowbird," Valentina stated. "You'll fit right in. Lots of Buckeyes here—especially in the winter."

Alison parked in the public parking area, glad her friend was with her so she'd only have to make one trip to the cottage. Not to mention she really enjoyed her company. More than ever, she wanted that darn driveway finished. Maybe she'd bite the bullet and call Gib. See what kind of price he offered, maybe hire Hal to do the entire job, if he was up for it.

"What do you know about Hal from Gibbons Hardware?" Ali asked.

"Everyone around here knows Hal. He's as sweet as sugar and would do anything for anyone. His father orders him around like he's some kind of robot."

"Who's his dad?"

"Gib, the owner of the store. He's been here as long as I can remember. His wife died when Hal was young, not sure of what. He's been a mainstay at the hardware store for as long as I can remember."

"I'm thinking about hiring Hal to clear out all the overgrowth in the drive. I can't imagine having to tromp back and forth from the house to the public lot every day."

"He's an excellent worker. He's helped me with a few things throughout the years. I'd hire him again in a heartbeat."

They each carried the bags to the cottage, dropping them on the front porch while Ali unlocked the key box. "I'll be glad to get rid of this thing. Kimberly is supposed to stop by later to pick it up."

"That would get tiresome after a while," Valentina noted.

As soon as Ali stepped inside, she knew immediately something was off. "Can you smell that?" she asked.

They both walked into the kitchen, where the stench was much stronger. "What the hell?" Ali saw the freezer door was wide open, and a smattering of gray, red, and pink covered the entire bottom.

Valentina pinched her nose as she peered inside to see where the horrid odor was coming from. "That's disgusting—it looks like fish guts." She leaned in closer before saying, "Be right back."

Who had been in her house? Was this a message?

"Here," Valentina said as she returned with some paper towels and a bottle of spray disinfectant.

"I'll do it," Ali said. Taking the roll of paper towels from Valentina, she spread them out in a couple of layers to absorb the blood, then took the yellow shopping bag Valentina held out for her and dumped the now foul-smelling paper towels inside. She did this three more times, then sprayed the surface with disinfectant. When she finished cleaning the mess, she turned to Valentina. "Who would do something like this?"

"I wish I knew. This is disgusting. I think you should call the police, Ali."

Ali shook her head. "No. I have an idea who might've done this, I just don't know how they were able to get inside. I checked all the windows and doors. They were all locked when I left earlier." She took the bag of fish guts and soiled paper towels and set it on the porch. Valentina followed, and they brought the rest of the bags inside.

"Who picks up the garbage? I guess I should've asked Kimberly." Ali was new to the ins and outs of being a homeowner; she'd never had to deal with this sort of problem.

"You should have a couple of cans outside. The county waste company comes to the island once a week."

Alison went outside to see where the cans were. "Nothing out there," she said to Valentina, who'd unpacked the supplies and placed them on the kitchen counter.

"You'll have to call the city. I'll take the garbage to my house. The cans aren't full."

"It's too nasty. I can't have you do that. I'll find a place to dump this. Maybe by the bridge? Fish eat other fish, so why not give them an extra treat?"

"Don't let anyone see you, or they'll raise nine kinds of hell. Specifically Rummy. He owns the seafood shop and uses this yuck to make fish stew. I've never tried it—and won't. I hear it's best to dump fish guts in the deep, so all that grossness will decompose. If folks see entrails and guts in the shallow waters, Rummy will get wind of it. He'll tell you what a wasteful person you are, blah, blah, blah."

"Screw Rummy. I don't care what he thinks. Actually, the tide is out now. I can toss this mess into the gulf and be done with it."

"Good idea. I was going to suggest it, but I wasn't sure if you were one of those eco-nuts we have around here."

"No, but I'm thrifty, and don't waste food. However, I have my limits, and that crap on the porch is going back where it came from. This is disgusting, but I have to ask—can you tell what kind of fish it was?"

"Maybe redfish? I'm not sure," Valentina said. "You mentioned you might know who did this? Tell me if I'm being as nosy as my daughter, but is it someone I might know? If so, maybe I can . . . I don't know, tell them off." She gave a half laugh. "Not much help, I know."

"He drives a taxi in Fort Charlotte. I ran into him my first morning at the hotel, then bumped into him again at Mel's Diner and the Daily Grind. I couldn't tell you why, but he has it in for me. He's disgusting, so I'm sure you wouldn't know him."

"Are you kidding? Everyone knows Tank. He drives a cab most of the time when he's not working on a shrimp boat. He's a piece of work. He lives with his mom, I think. Smelly and the size of a broomstick. Everyone around the Pass has a story about him. Personally, I think he might be a little slow, but who am I to judge? He was able to get a driver's license, so I guess he can read traffic signs." Valentina grinned.

"That definitely sounds like the man I met." She sprayed the inside of the freezer again. "I'll take care of those guts once the power is turned on. It shouldn't be too late—at least that's what the clerk at the power company told me. You don't have to hang around here. It's hot and smelly."

"I don't care. I'm enjoying myself. Are we still on for dinner? I haven't had a good neighbor in forever, let alone one who invites me to dinner. Most folks are renters; they come and go. Of course, there's John, but I stay away from him. You should too. I know I told you this, but seriously, he scares me. I wouldn't be surprised if he was involved with those bones they found a few years ago."

"Absolutely, I didn't forget about dinner or John! Though I hope he isn't responsible for burying that bone I found earlier. Do you really think he was involved in any way? I'd hate to think I'm buying a home where someone was killed."

Valentina's words were laced with bitterness. "There are reasons I don't want my daughter around him, though I couldn't say for sure he was involved. If he was, his family would step in, pay off whomever, then he'd be right back where he is now."

Briefly, Ali wondered if her new friend had been personally attacked by John. "He sounds like bad news."

"Speaking of bad news, did you have some kind of altercation with Tank?" Valentina asked. "Not my business, I know."

"At the Courtesy Court, Tank picked me up when I was walking. Long story not worth repeating. I think he's got some sick fixation on me."

"That sounds like him," Valentina said. "His mother is strange, too. That place has been shut down so many times by the health department, I've lost count. It's always in the back of the paper."

Ali thought maybe Valentina was mistaken. "The place was immaculate. At least my room was. Very modern, too."

"Let me guess—you were in room number two?"

"How did you know? Did you use your gift?" Ali asked.

"Nope, just a known fact. When you're here long enough, you'll learn no one around the island can keep a secret. North Fort Charlotte, too. That motel's in a bad part of town."

It had seemed decent enough to Ali. She didn't remember seeing anything out of place—no homeless folks living under trees or on the side of the road, no crackheads trying to rob her. "So what's wrong with the other rooms? Are they being remodeled?"

Valentina looked away, a shadow dimming her blue eyes. "I don't gossip. It causes too much trouble."

"There's a 'but' in there somewhere," Ali prodded.

"Yes. There's been talk about that motel for years, about strange happenings there. I didn't want to say when we were talking to Kit earlier, but most folks on the island do think Betty is involved in a cult." Valentina gave a half-laugh.

Stunned, Alison said, "You're kidding? I'd find that hard to believe." Then she remembered how sick she'd gotten her one night there. "Never mind—forget I said that."

"No wonder Tank's fixated on you. Maybe he thinks you're on to them. Did you see anything, hear anyone? Maybe someone in distress, trying to ask for help?" Valentina's words echoed Ali's own fears.

"No, nothing like that." Ali's thoughts were all over the place. "Is Betty Tank's mother?"

"Yes, I assumed you knew that. Sorry I didn't elaborate," Valentina added.

"Now I wish I would have called the police. If she's involved in a cult, what's her role? Do you think Tank is involved, too?"

"I don't have an answer for that, though I wouldn't put it past her, or him, given the reputation of that hotel. Do you think she might've laced your tea or the cookies with something?"

"Probably. The cookies were sickeningly sweet enough to mask a bad taste, say a crushed pill, and the tea had enough sugar to kill a diabetic. If I had to guess, I'd say she put something in the tea." The more she thought about that night, the more convinced she was that Betty had doped her. "Kit implied he's investigating a cult, in Estero, right? What I don't get is why he needs to look around my property, besides the bone I found. How does that figure into the picture?"

Valentina glanced at the diamond watch on her wrist. "He knows more than he's telling us, which is what a good reporter does. At least on the *Columbo* re-runs I watch." She looked at her watch again. "I need to check on Renée. She should be home by now."

Ali nodded. "Yeah, I need to make that call to Miami. You still have his card?"

Valentina took Kit's card out of her pocket and gave it to her. "Thanks," Ali said, then stepped outside to give them both a few minutes of privacy.

Ali could smell the bag of fish guts on the porch. She walked around to the back of her house, then dialed the number on the card.

"*Miami Journal*; this is Carla. How may I direct your call?"

Surprised that such a large newspaper would actually have a human answering their phone rather than the usual mechanical message that'd become the norm, Ali took a couple seconds to respond. "I'd like to speak with Kit Moore," she said.

"Yep, I'll put you through to his voice mail."

"Kit Moore here. I'm unavailable, so call my cell."

The number he then recited was the same one he'd written on the card. So okay, the guy was legit. Relieved that he wasn't a stalker or pretending to be someone else, she returned to the front porch. She once again saw the disgusting yellow bag of fish, so she grabbed it and quickly jogged down the well-worn path to the beach, checking to make sure there was no sign of John. No one as far as she could see. She tossed her shoes aside and walked toward the waves, stopping when the warm salty water hit her just below her knees. This was deep enough, she thought. Dumping the contents of the bag, she dunked it into the water to rinse it out. As soon as she finished, she grabbed her shoes and headed back to her house with the empty bag. Ali smiled. *Her house.* Finally, she'd achieved her dream, and it felt damn good just thinking the words in her head. She left the wet bag on the porch, brushed the sand off the bottoms of her feet, then slid her shoes back on.

She heard Valentina talking inside, and she sounded upset. Ali waited for her to finish her call, and when she no longer heard her speaking, she went to the kitchen, where she found Valentina pacing.

"Are you okay?" Ali asked.

Taking a deep breath, Valentina shook her head. "I'm not sure. I called Renée's cell, and it went straight to her voice mail. Then I texted her our special code, and she hasn't replied. I'm worried, because she always responds to me immediately when I use the code."

"Maybe her cell battery is dead?"

"You're probably right. After a day at the mall with Danielle, her best friend, she's probably snapped pictures all day to post on Instagram and didn't bring her charger with her."

"Can you view her page on your phone?" Ali asked.

Valentina rolled her eyes. "Of course. I don't know why in the heck I didn't think of that. I'm the mother, and you're the gal without kids. Let me check," she said, using both thumbs to type.

Ali busied herself by wiping the cabinets out, using the same disinfectant she'd used earlier for the freezer. She needed to line her cabinets. Next time she was in town, she'd purchase a roll of pretty liner.

"There aren't any pictures, and she hasn't checked in," Valentina said. "I should go to the house and see if she's in her room. Would you walk over with me?"

"Absolutely—let's go." Ali dropped the dirty paper towels in the sink, grabbed her keys, and together they raced to Valentina's house.

Running up the three flights of stairs to the deck, Alison was surprised when her friend opened the door without a key. "Shit," Ali said out loud. "I forgot to lock the house."

"Renée," shouted Valentina. "If you're in your room, you'd best get your ass downstairs now!" She turned to Ali. "Your place is fine unlocked during the day. I forget to lock mine sometimes, except at night, when I turn on the security system. I'll be right back," she told her before racing upstairs.

Ali waited in the main room, walking to the window to look out at the view. "Amazing," she said to herself. While her place didn't have this view, she was still able to see and hear the waves, probably more so if she were to leave the windows open.

When Valentina returned, her face was as white as the walls. "I don't think she's at the mall. Her purse and cell phone are lying on her bed."

Ali took a deep breath. "Can you call the girl she

was with, Danielle? Her friend. Maybe they've met up with some guys. Renée told me she had a crush on a football player, though I can't recall his name."

Valentina nodded, then used her landline to make the call. "Hey, Beth, it's Val. I'm worried sick. Renée's phone and purse are in her room, and there's no sign of her. Please tell me she's with Danielle at your house. She left me a note saying they were spending the day at the mall."

Waiting for some sign that Valentina heard good news on her end, Ali watched her as her look went from worried to disbelief. "Are you sure? She said they were both going. Yes, of course I'm sure. Call my cell as soon as you talk to her." She hung up the phone, her hands shaking.

"She's not with Danielle. According to Beth, Danielle spent the night in Naples with her grandmother and was there most of the day. I can't just sit here; I need to find her. Something is wrong. I know it; mother's instinct. The note was typewritten, printed off her computer. That's not like her."

"Let's go find her," Ali said. "I just need to lock up beforehand."

"I don't want to wait. I'll go by myself. Maybe you could stay here and answer the phone if it rings. And here is mine and Renée's cell numbers. Call me if she comes home or calls." Valentina jotted the numbers on a pad by the landline, then disappeared before returning with a designer handbag and a set of keys. "Say a prayer she's all right."

Ali nodded. "I will. You let me know too, okay?" She was truly worried now.

As soon as Valentina left, Ali wished there was a way she could help her friend. She trusted her, which meant more to her than Valentina would ever know. The joy from the view gone, she sat on a stool by the phone so she could answer the second it rang.

Chapter Eleven

Valentina had been gone for over an hour. Wishing she could be of more help, Ali went out to the deck to look over at her house to see if the electric company had arrived. If she wasn't home, most likely they'd leave. She'd reschedule. Renée's safety was much more important.

Cramming her hands in her pockets, she pulled out Kit's business card. Debating on whether to call him again, and what she'd say if she did, Ali swallowed her pride and dialed his cell number.

"Kit Moore," he answered immediately.

"Hey, it's me," she said, then added, "Alison Marshall."

"You've decided to take me up on my dinner invitation?" he asked.

Hearing the humor in his voice, she smiled. "Uh, no, I can't. Yet."

"So you're calling to tell me what?"

Feeling like an idiot, she explained. "My friend Valentina, the one with me today, her daughter is missing." Saying the words out loud made them much more real to her.

"Has she called the police?" he asked, his tone going from humorous to professional.

"I'm at her house now. She drove into town." Had Valentina actually said she was going to the police department? "Actually, she left in such a hurry, I'm not sure. Maybe she was going to search for her. Renée, that's her daughter, told her mom she was hanging out at a mall with a friend, but her friend was at her grandmother's house in Naples." She gave him what little information she had.

"I'm glad you called. Where is this house you're at now?"

"It's by the cottage—it's the three-story pale blue house on the beach. You can't miss it," she told him. "I told Valentina I'd stay here in case Renée came home or called."

"I can be there in twenty minutes," he said.

"Thanks," she said. "I'll be here waiting." Ending the call, she wasn't sure if Valentina would approve of her inviting Kit to her house. But these weren't normal circumstances. He might be able to help locate Renée, or possibly he had contacts in the local police department.

Her mouth dry from nerves, she opened the massive refrigerator. Bottles of water, tea, and every kind of soda one could ask for filled the bottom half. She chose a bottle of spring water. Gulping half of it down, she returned to the stool by the phone. On edge, she picked at her cuticles, an old habit from long ago. Ali wondered if she'd made the right decision staying on Palmetto Island. It seemed trouble had followed her everywhere since she'd checked into the Courtesy Court. Had Betty really put a drug in the cookies or the tea? She recalled eating two or three, then drinking more tea. She'd been dizzy. Try as she might, she couldn't summon up much more than that. No memory of returning to her room, absolutely no recollection of Betty taking care of her or the kittens. Or so she'd said that's what had transpired. If Betty was involved in this cult Kit was investigating, she sure as heck put on a good show acting like the poor little old lady without friends or family.

The sound of footsteps running up the stairs jolted her back to the present. After there was a tap on the door, she hurried across the massive front room to let Kit inside. "Thanks for coming," she said, standing aside as he entered.

Kit still wore the same clothes he'd had on earlier. The only difference was he now had a five-o'clock shadow. His windblown hair made him look as sexy as a male model in a magazine. Even sexier, if she were being honest, because he didn't look *too* perfect. She realized that she liked that about him.

He glanced around at Valentina's house but didn't appear overly impressed. "Tell me everything you know," he said.

"Have a seat." She directed him to a barstool in the kitchen. She stood across from him, only a few steps away from the landline, should it ring. "There's not much other than what I told you over the phone." Ali repeated what she knew.

"Is there anything else that seemed off, at least in your mind?" Kit said when she was done.

"Yes, the fish." She'd forgotten all about her ordeal with the smelly guts.

"You'll have to explain that one in a little more detail," he said, though he was smiling. His deep emerald eyes glistened, assuring her that he wasn't being sarcastic or condescending.

"Valentina and I stopped at the store to pick up a few items for my place, mostly cleaning stuff. When we returned and went inside, there was a horrible odor coming from the kitchen. I saw the freezer door was open, saw a massive amount of fish guts there. Before I left, I made sure everything was locked, so someone had to figure a way to get inside, or they knew the code on the key box. The real estate agent was supposed to pick the box up today. She should've been there by now. I was supposed to be there waiting for the electric company, then Valentina couldn't find Renée, and here I am."

Kit shook his head as he took in what she said. "So you need someone at your house now?" he asked.

Sighing, Ali nodded. "I don't care about the electricity, though I would like to get rid of that key box so I can at least lock my door with the key. We ran out so fast I didn't have a chance to lock up."

"What if I go and have a look around? I can wait for the power company and your real estate agent. Do you know what kind of fish was put in your freezer?"

"It was just guts; there were no actual fish. No heads. Just guts and scales. Maybe redfish, according to Valentina, though she wasn't sure. Does it matter?"

"It might, though if you let me have a look, I'm pretty sure I can tell you what kind of fish it is. Was," he added.

"Can't do that. I cleaned the freezer out, took the mess to the beach, and dumped it in the water. A treat for some other fish, I suppose," she said.

"Can't say I wouldn't have done the same. Do you know why anyone would do this? Did you piss anyone off?"

"You mean besides Tank, the idiot from the coffee shop? No, I've only been here a few days—and I'm starting to regret it, too."

"He's trouble, but I don't believe he'd go to such lengths to piss you off. He seems to feel free to do so in public," Kit said.

"I don't care about that now. I just hope nothing has happened to Renée. She's a remarkable young girl. Super sweet."

Kit didn't say anything for a few minutes. Ali was beginning to feel uncomfortable.

"You said she went to the mall with her friend? I assume her mother tried to contact the friend's parents?" Kit finally said.

"She did. Her daughter spent the night with her grandmother. Apparently, Renée left a note in her room, but she left her cell phone and purse behind. Valentina has a safety code they use in case of an emergency and said Renée always responds when she sends this code, which she didn't receive, obviously, because her phone is in her room."

"I'd like to see her room, but I could contaminate

evidence. Though I'm sure you're not naïve where young girls are concerned. Who knows what's actually going on with teenagers? Lots of strange stuff."

Stunned at his statement, it made her wonder if he knew things about her that she'd kept secret since the night she'd graduated from high school. "I don't have children. I know bad things can happen to girls and boys. Why would you suggest I'm 'not naïve' on this particular issue?"

"You're a young woman yourself. I would assume you know the dangers in this world. Most women do."

Ali didn't believe his statement was quite that simple, but now wasn't the time to dig into what he did or didn't know about her past. "Of course I know that. I've been on my own for a while now," she said, not willing to elaborate further.

"I'll go to your cottage and see what I can find. If you'll give me the code to your key box, I'll lock up."

She used the same pad of paper Valentina had to write the code down, then gave him her keys. "If Kimberly the real estate agent shows, you'll need these to lock up."

"Of course. Call me if you have any news about your friend," he said.

"I will," Ali said, walking him to the door. "Thanks for doing this."

He looked at her, his eyes searching hers. "It's my pleasure, Alison." He walked out to the deck. She watched him walk as far as she could see, then returned to her spot by the phone.

It was close to six, probably too late for the power

company; too late for Kimberly, as well. It really didn't matter now, she told herself. All that mattered was Renée and her safety. Debating whether to call Valentina to see if she had any news, she decided against it in case she had an incoming call. Patience was something she had an abundance of, but she felt restless, fearful. There was something about Renée that had touched a part of her that she'd never known existed—true, heartfelt emotions. If she felt this way about someone she barely knew, she couldn't begin to imagine what Valentina was feeling right now. If she had children, she wouldn't let them out of her sight. From experience, as Kit had intimated, she knew what could happen to young girls. Could she bring a child into the world knowing their future could be in constant jeopardy? Maybe she wasn't cut out for the mom stuff, but she cared about Renée and her mother a lot. Was it because they were the first people she'd met that treated her kindly? They didn't treat her like she was worthless. If they knew her past, would it change either of their opinions of her? She didn't think so, because they were good people. So far.

And Kit? Besides being a reporter searching for his next big story, would he think less of her if he knew her past? It didn't matter. At least not yet—maybe she'd tell him more once he solved his mystery. He'd return to Miami and forget he ever met her, unless she was truly a part of his investigation. Then he'd move on to the next big story. Her thoughts raced. She knew it was nervous energy, as she'd felt it many times before, after her many escapes from the broken homes she'd been forced to live in. She glanced at her cell phone to see if she'd missed a call. No one had actually called her number before, so she was clueless to the ringtone. She didn't see a missed call.

Antsy to the point of pulling her hair out, she got off the stool and went to the deck. She could see her yellow cottage. Apparently, the power company had been there, and Kit had turned the kitchen light on. Deep in thought, all she cared about at the moment was locating Renée, praying she was safe.

From her view, she watched the sun make its slow descent, noting the pale yet striking palette of colors streaking across the blue sky. Pink and violet—some deeper, others a pale pastel—blended into so many shades, Ali felt like she'd stepped into a painting, a masterpiece. Amazed, she walked to the floor-to-ceiling window, gazing out at the beauty marking the end of the day. She almost had to pinch herself when she realized she could now see this any day she wanted. Taking her cell from her pocket, she noted the time. It was just after eight o'clock; she'd been waiting well over two hours, with no news of Renée and nothing from Kit, though she saw her lights were still on when she stepped out onto the deck. The cooler evening air emitted a briny scent, reminding her of seaweed. While it wasn't a horrible smell, it wasn't exactly pleasant. Could have something to do with the tides, she thought.

As she returned to her perch on the stool, hunger pains gnawed her stomach, reminding her she hadn't eaten all day. With no word from Valentina, and the dinner they'd planned now out of the question, she peered inside the refrigerator again, searching for something to eat. Taking an apple from the produce drawer, she walked across the room to the dining area. The view was just as spectacular from this angle. Munching on her apple, gazing out at the view, she jumped when she heard a knock on the door.

Kit.

"Any news?" he asked once he was inside the house.

"Nothing. No calls. I'm beyond worried," she said. "I saw the power is turned on at my place. I hope I didn't inconvenience you."

"Your real estate agent didn't show," Kit said. "You can have these back." He placed her keys on the kitchen counter by the phone. "And it wasn't an inconvenience."

"I'll call her tomorrow. Were you able to find whatever it is you're searching for on my property?" Ali loved the sound of those words: *my property.*

"I'm afraid I didn't have enough time, or light, but the smell is still lingering," he told her. "Are you sure you removed all the fish?"

"Of course. The smell is still bad?"

"It is, probably because the place is closed up. Once you open the windows and let some fresh air inside, it'll go away."

"I'll do that tomorrow."

Kit leaned against the counter, his eyes scanning the room, stopping on the refrigerator. "You hungry?" he asked.

"Yeah, I just finished an apple. You want one? I'm

sure Valentina won't care." She'd offer to make him a sandwich, but she wasn't one-hundred percent comfortable even taking the apple she'd had. Having been on her own for so long, she didn't have the best social skills.

Grinning, he said, "I can order a pizza if you'll share it with me."

Would that count as a dinner date under these circumstances? She didn't dare voice this thought, but a pizza would be good no matter what. "Sure, but only if you let me pay half," she said, just to see if he'd insist on picking up the tab. If so, this would be her first real dinner date—ever. With the few men she'd dated, if you could even call them dates, she'd always paid for her own dinner.

"Nope, I refuse. What do you like on yours?" he asked as he scrolled through his smartphone, one of the latest models. She only knew this because last night, when she'd been watching a movie, the same phone was being advertised as the most current of its kind on the market.

"Anything. I'm not picky," she told him.

"I'll get the works," he said, then ran his finger across the phone, tapping on the number. She wondered how he knew there was pizza delivery on the island. She hadn't seen any pizza joints, but that didn't mean much. These days, you could get pizza anywhere. When he spewed off Valentina's address, an alarm triggered in her head. How did he already know her address from memory?

He placed their order, then clicked end.

"I can guess what you're thinking by the look on your face. The house numbers are on the front of the house, and there's only one main road. Plus, Terri's Diner makes a mean pizza."

That was the diner that advertised in the paper. "Sorry," she said.

"Don't worry about it. I'm glad you're aware of what goes on in this insane world."

Ali nodded in agreement. "Are you going to tell me what you're searching for? I'm intrigued, to say the least." Not much of a conversationalist, she was trying her best to maintain what little social graces she possessed.

"The cult story goes way back. I can tell you about this part without revealing too much. It's just my job, nothing personal. It's not that I can't trust you, it's just crucial I keep a few things to myself for now."

"I understand. You're not obligated to tell me anything you don't want to," she said. Though Kit didn't know it—at least, she didn't think he did—she was very, very good at keeping secrets.

"This particular cult, the Koreshan cult, was founded by a young guy, Cyrus Teed. This was back in the late 1800s. He was into different types of pseudoscience—eclectic physics and alchemy. Story goes, he was messing around with an experiment that involved electricity and shocked himself to the point of passing out. During his so-called unconscious state, he believed he became the messiah. From that moment on, his mission was to save humanity through science. Not too far off the mark in those days. Everything was new, unexplored. Cyrus changed his name to *Koresh*, the Persian word for Cyrus, and from there, he started the Koreshan Unity organization.

"Cellular cosmogony was Cyrus' theory that the earth and the universe were contained in a concave sphere or a cell. They did all kinds of experiments. Their most famous, or infamous, if you will, was in Naples on the beach. I won't bore you with all the scientific details, or what they believed to be scientific at the time. Fast forward to the early twentieth century. Cyrus proposes his movement live on through his creation, calling it the new Jerusalem. His followers, or rather his cult members, had what one considered strange beliefs. Sacrificial stuff, not unlike more modern-day cults. They formed a commune in Estero. Everyone shared the work, and no one received any form of payment, all working in order to keep this new faith, *Koreshanity*, active and thriving. Cyrus bit the dust in the early part of the twentieth century. In the sixties, there were still four remaining members. These folks deeded the land to the state, which is now known as Koreshan State Historic Site. I believe the cult is still active today. They've changed locations and methods, though now they're eviler than they were then."

Ali listened intently to his story. "So you believe this Cyrus still has followers, and they're here? On Palmetto Island?"

"I can't say where the cult is, but I know they're still active. I'm sorry I have to keep repeating myself. It goes with the job."

"So you're here to . . . what? Bring them to justice for whatever it is they do? Or what?"

He laughed, his jade-green eyes shining. "You're a tough nut to crack, aren't you?"

She smiled. "Maybe."

There was the sound of footsteps, then a knock on the door. Ali got up to answer, but Kit stepped in front of her, preventing her access to the door. "My treat, okay?"

"Sure," she said, unused to this kind of behavior from a man. He was a little bossy, or assertive, she wasn't sure which, but she liked him. He was handsome, intelligent, and had an important job; plus, he'd won a Pulitzer Prize for his work. She knew he was out of her league. For now, she would take pleasure in the few minutes it took them to eat the pizza. She could pretend they were a couple, just having a casual conversation over dinner.

He returned to the kitchen with a giant pizza box. The aroma of roasted tomatoes and garlic penetrated the cardboard, causing her stomach to grind in hunger. She'd been used to being hungry for so many years. Now, however, it reminded her of the past and how far she'd come.

"I'll find plates," she said. She opened a few cabinets before finding a large supply of paper products. She took two paper plates and paper napkins, placing them on the counter. Kit put a slice on a plate, gave it to her, then did one for himself.

Alison bit into the crusty dough topped with thick mozzarella cheese, bacon, ham, and sausage. There were also black olives, onions, and green peppers. She could only imagine what her breath would smell like after she finished eating. Not the time for a first kiss.

Why was she having these kinds of thoughts—and now, of all times? She should be focused on Renée and Valentina, not knowing if either was safe. Instead, she was in another woman's beachside mansion with a man she barely knew, eating pizza.

Is this what normal people do during a crisis? Alison didn't know for sure, but instinctually, she knew Valentina would insist she do exactly what she was doing if she were here.

"You're too quiet," Kit said between bites.

She swallowed before replying. "I don't like to talk with my mouth full."

"Good manners."

"I suppose," she said before taking another bite. "Whatever that means to you."

"You're not cramming pizza in your mouth, nor is there sauce on your face." He stopped, then leaned so close to her she could smell his aftershave. "Oops," he said, "there is a little speck right here." He used his thumb to wipe the sauce from her chin, his eyes focusing on hers.

A trickle of excitement ran down her spine as he continued to stare at her. Ali couldn't stop herself from returning his gaze, but after a few seconds, forced herself to look away. She stepped around him to get them drinks from the refrigerator. "There's a variety of tea and soda if you want," she said, taking another bottle of water for herself.

"I'll have what you're having," he responded.

She took another bottle of water, handing it to him.

"Thanks. You like the pizza?" he asked as he placed another slice on each of their plates.

"It's delicious," she said, and it was. When life quieted, maybe she'd order a pizza and sit on the beach and watch the sunset. Ali forced her attention back to the present. "I'm going to call Valentina. She would've called by now if she had good news."

"You probably should. I don't have kids, but they're a tremendous responsibility. My brother Rhett has a couple kids. They are super cute, but man, what a workout I get when I visit them."

She supposed this was just small talk, him trying to ease her worry. She took the piece of paper with Valentina's cell number, and took the house phone, then thought better of it and hung it up. If Valentina hadn't found Renée and saw her home number come up on her cell, it would give her false hope, and she didn't want to do that. Ali took her cell out of her pocket and dialed Valentina's number.

"Hello," Valentina answered. Her voice sounded like she'd been crying.

"Hey, it's me. I just wanted to find out if you've heard anything," Ali said as gently as she could.

"Nothing. Not one call or text. I'm in Fort Charlotte filing a missing person's report now."

"Oh my gosh, Val. I am so sorry. Do you want me to come down there? I could sit with you?" Ali realized she'd used the shortened version of her friend's name, as she'd heard her use it when she'd been on the phone with Beth earlier.

"No, but thanks. If you can stay at the house a while longer, I'd appreciate it. The police want to search the house. See if any of her clothes are missing, or other things she'd take if she were leaving. I told them absolutely not, that she would never leave without her cell phone or her purse, but they seem to think she's a runaway."

"I can stay here as long as you need me to. I called Kit. He's here now. I hope I didn't overstep any boundaries."

"Good. I'm glad he's there with you. I believe he's a good guy. I just want my daughter back." Valentina broke down then, her cries pitiful.

"Are you sure you won't let me drive you home? Or Kit?" She looked at him, and he nodded. "You're upset; you shouldn't be driving."

"No, I can manage. I'm going to drive by a few areas where some of the high school kids on the island hang out. See if anyone is there or if they might know something. Maybe I can find her. If I'm not back before the police arrive, let them in Renée's room, but don't let them remove anything unless I'm there."

"I promise," she said, then hit the end button. To Kit, she said, "She's filed a missing person's report. The police will be here soon to search Renée's room. Valentina's returning, though she has a few stops to make on her way back. Apparently, there are a few high school hangouts she wants to check first."

"Dang, I was hoping for good news. I wish there was something I could do. The Fort Charlotte police department and the sheriff's office around here aren't very well-liked. The sheriff is crooked, and the police chief spends most of his time on the golf course."

"I wasn't impressed with the sheriff's department,

either. The forensics guy tried to tell me that bone I found wasn't a femur. Said he had to do some testing. I'm no medical expert, but that bone was a femur." She paused. "Do you think the bone and the others that were found are connected to your cult story?"

Kit tilted his head. "I don't know. Strange stuff is going on with this story, so nothing would surprise me at this point."

Her decision to live here hadn't been the least bit smooth. If anything, she felt like she was toxic. There were too many bad vibes, weird people, and now, Renée was missing. Add in Kit's story of a cult here on the island, and she would be smart to put the cottage back on the market and hightail it south to the Keys. She never really thought of herself as smart, unless street smarts counted. Those she had in abundance. Common sense told her she couldn't put the house on the market. She'd barely spent a couple of hours there. House flipping wasn't her thing.

Kit took a third slice of pizza for himself. When he offered her another slice, she shook her head. "That was delicious. I've had plenty, thanks."

Her thoughts drifted back to hard times, when a bite of pizza from a garbage can had been her meal for the day. So many struggles that should have never happened to a teenage girl. She'd endured more than most adults would in a lifetime. Sleeping outside in freezing temperatures, going days without anything to eat, shoes with the soles worn down so thin she'd had to stuff them with newspapers. And now, just when she thought better times were ahead, everyone she came in contact with seemed to have some kind of trouble. She wondered if she was a jinx. Her nomadic lifestyle hadn't been perfect, but she'd never allowed anyone to get too close to her. Now she had Valentina, Renée, and Kit as friends, though they didn't know one another well. She felt guilty for bringing her bad mojo to Palmetto Island.

"You're quiet. Deep thoughts?" Kit asked as soon as he finished his pizza.

She walked over to the window, looking out at the water. "I don't have deep thoughts. I think on something for a bit. That's all," she said.

He walked across the room and stood beside her. "You don't have a very high opinion of yourself, do you?"

She watched the ebb and flow of the gulf. The moonlight shone on the wet sand. Closing her eyes, she imagined the feel of tiny granules of sand beneath her bare feet, the warm water rippling across her as she wiggled her toes in the sand. Somewhere, she'd heard it was therapeutic for one to dig their toes into the sand, to walk barefoot on the water's edge. She didn't know if it were true or not, but right now, it sounded good to her. Alison wanted to go outside and feel the humid night air moisten her skin, the salt air tangle her hair.

"Alison? Are you all right?" Kit asked.

"Sorry, just dreaming," she told him.

"Good or bad?"

She turned to face him. "A bit of both. I was thinking how it feels when you're standing on the beach, digging your feet in the sand, the warm water rolling over the top of your feet. Silly, huh?"

"That's the good part. Care to tell me the bad?" he asked.

Ali wondered if she should tell him a small truth. No, now wasn't the time. This evening was all about finding a young girl.

"No, nothing worth hearing," she said as casually as she could manage.

"You wanna go down to the beach now?" he asked.

"I have to wait for the police and Valentina. In different circumstances, I'd love to. This has been my dream for so many years. I keep pinching myself so I know it's real, living here and all," she told him.

"I love the beach myself, though I don't get to spend as much time as I'd like with my work schedule. Though I had a lot of good memories growing up here," he said.

Ali turned to look at him. "Here, on Palmetto Island?"

He stared down at her. His height should've been intimidating, but it wasn't. He had kind eyes and a gentle smile. "Yes, I lived here for a while growing up."

"Is that why you're working on this cult thing?" she asked, wondering if he or any of his family had experience with the cult.

"Let's just say I've known about the cult's existence for a while. When I left for college, I forgot about it for a time. I wondered if it was even true. Kids make up all kinds of stories, especially a bunch of teenagers on the beach at night, along with a campfire and a few beers stolen from our parents. Later, when I started working as a journalist, I was assigned to do a story on a cult, though it had nothing to do with the Cyrus story. While I was researching, I came across a few tidbits about the island, always telling myself I'd come back and find out the truth. Without revealing too much, in my research I discovered a very disturbing group of folks. I'm sorry I can't tell you more. I respect my sources' privacy."

"This might sound far-fetched, but could the cult be responsible for Renée's disappearance?"

He sighed and stepped away from the window, taking a seat on the large, lavish white sofa. She sat across from him in a matching white chair.

"I wouldn't know. Let's just cross our fingers that isn't the case. Maybe Renée just had a fight with her mother and decided to give her a scare."

She shook her head. "No, she wouldn't do that. I haven't known either of them very long, but I think they're more like sisters. They seem to have a good mother-daughter relationship, as far as I can tell. They tease one another, yet Valentina is strict with her. Won't let her go near John Wilson, who lives a couple houses down. From what little I observed, Renée always obeys her mom."

"I can't believe John is still around here," Kit said. "A total loser, if you ask me. He's a few years older than I. Was always starting trouble, with his parents bailing him out."

She was unsure whether or not to tell Kit what she'd been told. She didn't like John, plus she didn't feel she was saying anything he couldn't hear in one of the bars at the Pass. "Valentina says he messes with little girls. Very little, like eight or nine. His parents would do what they could to pay off whomever was needed to keep him out of trouble. I had a couple encounters with him. He's a real ass."

Kit listened to her, and she watched his expression change as she told him what she'd heard.

"John is an ass, but a pedophile? I don't know. I never heard that about him. Do you know if charges were ever brought against him?"

"Like I said, Val told me his parents paid his way out of any trouble he got himself into. I assume he had to be doing something if he's being accused of molesting a child. That jerk makes me sick," she said, anger giving her a second burst of energy. She got up and stood at the window. Shouldn't the police be here by now? And Valentina, too?

"I've been away a long time. But I don't recall any rumors about that when I lived here. Gossip spreads like melted butter on the island and in Fort Charlotte. That's a fact that hasn't changed."

"It was like that when you lived here, too?"

"Yes, people running their mouths with nothing better to do. Off-season was quiet, so people needed entertainment. Not my kind of fun, but the fishermen and the shrimpers ate it up. Many of them weren't from around here, so listening to the locals tell tall tales about whomever, whatever, seemed to be the gig then."

Ali considered what he said. "Were these tall tales

hints of what might've been happening on the island then?"

"Maybe. No way to know. I was a teenager, so I didn't pay too much attention then. Though Rhett might've heard. He was hitting the bars up starting on his eighteenth birthday. That was the legal age at the time."

"Too young," she said, thinking back to when she was eighteen. Nightclubs hadn't been her thing and still weren't. "Your parents were readers?" she said out of the blue.

"Yes, my father is. Mom, not so much. She spent what little time I knew her in bed. Sick. She passed when I was ten, during Rhett's first year of high school. Bad times."

"I'm sorry," was all she could come up with. She was, though. Losing a real parent had to be as tough as it got, especially when there was love in the family.

Kit nodded, then raked his hand through his hair. "Thanks. Time heals old wounds, I guess. Dad remarried when I was fifteen. We moved off the island after Rhett graduated high school. Couple years later, I had a baby sister."

She smiled. "How cool, especially for your parents, with two built-in babysitters."

"Both of us doted on Jane," he said, a sad look on his face.

"Another literary name?"

"My stepmom loves books as much as dad does. They met through a book club," he said. "They're a good match, but they've never been the same since they lost Jane."

"Your sister? I'm so very sorry. How horrible for you and your family." She wasn't expecting to hear such sad news. Especially now that Renée was missing, she wasn't sure she could deal with more bad news.

Kit had a faraway look in his eyes, as though he'd traveled back in time to his family's tragedy. "She was only six," he told her.

"Would it be rude of me to ask what happened to her?"

He raked his hand through his hair again. She supposed it was a habit of his, as she'd seen him do it before. "We don't know."

"Was she sick?" she couldn't help but ask. She wanted to know as much as she could about Kit's family.

"You'll keep this to yourself?" he asked.

"Of course," she told him, but wondered why it mattered, since Jane's death had happened so long ago.

"She's been missing for more than twenty years. I'd been out of college for a year or so. My stepmom, who raised us, was younger than Dad, but it didn't matter, because they're like two peas in a pod. I was seventeen when Jane came along. Cutest little girl. Rhett and I adored her. Spoiled her constantly. This is the part I can't tell you, but suffice it to say, Jane's disappearance is relevant to what I'm working on."

In a soft voice, she asked, "The cult story?"

"Let's leave it at that for now."

"Okay." Unsure what else to say, she tried wrapping her mind around the strange events that took place here and in town.

Through the window, Ali saw red and blue lights flashing but didn't hear a siren. "Looks like the police are here," she said. "I dread this. I can't begin to imagine what Val's going through."

"I have no doubt this is the start of her worst nightmare," Kit said, then stood up, walking to the door. Ali joined him, waiting to let the authorities in to do their job. Sending up a silent prayer this nightmare would have a magical ending, she prepared for a long night ahead.

Chapter Twelve

When Alison saw Ricky Sanders from the sheriff's department, along with three others she hadn't met, her stomach sank. She knew he wasn't the most experienced or the brightest star, even though he wore two actual gold stars plastered on his shirt. Was his presence a sign of a bad outcome?

Kit took charge as soon as the cops entered.

"Well, well, now look at this," Sanders said when he saw her standing beside Kit. "Trouble follows you everywhere, don't it?" he said between snaps of bubble gum. "You do something to the kid? You wantin' some ransom money?" He laughed, while the other three deputies reminded her of Larry, Moe, and Curly as they waited silently for direction. The three deputies looked to be in their early twenties. Most likely, this was their first real investigation.

"Don't speak to Alison like that," Kit warned. "Do you what you were sent here to do."

"I gotcha. You two got a thing goin' on. You don't waste time, do ya, girl?"

Kit stepped as close to Sanders as he could without touching him. "I asked you not to speak to her like that. Are you deaf?"

Ali watched the three deputies snicker at Kit's comment to Sanders, who must be their superior, which was the biggest joke of all. Renée didn't stand a chance if this idiot controlled the investigation.

"I see we got a smartass on our hands." Sanders spoke to the three idiots, stepping away from Kit, who towered over him by nearly a foot.

"Listen, you're not here to decide what I am or not. A child is missing, or have you forgotten why you're here?" Kit's words were laced with unreleased anger. Seeing him stand up to the deputy, Ali was proud he wasn't frightened by a badge.

Inwardly, Ali laughed. Sanders would be no match for Kit, unless he used his weapon. He would be the kind to use a gun just to bully others.

"She's probably run away with some boy. Girls her age oughta be locked up till they're old enough to marry," Sanders said to no one in particular.

Alison saw headlights reflecting on the windows. She hoped it was Valentina with good news.

"I see you have a high opinion of women. Men like you make me sick," Kit said. "Do your damned job, or I'm going to make a phone call, and it won't be to your uncle."

"You threatenin' me?"

"Call it whatever you like. Do your job and quit wasting time showing us what an ass you are," Kit said, his fists clenched at his side.

Valentina came through the door, her blonde hair a

tangled mess, eyes red from crying. She glanced at the deputies. "Is this how you search for a missing person? Get out. Now!" she said. "I refuse to allow you in her room. Go!" She pointed her finger toward the door.

"Hey, woman, you need to calm down. You're the one that called us, remember?" Sanders said.

"I didn't call you," Valentina said, "your stupid-ass uncle sent you here. This is my house, and I'll give you to the count of five to get out of here!"

Alison went to Valentina, placing an arm around her. "You heard what she said. Go. Now."

"You better not call the department again, cause we ain't gonna waste any more time on you, you got that?" Sanders smirked. "Go on—she can find her kid herself. Probably out screwin' around anyway. Girls like her, well, if you ask me, they deserve whatever they get."

Kit grabbed Sanders by the shoulders. "Get out before I toss your puny ass over the balcony for the fish to feast on. I'm not the least bit intimidated by you or the uniform that you're a disgrace to. Go." He turned Sanders toward the door.

"Let's get out of here," Sanders said to the three silent deputies. "Let 'em find the kid on their own."

Finally getting the message, Sanders stomped out, his crew following behind like baby ducks. When they drove off, not only did they turn their red and blue lights on, but they also turned up the sirens, too. All for show, Ali thought.

"Have you heard anything?" Ali asked Valentina.

Valentina shook her head. "Yes, and it's not what any mother wants to hear."

Without offering an explanation, Valentina went to the kitchen and took a soda from the refrigerator. "Y'all help yourselves; then we'll talk." She sat on a barstool, no longer the confident woman Ali had gone shopping with just a few hours earlier.

"I'm good," Ali said. "Kit?" She motioned toward the fridge.

"Nothing for me," he said.

"Renée is fine. At least, I hope she is." Valentina sighed, pinching the bridge of her nose with one hand, looking down. "I thought we had a close relationship. I thought she told me everything, at least things a mother needs to know. Apparently, I've been blindsided by her the past few months."

Ali and Kit waited for her to continue explaining what had become of her daughter.

"This is so unreal, it's hard for me to speak about it."

"Then don't," Ali suggested. "If Renée isn't in any danger, you don't need to explain anything. Right?" She turned to Kit.

He took a deep breath, letting it out slowly. "Actually, I think she should."

Valentina nodded. She took an unused napkin left on the bar, wiping the fresh tears from her face. "It's embarrassing. Moms should know stuff about their kid, right?"

"Not always," Kit told her. "Is she with someone you don't like?"

She looked at him. "Yes. Someone I despise."

"All girls date at least one guy their parents don't like," Ali said. Though she'd never personally experienced it, she'd spent a lot of time reading young-adult novels in her youth, and many shared this theme.

"It's that son of a bitch who's old enough to be her father!" Valentina blurted out, another round of tears streaming down her face.

"Who?" Ali asked with a sinking feeling in her stomach.

"John Wilson, the island idiot," Valentina answered.

Neither Ali nor Kit spoke for a few seconds. Finally, Ali managed to say, "But she hates him. She told us that at lunch, remember? Maybe you're mistaken?"

"No, I'm positive. She's with him now. The story about going to the mall with Danielle was a lie. I had to practically threaten Danielle's life to drag the truth from her, but she broke down. She told me and Beth how Renée and John have been friendly for a while. Said they were more than friends." She shook her head. "Can you believe that? She's barely sixteen, and he's in his thirties! Yet, there's more to this. Danielle was afraid of something; I sensed that. I don't know if she was threatened as well."

"You can bring charges against him," Kit said. "He'll go to prison for a very long time. There are laws to protect young girls from predators like him."

"If she's having a consensual relationship with the piece of garbage, how can I do anything? She'll never forgive me," Valentina said, more tears running down her face.

"You don't need her approval to file charges against him. Renée is underage, and in your care. I wouldn't worry about what she thinks. You're the mom, and as long as she's in your care, you're responsible for her." Kit spoke confidently, and Ali guessed he'd had experience in this area, dealing with his missing sister.

Maybe he'd written a story on the topic. Either way, he was right.

"I trusted her. I've always warned her about guys. She knows about her father. He was much older than I was. I'd lost my parents, had a fortune at my disposal. Andre was a friend my family met in Paris long before I came along. He didn't care about me. He just wanted my money. He took advantage of me. He was supposed to be my guardian. I got pregnant, just turned eighteen, and things got out of hand. Then, boom, he insisted we marry. The rest isn't hard to figure out," she said, blotting her eyes. "I didn't instill enough in Renée. I've tried to protect her from men like her father. I thought she knew John Wilson is a lowlife scumbag."

Kit looked at Ali. Maybe she needed to step in, add a female point of view. "He took advantage of her age and her naïveté, Val," she said. "You've sheltered her, and that's good. It doesn't take much to turn a young girl's head. Pretty words, offering them undying love . . . all that garbage guys say to have their way with girls. It's no wonder she was . . ." She wanted to use the word "seduced," but didn't know if their relationship had gone that far. She prayed it hadn't. "Impressed. He's older, and he's really not bad-looking, if you can get past the grunge."

Val gave a half-hearted smile. "Apparently he cleaned up for my daughter, because she's a fanatic about cleanliness."

"None of that matters now. What does matter is we need to find her, bring her home, and do as Kit suggested. Renée will thank you for this when she's older and more mature."

"According to Danielle, they're in Orlando at one of the theme parks. That's why she didn't take her phone. I have an app that allows me to see where she goes, but if she doesn't have her phone with her, it's useless."

"Look, let's contact the Orlando police. They're not idiots like those that just left. Do you know what kind of car they're in?" Kit asked her.

"He's got several cars. Or rather, his family does. Danielle didn't know for sure, but I asked her."

"Did she happen to tell you what Renée is wearing? Any plans about where they might spend the night?" Kit took a deep breath. "I know this is hard to hear, but if it helps, we need to know."

"I have no clue what she wore today. She left me a typewritten note, which still doesn't make any sense to me. Maybe she wanted me to think she'd been taken or forced. Who knows? When she returned, she wouldn't need an explanation, because she'd know I would be so relieved that she was home safe. Danielle said she'd offered to cover for her if she didn't make it home tonight, and I'm sure she wasn't telling me the complete truth. Danielle was frightened. Not in the way she normally would be if she were covering for Renée," Val said.

"All the more reason to call the police," Ali said. "I'll stay with you as long as you need me to. Kit, do have a contact in Orlando? Maybe?" she asked hopefully.

"I do, but he's not a police officer. I'll call my friend at the *Orlando Sentinel*. He's an investigative reporter with access to all the data most police departments have. Let me make the call." He walked out to the deck, closing the door behind him.

Ali sat on the stool next to her friend. "I know this isn't what you wanted to hear, but think of it like this—she's alive. She may be ticked off big time when she finds out you know her secret, but it's not the end of the world."

Valentina shook her head. "I know, but I feel like I've failed her. Since she was old enough to know, I've told her about boys, *men*, and how they can influence girls, especially at her age. She knew about her dad, and thank goodness he was out of the picture shortly after Renée was born. He passed away when she was a baby, but I was glad. I knew what he would do once he saw his daughter. It's always been just the two of us. I thought we shared everything. Boy, was I ever wrong." Elbows on the bar, she cupped her chin in both hands, a fresh batch of tears rolling down her face, splattering on the counter.

Ali wanted to tell her about her experience, how she'd turned out okay, or she thought she did, but decided against it. Valentina needed her support, not stories of her past. "Parents make mistakes, Val. You're human," she said. "Times are different now. So are teenagers. Their ideas are often nothing but fantasies. I would bet Renée was just taken in by John's charm."

"The man has no charm, Ali. He's a pervert."

"Why hasn't he been charged? Seriously? I know you said his family bails him out whenever he's in trouble, but who are his victims? Have they ever come out of the woodwork? Maybe some of the parents have and you're not aware?" Ali's thoughts were going in a direction they shouldn't, but what if Valentina's accusations weren't true? Kit grew up on the island, and he'd seemed surprised when she told him what Valentina accused John of.

"His family probably threatened them if they did, or offered money," Valentina said, her voiced filled with disgust. "He's been a thorn in my side for as long as I can remember."

Kit came back inside. "My buddy says we don't have enough information to issue an Amber Alert. We can't prove she's been abducted or that's she's in imminent danger. No description of what she's wearing and no idea what kind of car they're in. All requirements to issue an alert."

Valentina got up and took another soda out of the fridge. She popped the tab on the can, the hissing sound the only noise in the room. She took a couple sips before she spoke. "No, we can't do that. Even if those requirements are met, Renée would kill me if I did that. She'd be so humiliated."

Ali directed a glance toward Kit.

"You just want to wait then? See if she returns on her own? Act like nothing happened?" Kit asked Val. "I'm not a parent, so I don't know what else to suggest, other than calling the Orlando police. Tell them she's a runaway, maybe she was taken against her will. They'll contact the theme parks," he said. "Check with their security."

"I'll call them myself," Valentina said.

"Here's the number to the main office." Kit recited the number. "Ask for Detective Charles Bice. He's friends with my buddy. He said he's the one you'd want to handle this."

"She's going to hate me for the rest of her life," Valentina said as she dialed the number on her cell phone.

"Better than never seeing her again," Kit added.

Val nodded, then stepped outside.

Ali didn't understand Val's hesitancy to do what was needed to protect her daughter. So what if Renée got pissed? She should be home right now. It was after ten; the parks were closing. If they were leaving, maybe one of the security guards would recognize her or that evil, sick John who'd taken advantage of her. The thought hit her out of the blue that people on this island had many secrets. If a sixteen-year-old girl could keep a relationship with an older man from her mother, then who knew what else lay hidden in the minds of these island folks? Yet again, Ali questioned her decision to remain on Palmetto Island.

She and Kit waited inside as Valentina explained the situation to the Orlando police detective. After speaking on the phone for a few minutes, Val ended her call before returning inside. "He's going to make a few calls, then he'll get back to me. Never in a million years did I think my daughter would do the exact opposite of what I've practically beat in her head since she was old enough to know the basics about relationships between men and women. Maybe I should've kept my experience to myself? Had someone told me about men like Andre, I wouldn't have allowed him to take advantage of me. He just wanted my family's money. John's family has plenty of money and contacts. Why would a man his age be interested in a young girl?"

Ali knew a number of reasons but kept them to herself. Now was not the time or place to bring up her past, if ever. She'd survived but didn't believe Renée had the capability to live through the torture she'd suffered at the hands of another sick man like John Wilson.

"Sadly, there's bucketloads of sickos in the world who are obsessed with young kids. Girls, boys, it doesn't matter," Kit said, as Ali observed him. He had more to say, but for one reason or another, he kept it to himself. He was easy to read. Now that she knew what happened to his sister, she understood his forcefulness.

"You've never picked up on any of this with your gift?" Ali had to ask.

"No, I haven't, and that's okay with me. People like myself aren't always psychically in tune with our own family members. I do have a mother's intuition. I really don't want to know my daughter's future, at least not in the way I sense others'."

Briefly, Ali wondered if Valentina had any kind of premonition of her parents' death. She said they died in a fire, but never offered up any details. It had to be incredibly difficult to share the details. Fire had to be one of the most horrific ways to die.

"Have you ever had bad vibes about John? Any visions?" Kit questioned her. "Maybe some that alluded to your daughter?"

Val got up and tossed her empty soda can in a recycling bin beneath the cabinet. "Never. If I had, I would've acted on them. I should send her to Switzerland to finish high school. I spent my first year of high school there. It wasn't so bad."

Ali realized she knew very little about her friend. "That's pretty drastic, though not my business," she said, wishing she'd kept that to herself.

"I know it is. I was there because I wanted to give it a try. I'd had this silly fantasy after a movie I saw in seventh grade. I just had to go to an all-girls' boarding school in Switzerland. I begged my mom and dad to let me at least start high school there, and if I didn't like it, I'd come home."

"Did you like it?" Kit asked.

"Not as much as I thought I would, but it was quite an experience for a fourteen-year-old. When I came home for the summer, I realized how much I missed living on the island, having the beach at my doorstep. Plus, I never did learn how to snow ski. My parents were thrilled, to say the least. I came home, and the next year, they died in an explosion, a gas leak on their boat. I'm told they didn't suffer. I'm not sure I believe that. It's certainly not the ending I expected for them."

"I'm so sorry," Ali repeated.

"Thanks, but I'm okay now. It took a while for me to come to terms with their passing, but it was simply a freak accident. I believe our destinies are predetermined, and it was their time to go. Dad took that summer off; no traveling to his clinics. I remember him telling me and Mom he just wanted to spend the summer with his girls. That's how he referred to us." Valentina walked across the room to stare out the window. "They'd taken the boat out. They were planning to sail over to Sanibel Island for dinner. They did that a lot during that last summer. It was always so cool to me. Even though I'd sailed numerous times with them, I just got a kick out of taking the boat to dinner, seeing the island from a different perspective."

Kit remained quiet, maybe lost in thoughts of his own. After a moment, he said, "I remember reading about that in the paper. I'm sorry I didn't put two and two together sooner," he told Valentina.

"Don't be sorry for me. I've had a decent life. It's Renée I'm sorry for. I swear I'll send her to Switzerland. Anywhere that's far away from that perverted piece of garbage."

"You'll do what's best for her," Ali said. "Renée is a good kid, just young and impressionable."

"I get that, but why *him,* of all people? He's old enough to be her father! It's sick!" Val said, then stepped away from the window. "I've always disliked him. She knows this. He knows it, too."

Ali rubbed the old scar on her temple, thinking back to when she was Renée's age. She had been hardened, wise beyond her years. No way would she have been intimidated by a freak like John Wilson. But before the final experience that sent her running, she'd always held a shred of hope that her life would turn out to be normal, happy, if only the state would find a nice foster family for her to spend the last two years of high school with.

Chapter Thirteen

Covered in blood—her own and his—Alison reached the bus station and saw that it was empty, except for a clerk who appeared lost in his video game. She hurried to the ladies' room before he could spot her.

Seeing herself in the mirror, then quickly looking away, she turned the faucet on with her uninjured arm. Alison was grateful it was her left arm that was injured, since she was right-handed. She caught the icy cold water in her right hand, splashing her face several times before she dared to look in the mirror again. A cut on the left side of her head oozed blood. She leaned in closely to get a better look. The cut was deep; it probably needed stitches. She also sensed her arm was broken, but medical attention was out of the question. If she showed up at the emergency room at this hour, with her injuries, it wouldn't take long for someone at the hospital to call Child Protective Services. She'd be returned to the Robertsons', where she was unprotected by those who were paid to protect her and three other girls.

Each pulse of her heartbeat magnified the pain in her head and arm. Knowing she had to take care of her injuries on her own, she went inside one of the three stalls, choosing the handicapped one, because it was biggest. She slid down onto the dirty tile, not caring there was urine on the floor. She'd seen much worse. With the small amount of cash she'd saved, she had enough for aspirin and some kind of arm bandage. Alison stayed in the stall for another hour before the pain sent her out into the night, searching for relief. Pretty sure IGA was open twenty-four hours, she made her way out of the bus station undetected.

It took an hour for her to walk the three miles. She kept telling herself all the pain in the world was better than being around him. Inside the IGA, the scent of the bakery's yeasty sweetness filled the air. The tasty donuts were famous around town. Alison wanted one so badly she could taste it. She hadn't eaten anything since lunch yesterday. Finding the aisle where the pain relievers were, she chose a generic bottle of extra-strength acetaminophen, a bottle of hydrogen peroxide, and a box of Band-Aids. Unable to find a brace, she opted for an Ace bandage. She'd figure out a way to use it. Next, she headed to the bakery, where the donuts still smelled like heaven. She took a box of six, along with a small carton of chocolate milk, not knowing when she'd have another chance to eat.

She dropped her purchases onto the conveyor belt. The cashier, an older woman, shook her head. "Girl, you look pretty beat up," she said as she bagged her items. She took her cash but didn't speak again. Alison was grateful. Yes, she was beat up, but more mentally than physically. As soon as she left the store, she headed back to the bus station, and again she slipped in without anyone paying attention. She'd had three of the donuts and all of the milk on her walk back. Now back in the handicapped stall, she swallowed four of the pills, using water cupped in her good hand from the faucet.

Next, she removed her shirt, careful of her injured arm. When she saw the extent of the damage to her arm, she realized the Ace bandage wouldn't do much save hide the cuts. Taking a deep breath, she eased her arm under the cool water, carefully wiping away the blood from the cuts; then, she doused her wounds with peroxide, cringing at the sting. Once she'd cleaned up as best she could, she added Band-Aids, then wrapped the Ace bandage around her arm loosely before pulling her shirt back over her head. Another glance in the mirror revealed she looked hideous, but she'd cleaned up most of the visible blood. Knowing it was now or never, she went to the clerk, a woman this time, and asked her what time the next bus left.

"Ten minutes," she told her.

"How much?" Alison asked, not caring where the bus was headed, as long as it was out of the state of Ohio.

"Fifty-five for a round trip to Atlanta is all we got now," she said, adding, "each way."

"What's it cost for one way?"

"Sixty dollars," she told her.

She counted out the money and gave it to the woman, realizing after her purchase at IGA and this ticket, she only had eighteen dollars left. The lady handed her a small booklet with a number of pages. "Each stop, you'll need one to show the driver. You'll change buses in Tennessee."

Alison had never left the state of Ohio. Acting like she'd done this before, she said, "I know." She flipped through the booklet. She also held onto the IGA paper bag, thankful it was light.

"You want food, you gotta bring your own," the clerk told her.

Alison knew it was obvious she'd never traveled before. She held up the box with three remaining donuts. "I'm good," she said, even as hot shards of pain shot up and down her left arm.

"Then have a safe trip," the lady added.

Alison took a seat on a highly polished wooden bench, long enough to seat at least a dozen or more. As soon as she settled on the bench, she heard hissing, a squeal, and a slow grind as the brakes from the bus came to a complete stop in front of the station. She couldn't wait to get on the bus and on the way to a brand-new life. As soon as they allowed her and the six other passengers to board, she chose a seat in the middle of the bus. If she sat in the back, she'd stick out like a sore thumb, the same if she was in the front. Laying her IGA bag on the aisle seat, hoping to deter anyone from sitting beside her even though the bus had plenty of seats, she waited. No one got off in Middletown. She didn't pay much attention to her fellow passengers, as she was trying her best to appear normal and go unnoticed while waiting to depart.

Feeling safe for the first time since she left the Robertsons', she leaned her head against the window, then jerked away. The cut on the left side of her temple still hurt, and her left arm was useless. Knowing she needed medical care—and soon—if she hoped to use her arm again, she'd have to see a doctor. Searching through the ticket booklet, she saw several stops. If she could make it to an emergency room during one of the stops, she'd get the bone set, a cast or something, then hurry back to the bus station and continue on to Atlanta. Once in a new town, she hoped the hospital wouldn't ask too many questions. Right now, all she wanted to do was sleep, but pain and fear kept her alert. She wished she had a book or a magazine. Never in a million years did she imagine that the day after high school graduation, she'd be on her own, heading to parts unknown.

The constant hum of the bus's wheels lulled her in and out of sleep. Finally, she gave in to the need to rest. In spite of the intense throbbing in her arm and head, she allowed herself to drift in and out of a pain-filled state of grogginess.

She was unsure of how much time had passed when the sound of people's voices startled her awake. The driver was in a heated argument with someone at the front of the bus. It was a voice she recognized, becoming louder with each angry word.

"You better let me on this bus, or I'll kick your ass!" he said.

Alison cringed, then did her best to lower herself onto the small area where she'd barely had enough room for her feet.

"With no ticket, sir, I can't allow you to board," the bus driver stated.

Crouched in such a small space, Alison's arm hurt even more. How in the heck did he find her? How long had it been since they'd left the station in Middletown? She wanted to ask someone where they were, but couldn't, because the second he saw her, all hell would break loose.

"I'm gonna follow you, buddy. Your ass is mine next stop," he said.

The bus driver returned to his seat, then reached for the handle to close the doors. He practically fell backward into his seat, or at least that's what it sounded like. When the bus finally pulled out of whatever town they were in, Alison pulled herself up and sat back down in her seat. Looking out the window, she saw they were only in Monroe, just a few short miles from Middletown.

A tap on her shoulder from the person sitting behind her almost caused her to bolt out of her seat. She turned to look at the person behind her.

"I know that guy was after you," said a sweet older woman. "I'll keep my eyes open."

Alison nodded. "Thanks." She couldn't deny it, and in a way, she was glad someone was looking out for her, even if it was only temporary.

"He the one that hurt you?" she asked.

Not wanting to go into details about what had happened to her, she said, "Yeah, but he won't do it again." Where this newfound confidence came from, she hadn't a clue, but she'd keep up the pretense.

"Well, let's hope not. This bus makes a dozen other stops that aren't listed in your ticket voucher."

Dang, she hadn't realized that, but she was not a

seasoned traveler by any means. "It doesn't say that," she said.

"Never does. They never list the small towns, only the larger cities, which means it'll take at least three days before arriving in Atlanta."

Could she remain hidden long enough to leave Ohio behind? Alison knew he wouldn't follow the bus that far. He didn't have gas money; plus, the hunk of junk he drove couldn't make it that far. Assured that she was safe until the next town, she took four more pills from the bottle she'd put in the IGA bag. She chewed them up, then took a bite of the donut to rid herself of the bitter taste, wishing she'd bought a bottle of water.

"Here," said the older lady. She must be a mind reader, as she offered Alison a large bottle of water. "This should hold you over for a while."

"Are you sure? I don't want to take your supplies," she said. Wincing in pain, she did her best to smile at the kind lady.

"I've plenty more where this came from," she said. "You rest up, and I'll let you know when we reach the next stop. Should be about thirty minutes, if I remember."

"You've been on this route before?" Alison asked.

"More times than I can remember. My son and his wife live in Atlanta. I refuse to fly, so I ride the bus. It's not so bad as long as you're not in a hurry."

Alison hoped he wasn't following them to the next stop. If he was, she'd get off the bus and hitch a ride to Atlanta.

Chapter Fourteen

"Alison, are you okay?" asked Kit.

Lost in the past, Ali refocused her attention on the present. "I'm good. I was just thinking," she said—but certainly wouldn't say what it was she had been thinking of.

Valentina returned to the window, staring out at the gulf. "Wouldn't this Bice guy have called by now if he found her?" she asked.

"I don't know. These things could take a while. Remember how large the parks are. And Danielle wasn't sure which park they were going to. I know it's hard, but try to stay calm," Kit told her. Ali had a different view, but it didn't matter at this point. All that mattered was finding Renée.

Valentina walked away from the window again, sitting down on the sofa. "That's not so easy when you're the parent."

"I know," Kit told her. "Not in the sense of being a parent, but I know what it's like to fear for a loved one."

Ali knew what he meant. It could be due to a number of different reasons other than his sister. His mom had passed; maybe there was more to the story than he told her. That was his story, and any other loss he'd been through that she wasn't aware of wasn't her business, anyway. She went over and sat beside her friend on the sofa. "I can't begin to imagine what you're going through, but I'm here for you. Whatever I can do, consider it done."

Val reached for her hand, giving it a squeeze. "Thanks, Ali. I'm glad we're friends."

Ali had been sitting with her for a while when the jarring sound of Valentina's cell phone sent her jolting upright.

"Hello?" Valentina said, answering immediately.

Only hearing one side of the conversation, Ali crossed her fingers, praying whatever Val heard was good news.

"I see," Val said. "I don't have a problem with that."

Alison and Kit waited until she ended her call before bombarding her with questions.

"Have they found her? Is she all right?" Ali asked.

Val nodded, a round of fresh tears snaking down her face. "Yes, they found her, and they said she told them she was fine. Upset, but I wouldn't expect her to be any other way. They're going to keep her in custody at a juvenile center for the night. I'll drive to Orlando first thing tomorrow morning to pick her up."

"And John?" asked Kit.

Val smiled. "He's going to jail. Not sure if he's made his one call to Mommy or Daddy yet. I'm sure they'll send their private jet to pick him up the second he's released."

"Wait a minute—if my understanding of Florida law is correct, there is no bail for abducting a minor and who-knows-what-else he's done," Kit said.

"I guess I should call my family attorney and see what he advises. I'll call him first thing in the morning. Now, all I want to do is take a long, hot shower and call it a night. You two stay with me, okay? There are plenty of rooms. Find one you like and make yourself at home. They're stocked with jammies and tooth-brushes, everything you'll need." Valentina took her cell phone, purse, and a bottled water from the fridge, then headed to her room. "Good night, and thank you both. I appreciate all that you're doing for me and my daughter."

"Sure," Ali said, "get some rest."

Now that she knew Renée wasn't in immediate dan-ger, Ali went to the door and stepped outside. The night air was warm, the breeze from the gulf just enough to keep her comfortable. Kit followed her outside.

"You want to take that walk on the beach?" he asked her.

"Sure," she said, seeing no reason not to.

When they reached the stretch of beach in front of the house, Kit reached for her hand. She didn't resist. As they walked along the water's edge, neither spoke, yet she didn't mind the silence between them. If asked, she'd describe it as comfortable.

As they neared the curve of beach close to the bait store, Kit stopped. "What are the odds of the two of them pairing up? Renée and John, I mean. I'm not so sure the girl wasn't forced into this so-called relation-ship with him." He nodded toward the bait shop.

"She knew Val would be totally against it. Any adult

in their right mind would. I just find it hard to believe Renée would be so reckless. From what I observed, she's a great kid." She didn't add that her gut was telling her this situation was much more than Renée having a fling with John. She'd told her about the guy she was crushing on, and it did not appear to be an act.

"Old cliché, but appearances can be deceiving," he said. "Are you tired?"

She smiled. "Not in the least. If anything, I'm so wired, I doubt I could sleep, even in one of those fancy bedrooms of Val's."

"Same here. What would it take to persuade you to partake in a little breaking and entering?"

"The bait shop?"

"Yes. It's dark, and we know the owner isn't nearby. Might be a chance to find if there was any type of communication between his sick ass and Renée."

"What if we're caught?" she asked, not relishing the idea of having a criminal record. "I've never been in trouble with the law," she added, wanting him to know this wasn't something she took lightly.

"Me either, but I don't plan on getting caught," he said. The moonlight was just bright enough for her to see the smile on his face.

"I suppose there's a first time for everything," she said. Breaking and entering wasn't her first choice, though she knew there was somewhat of a noble reason behind their actions, and it didn't really seem all that bad when she thought of it in those terms.

"Consider this a favor to Val," Kit said, still holding onto her hand. "Come on—let's do this before anyone sees."

She followed him to the bait shop. No lights were on inside, at least none visible from their position. She followed Kit to the back of the shop, the smell familiar. "This is what I smelled in the freezer," she told him, holding her free hand over her mouth and nose.

"Redfish," he whispered.

How he or Val could identify such a sickly fish odor was beyond her sniffing skills. "Doesn't he sell *live* bait?" she whispered back. "Why the stench?"

"Supposedly. Maybe it's dead. Who knows?" Kit said. Releasing her hand, he used both of his to clear away an empty bait bucket, a few reels minus the rods tangled in fishing line, a shovel, and a bag of lime from the top of the outside air-conditioning unit. It was quiet, so Ali assumed it was turned off.

"Who doesn't leave the air on in a freaking bait shop?" Kit asked as he climbed on top of the unit.

"I was just thinking that myself."

"Great minds," he said as he grabbed the shovel.

That reminded Ali of the bone. She hoped her discovery wasn't connected to Kit's cult story. "Yes," she finally said, though she didn't agree with the great mind theory.

She watched as Kit wedged the end of the shovel between the window and the frame. It didn't take much to pop open the window.

"I don't think this was even locked—more like stuck." He slid the window, which opened horizontally, to the side. "No one has these kind of windows anymore." She didn't have that type of window at the cottage, so hopefully hers were old, but still sturdier than these.

As Kit eased his large frame inside, he said, "I don't

want you inside, but keep watch for a few minutes while I search his place."

"Okay," Ali replied in a quiet tone. Scanning the area around her, she didn't see anything unusual. The place stunk big time, but possibly the bait tanks were off. Maybe John hadn't paid his utility bill. Doubting that was the case, she thought maybe there was a short in the electrical wiring. Either way, it couldn't be blamed on one of Florida's famous lightning storms, because the weather had been as dry as a bone.

Dang, she was glad no one could read her mind. Everything came back to that bone. She knew it was human; she didn't care what Dr. Ray Bruce, aka Sharp, said. For all she knew, he could be involved in this cult that Kit was investigating. Maybe the bone actually belonged to Jane. Again, she questioned her decision in making this island her forever home. While it was never too late to leave, she'd used up a chunk of her savings buying the place. If she headed to the Keys, she'd still have enough money to purchase a home, but it sure as heck wouldn't be on the beach. For now, she'd stick to her plan. If she decided later this wasn't the place for her, she'd sell the cottage. Kit lived in Florida. She assumed Miami, since he worked for the *Miami Journal*. Did he have a girlfriend? Had he ever been married? He seemed sincere and honest, though she did not have much experience with normal relationships, so there was nothing to compare it with.

A loud clinking sound jarred her from her thoughts. As quietly as possible, she walked the perimeter of the bait shop but didn't see anything or anyone. She went to the front of the shop and walked up the wooden walkway to the entrance. Placing a hand on either side of her face, she leaned as close to the door as she could without actually touching the glass. She saw large bait tanks against both walls. The center of the store had freestanding displays of fishing gear. Bright yellow bait buckets stacked inside one another were shoved between the tanks. That all made sense, she thought, as she continued to look through the door. She wondered why she didn't see Kit. He must be in an area that couldn't be viewed from the front. She stepped away from the door and almost cried out when she bumped into Kit.

"Shhh." He held his finger against his lips. "I think I heard someone inside. Let's hurry." He took her hand, and they ran as fast as they could. When they reached the curve of beach where the bait shop was no longer in sight, they both dropped down on the damp sand.

When she got her breath, she told Kit what she heard.

"That was probably me tossing the shovel out the window. I didn't get a chance to look in his office. Pretty sure someone is camping inside. I saw a few food wrappers. No power, either, hence all the dead shrimp and minnows. Whatever bait he had, it's useless now."

Not that Alison cared, but still curious, she asked, "Why?"

"Fish like live bait. That's the general rule around here," he said, then touched her cheek with his fingertip.

"Oh," was all she could come up with. Her entire body felt electrified by his touch. Never in her life had a man had this effect on her, and so instantaneously. Before she could overthink what she felt, his mouth came toward hers, his lips soft against hers. Leaning into his kiss, her body yearning, she placed her hands on his shoulders, pulling him close to her. Kit's hands gently touched her face as he deepened their kiss. She was unsure of how long they had kissed when Kit's mouth eased from hers. He gazed into her eyes.

"Alison Marshall, what have you done to me?" He smiled, then wrapped her in his arms as though it were the most natural thing in the world, as though they'd both done this many times before.

Her lips tingled. They felt bruised, but in a good way. Uncertain how to respond to his question, she opted to remain silent. Someone, though she couldn't recall who it was, had told her long ago that if you didn't know an answer to a question, say nothing. To act as though you did understand only made one appear ignorant. Or something to that effect.

"So," Kit said, "what are we going to do about this?" He nodded at her.

She responded truthfully. "I don't know what you mean." She remembered he was a Pulitzer Prize–winning author, so he must think her dumb as a box of rocks.

"Us. Me and you."

"Oh, well, do we have to do something special or what? I don't get it." She was glad for the darkness, because she felt her face redden. Experience with men wasn't her strongest suit.

He laughed. "I, for one, like kissing you. I like you. Maybe a little more than like," he added.

Finally, she understood. "I liked it too. I like you back."

"Good, then it's settled. We like each other. I see no reason to keep our feelings secret; what about you?"

Ali's heart was beating so fast, she prayed she didn't suffer a heart attack right there on the beach. "I guess so," she said. "Why does it matter?"

"I'm working on a story that probably involves you, albeit indirectly. Folks around here gossip, as you know. It doesn't matter one bit to me, but I just want you to be okay with it if I decide to hold your hand or give you a kiss in public."

More than okay, she wanted to tell him, but just nodded.

He leaned close to her, giving her a kiss on both cheeks, then her mouth. "Good, because I'm an affectionate kinda guy."

He took her by the hand, and they stood up, heading back to Val's.

Feeling as though she could speak freely, she said, "Was it just me, or do you think it odd that Val didn't freak out when she finally found out where Renée was? I guess I thought she'd be more upset at the thought of her daughter spending the night in a juvenile home. I'm upset that she has to experience that at such a young age."

When they reached the beach house, they stopped. "I don't have kids, but if I did, I'd probably leave them to stew a while, too," said Kit. "Maybe make them rethink why they didn't follow the rules. Learn a lesson, I guess."

She sighed as she stared out at the gulf. The rushing waves, though slight, could be heard above the night sounds. The noises of frogs, birds' fluttering wings, and the occasional owl were a backdrop to her thoughts.

She'd been in foster homes that were worse than living in juvie. "If she were my daughter, I'd be on the road to bring her home."

"Do you want to tell this to Val? I saw the expression on your face when she decided to go to bed."

"It's not my place to tell her how to discipline her daughter, but it seemed out of character for her. She was upset to the point where I thought she would jump into action the second she heard any news. I'm not too sure this came as a big shock to her. As close as they are, I can't imagine her not knowing, or at least being suspicious. I'm not convinced Renée is even having any kind of relationship with John. Val gets very uptight when his name is mentioned, not that I blame her. Maybe there is more to this than she's telling us."

"I've just met the woman, but I trust you know her well enough."

"I just met her a couple days ago myself. For some reason, we clicked. Like we'd known each other a long time. She's a good person, I can tell. Maybe her gift allows her to . . . I don't know, relax now that she knows Renée is safe. Again, I'm just assuming most of this."

"I get it. As long as the kid makes it home safely, that's all that truly matters." Kit placed an arm across her shoulder. He was so tall, she had to lean her head all the way back to look up at him.

"We better get back inside before whoever was at the bait shop sees us lingering on the beach this time of night," Ali said, even though it was not what she wanted to do. She could spend all night listening to Kit or just being next to him. There was something special between them. Her question was: Was it special enough to survive a long-distance relationship?

"Let's go," he said, then guided her up the stairs to the deck. "You know what would be nice before we call it a night?"

Several images crossed her mind. "You tell me."

"A drink, maybe? A glass of wine."

"I guess," she said, then explained, "I'm not much of a drinker, so I'd be clueless as to what kind of wine is appropriate for this time of night."

"Whatever you like. And if it's not your thing, have a soda," he said. He was so unlike the few trashy dates she'd had who guzzled beer after beer, insisting she keep up with them, and then always stuck her with the tab. No more, she thought. Kit was a true gentleman.

"I'll see what Val has open," she said, quietly slipping into the house and opening the fridge door. Spying a bottle of white wine, she took a bottle of water for herself and found a paper cup among Val's supply of paper goods. She poured a generous amount into the cup before returning the bottle to the fridge. She hoped Val didn't think she was taking advantage of this unusual situation. She could replace the wine but didn't want to imagine losing her newfound friendship.

She found Kit seated in a deck chair with a small table beside it. She set the cup down, taking the deck chair beside him. "It's nice, huh?" she said, indicating the view.

"The best. This little strip of beach was my playground as a kid."

Surprised, Ali asked, "Did you live in one of these houses?" Most of them looked fairly new to her, though it was possible that any of the houses could have been updated.

"It's been torn down and remodeled. The empty place in front of yours was our land."

"I bet it's strange to see it all now, modern with all that glass," she said.

"Yeah, it's nice. Our place was old, like your cottage. If I'm not mistaken, both were built around the same time, in the early sixties. A little before our time." He took a sip of wine. "They don't build homes like those anymore."

Ali nodded, then took a sip of water. "I don't know too much about building or remodeling, even though I've spent plenty of time watching all those television programs that knock down dumps and rebuild mansions." Her words sounded doltish, and she felt ignorant.

Kit laughed. "I like how succinct you are. Don't see many women like you," he said, still smiling so she didn't take too much offense to his words.

"It's a good thing, right?" She just needed to confirm he wasn't making fun of her. Ali wouldn't be able to stand it if he were. She wanted him in her life. Never having had such sudden feelings for a man, she felt utterly and completely vulnerable.

"Very, especially because I appreciate the fact we're alike in that sense. No bull, just the two of us," he said, then took another drink.

She was relieved, but her insecure side needed to hear more—promises, details on their future, if this was going to be a summer fling or not. She'd realized they'd just met, and the circumstances weren't normal. Rushing into any kind of relationship with Kit probably wasn't a good idea, but for once in her life, she wasn't going to stress over what her future might be. Feeling such intense emotion was not her way. Yet here she was with a sexy, intelligent guy, secretly thrilled but afraid to say it, especially at such a horrific time.

"I don't mince words," was all she could come up with. If he knew what she was thinking, he'd probably run like a frightened animal. She smiled, remembering Peaches and her kittens.

"You know, you're beautiful when you smile," he told her. "That's about as cliché as one can get."

"What if I'm not smiling?" she asked, though she continued to smile at him.

"Stunning, mysterious, intriguing . . . I could go on if you'd like," he told her. "You want to tell me what made you smile? I hope it was me, but something tells me it wasn't."

She told him about finding Peaches and her babies. "It was sheer luck when I saw that Missing sign."

"You love animals."

"Yes, though I've never had a pet of my own. I plan on getting a dog when I'm settled in the cottage."

"Best friend you'll ever have."

She started to speak but suddenly stopped when she heard a scream. "Did you hear that?"

He nodded, motioning for her to follow him. Halfway down the steps, they heard a second scream. "That's human," Ali whispered.

"Stay here," he ordered.

"No, I'm going with you."

"Let's wait a minute," he whispered.

Another scream sounded; then they raced down the

steps to the beach. "Sounds like one of those screaming birds, a limpkin." They were rare birds in Florida, but she'd heard their screams a few times.

"Probably a domestic dispute," he said.

Ali tried to recall if she'd seen any occupants in the neighboring beach houses. "I haven't seen anyone, though that doesn't mean anything."

He took her hand. "Let's walk the beach and see if we can locate where the screams are coming from."

They retraced their steps from their last excursion. As soon as they were at the curve of beach leading to the marina and bait shop, there was another scream; only this time, it was much louder.

"We're close," Kit said, taking her hand. "Let's wait a minute more."

Ali nodded.

A few seconds later, they heard another scream, though this one was followed by the cry: "Help me!"

Chapter Fifteen

"Run," Kit shouted over his shoulder as he raced toward the bait shop. Alison's side pinched as she tried keeping up with him. When he reached the bait shop, he stopped, motioning for her to stay where she was.

They waited for what seemed like forever, but whoever was screaming had either got away or the unthinkable might've happened. "Should we go inside?"

"I'll get in the same as before, only stay put this time, just in case," he said as they quietly walked to the back of the bait shop. The items Kit tossed off the air conditioner were exactly as they'd left them. The only thing missing was the shovel.

"This is not looking good," he said.

"No," Alison agreed, wishing she'd brought her gun.

"Watch my back while I go inside." He told her as if this was something they'd done a zillion times before. She liked that he trusted her enough to ask.

"I will," she promised. This night reminded her of the times she'd spent throughout her life constantly looking over her shoulder, wondering if she could've done anything different. If so, would she have lived to tell what happened all those years ago?

Crouching down on the floorboards of the bus when they made another stop, Alison waited for him to come for her. Her lady friend said she'd tell her if she saw him again, but Alison knew it didn't matter. His loud, overbearing voice could be heard blocks away. Another fact she knew from experience.

The bus driver pulled the handle to open the door, allowing new passengers to board and others to leave. They were in Cincinnati and had a two-hour stop. Alison hadn't planned on leaving the safety of the bus while they waited for their next driver.

"I don't see him, dear," her friend told her.

Alison pushed herself up, flinched when she banged her injured arm on the back of the seat in front of her. Tears filled her eyes. The pills she'd bought didn't seem to be working anymore. She'd taken four of them about twenty minutes ago and felt no relief.

When she was able, she turned to the sweet woman. "Are the buses always on time?" she asked.

"Honestly, no, they're never on time. I've waited in the city for five or six hours before. Not sure why, but Cincinnati is always the worst and longest stop."

Knowing she needed medical attention, Alison thought this might be the stop where she could find a hospital. But because she was alone, underage, and practically broke, she didn't know if the hospital would treat her. Plus, he could be lurking right around the corner. He was sneaky that way. "Can I ask a favor?" She looked at the sweet lady, tears filling her eyes. She rubbed them away with her good hand. "My arm is broken, and I need to see a doctor."

"Then what are we waiting for?"

"Really? You'll help me?"

"We can catch a cab and head to Good Samaritan Hospital. They have an emergency room. Let's go before . . ." She paused. "Before we can't."

Alison knew exactly what she meant. She nodded.

"What's your name?" the woman asked Alison.

Debating whether she should give her real name in case the Robertsons were looking for her, she decided to be as truthful as possible. This woman was helping her, and she owed it to her to be honest. "I'm Alison Marshall."

"Nice to meet you, Alison Marshall. I'm Violet Danbridge."

"That's a pretty name," she told her.

As soon as they stepped off the bus, Alison saw a line of taxis. Violet waved her hand, and a yellow cab pulled up to the curb. "We need to get to Good Samaritan Hospital as fast as you can get us there. My granddaughter broke her arm at the last stop." Violet winked at her.

Alison liked this lady.

"I'll put the pedal to the metal, but if I get a ticket, you gotta promise me you'll pay for it," the cabbie

teased. Around sixty or so, bald, and with big ears and a pair of sunglasses resting on top of his head, he seemed genuinely nice.

Though she was in severe pain, Alison looked out the window, taking in the city. She'd never been this far outside of Middletown and had no idea what to expect. There were buildings, roads wrapping around one another, some crisscrossing over the top of the other, cars driving so fast she thought for sure they would crash into the taxi. Her eyes widened each time one car got close to the cab.

Violet must've sensed her fear, because she placed a hand on her lap. "We're safe, Alison. It's not much farther."

She just nodded, hoping they didn't get in an accident. She'd never been in a car that was going as fast as they were now. It scared her, but at the same time, despite the pain she was in, she felt a thrill, excitement at the thought of racing down this great highway. When she could, she'd buy a car of her own, and if she wanted to drive as fast as the cab driver, she would. If they made it to the hospital without crashing.

The taxi driver took the next exit, then a few minutes later, he pulled into the parking area of the emergency room. "Safe and sound," he said, then slid out from the driver's seat, opening the door for Violet. She reached inside a little dainty white purse with pink roses embroidered on the outside and took a wad of cash, handing it to the driver. "Thank you so much," she said.

"You got any idea how long you're gonna be inside? If you do, I can return and take you two back to the bus station."

Violet shook her head. "No, but thank you for the offer. If you have a phone number, I could call when we're ready."

He took a card from his shirt pocket. "Here, ask for Al. If I'm available, I'll be back in a flash."

"Very well, Al. Thank you," she said.

Alison couldn't believe her luck. First Violet, now Al, both going out of their way for her. "Thanks, Al," she managed to say. "It was a good ride."

"Anytime, kid," he said before returning to his cab.

Violet waved as he screeched out of the parking lot. "That man does know how to drive a car," she said with admiration. Alison smiled, even though she felt like she was ready to pass out from the pain. "Now, let's see what these doctors can do for you."

Inside, the emergency room throbbed with activity. People of all ages waited in the main room. Stacks of magazines were scattered around a large table. Alison eyed the soda machine and snack machine in the corner. She wished she had some change. She was thirsty, and a soda would be heavenly.

Violet touched her shoulder. "Let's register," she said, leading her to the admissions area.

"Okay," Alison said, feeling nervous. What if she'd waited too long to see a doctor? What if they had to amputate her arm? She hadn't had much medical care, except when she was little. She had been vaccinated so she could attend school.

Violet spoke to the admissions clerk with such confidence, Alison admired her even more.

"Let's get her to X-ray now," the admissions clerk said when Violet was done. "You'll need this," she said, tying a plastic bracelet on Alison's right arm and giving a sticker for Violet to place on her blouse.

The double doors buzzed, then automatically opened. A nurse wearing dark blue scrubs appeared, her hair twisted in a bun. She held a clipboard in her hand, glancing at the information. "Follow me," she said.

Alison heard sounds of moaning, crying, and in one area, a woman yelling at the top of her lungs. What had she gotten herself into? She'd rather suffer.

"Alison, don't be frightened by these folks. They're injured or sick. People tend to get a bit loopy in these types of situations," the nurse reassured her.

Relieved, though a bit puzzled that she knew her thoughts, Alison just nodded.

"In here," said the nurse in the blue scrubs.

The small area had a long bed with all kinds of buttons and handles. Behind the bed were various cords plugged into different receptacles. She'd never seen this stuff before.

"Have a seat," the nurse said. "Let's get your vitals before the X-ray team gets down here. They are pretty darn fast."

Alison sat on the bed, surprised at how hard it was. The nurse checked her blood pressure, took her temperature, then stuck something on her finger. As soon as she finished, she wrote on her clipboard. "Your stats are decent, though your blood pressure is a bit high for your age. But you're in pain, so that's very common; nothing to be concerned with. I'm going to get an IV going. We'll give you some meds and make you feel as happy as a lark." She removed supplies from a cabinet opposite the bed. She ripped open some packaging, *tossing it aside, then took Alison's right hand and cleaned it with alcohol. "This might pinch a little, but something tells me you're a tough cookie." She inserted a large needle, then added tape to hold it in place. A bag of something clear was attached to a pole above her right side. Tubing connected to her IV. Alison was scared, hoping they didn't inject her with poison.*

"You okay, hon?" the nurse asked.

Alison nodded, then directed her eyes on the giant rolling machine being pushed through the door. "You guys are fast," the nurse said. "We've got an open fracture, swelling, a few cuts," she told the X-ray team.

A tall African American man smiled at Alison. He looked at the bracelet on her arm and asked her to repeat her name and date of birth. She recited the information back to him, unsure why it mattered.

The second X-ray tech was a young woman with deep blue eyes and short blonde hair. She was so tiny, she reminded Alison of Tinker Bell. "Sweetie, I'm going to cut your shirt away, then Susannah, your nurse, will clean your cuts. But first, let's get a picture of what's going on with this bone peeping out."

"Susannah, go ahead and give her a little bit of morphine before taking an X-ray," a man standing in the doorway said, then stepped inside. "I'm Dr. Grant." He looked at her wristband before saying, "Alison." He wasn't very old, Alison thought, though he was bald, and in need of a shave. He wore the same blue scrubs as the nurse, plus a white jacket with the hospital's name printed on it and his name beneath.

Her nurse took a clear bottle from a red drawer that

reminded her of a toolbox. She inserted a needle in the top of the bottle, then injected the liquid into Alison's IV. Seconds later, she was dizzy, like she was floating on a cloud. She smiled, not caring about anything.

"Feel better?" Dr. Grant asked.

She tried to nod, but her eyes felt so heavy, she couldn't keep them open.

"Let's get a picture, then get her upstairs. This girl is going to need surgery. Stat."

Chapter Sixteen

Ali waited while Kit searched inside the bait shop. She didn't hear anyone screaming, but the missing shovel scared her more than the scream, knowing what it could've been used for.

On edge, she breathed a sigh of relief when she saw Kit climb out of the window, his arms clutched against his chest. "There's a laptop, and a really old cell phone," he said, handing her the items while he crawled the rest of the way out. He closed the window behind him. "Someone's definitely staying in the office. There's all kinds of crap in there. Pillows, blankets, empty fast-food containers. And the power is off."

As soon as he jumped off the air-conditioning unit, he took the computer and phone back. "Let's get out of here."

They ran as fast as they could, a repeat of their earlier jaunt. Reaching the curve on the beach, the bait shop out of eyesight, Ali plopped down on the sand, not caring that her shorts were soaking wet. Taking a few seconds to get her breathing under control, she waited while Kit opened the laptop. "There's still plenty of battery," he told her. "Check this—see if it's charged." He handed her the cell phone.

She fumbled with the buttons, and a small grayish-green screen came to life. "I guess it's working." She didn't want Kit to know how little she knew about technology.

"What's the last number dialed?" he asked as his keys flew across the laptop's keyboard. *Of course he types fast*, she thought. He was a reporter.

"I don't know how to search this. Sorry," she admitted, once again feeling ignorant at her lack of knowledge.

"No worries. Let me see what I can find." He took the phone and hit a few buttons before turning it off. "I don't want to waste the battery. No clue where I can find a charger that'll work on this antiquated piece of junk if I lose the battery power."

"Let's take it back to Val's. We can search there for whatever it is you're looking for. I'm not very good with technical stuff."

"Good, because this stuff controls your life. All the social media and text messaging can drive you up the wall."

Breathing a sigh of relief because he didn't tease her, she said, "Yeah, nothing I can't live without." And she meant it. Working as a waitress, she saw how people never communicated without their phones. No one spoke at the table, but to try and take their attention away from their phones, she'd had to raise her voice many times just to take an order.

They hurried back to Val's but didn't run this time. Once inside, Kit took the laptop, sitting down at the bar. Ali took two Diet Cokes from Val's plentiful supply.

"Thanks," Kit said, yet continued typing faster than anyone she'd seen, never taking his eyes off the screen. "I was able to get past the security, and now I'm reading a doc. But none of this makes any sense to me."

"What?"

"It's all about . . ." He paused. "Blood. Guts from fish. Redfish, specifically. Used in ways they shouldn't be."

She stood beside him, looking at the screen. She read a couple paragraphs. "Who does this belong to?"

"I don't know, but I'm pretty sure it doesn't belong to John, or have anything to do with the bait shop. Whoever this belongs to has major problems." He raked a hand through his hair.

Ali was alarmed, because she could see that Kit was, as well. Had they put themselves in jeopardy by taking this computer? Other than the breaking, entering, and stealing, what kind of crime could they be charged with, if it was discovered that they had this computer? Her thoughts raced. This island was unlike any place she'd been to in Florida. She remembered what Kimberly told her—she had said the island was a gem, because it hadn't been discovered by the big corporations wanting to build condos, houses, that kind of thing. Maybe they were smarter than Kimberly thought.

"What can we do with this?" she asked. "The blood stuff you found."

He sighed. "Take it to the police, but then we'd have

to explain how we managed to get our hands on this."
He tapped the computer.

"Maybe it belongs to a medical student who left it
behind, and, I don't know, maybe John found it."

"This isn't medical school terminology."

"How do you know?"

"Trust me, I know. Medical students wouldn't be interested in the innards of redfish. This is what I've
been searching for. I just need time to see what's on the
hard drive, see everything on it."

"So do it," she said. None of this made sense to her,
but right now, it didn't matter.

"I'm not that smart, but I know someone who is,"
Kit said, then took his cell phone from his pocket. "It's
late, but I need to make a call." He hit the green call
icon on his cell.

"Hey, Louie, what's up?" Kit said. "Yeah, I know.
Sorry about the time, but you know I wouldn't call if it
wasn't important."

Ali listened to the one-sided conversation. She
couldn't pretend to understand all the technical words
Kit used, but she was confident he knew what he was
doing. At least, she hoped so.

Today had been one of the best days in her life, and
also one of the worst, if that were even possible. She'd
made friends. Had a fantastic time with Val shopping.
She owned a home, and it was possible she'd finally
met the man of her dreams. Crossing her fingers behind her back, she offered up a silent prayer that Renée
would be unharmed emotionally and physically, that
Val wouldn't be too hard on her, and, somehow, she

hoped Kit could solve his mystery. And most of all, she hoped like hell there wasn't a cult in her new backyard.

Kit hung up, then made a second call. "How much will it take for you to fly to Miami? Tonight, both ways?" he asked the person on the other line, who Alison deduced was a pilot.

"I'm on Palmetto Island. I can meet you at Page Field in an hour," Kit said. "I'm on my way."

Ali waited for an explanation.

"My buddy Louie in Miami is a technological whiz. I need to see everything on this hard drive tonight. You want to fly to Miami with me or stay here with Val?"

"Are you serious?" She'd never flown in her life.

"I am."

"No," she said, shaking her head. "I think I need to stay with Val, just in case."

"Good decision. I was hoping you'd say that. If I have any news, I'll call. I'll let you know when I return. Meet me at The Daily Grind, if you can."

"Why there?" she asked, realizing how stupid she sounded.

"I have my reasons." He closed the laptop, then stuck the old cell in one pocket, his in the other. "The owner, Pete, is a good friend of mine, and my family's. Plus, I think we'll both need a large dose of caffeine."

"Fish-Eyes?" she said.

"Not what I call him, but yes, Pete owns the place. He's a good guy. Someone you'd want on your side if you're in trouble."

"Sorry, I didn't mean to insinuate anything rude. The first time I saw him, that impression came to mind, with his glasses and all. Pete. I'll remember that."

"No worries, Alison. Stop overthinking everything—you're perfect just the way you are."

She'd been on the defensive her entire life. It would take time for her to learn not everyone was against her. "Thanks."

"Try and get some sleep. Go with Val to Orlando in the morning if you want. A little moral support."

"Definitely," she said, even though she hadn't discussed it with Val yet. If Val invited her along, she would go, but she wouldn't force herself on her. Before she could say anything else, Kit kissed her on the cheek. "Promise you'll call me if there's trouble," he said.

"I will," she said, knowing he was referring to their breaking and entering expedition.

As soon as he left, Ali felt a void, not just physically, but emotionally, too. Before going upstairs to one of the lavish bedrooms, she cleared away the paper plates and the soda cans and folded the pizza box so it would fit in the recycling bin. Using damp paper towels, she wiped down the counters, then tossed the wet paper in the bin with the rest of the recyclables.

Quietly, she went upstairs, going to the bedroom next to Renée's, thinking she'd feel closer to her this way. Trying to put together details of what happened since she'd been on the island, she stepped into the shower, letting the hot water rinse the sweat and salt water off her skin. She shampooed her hair twice, then just stood beneath the powerful jets, the water easing the tension in her neck and shoulders.

When she finished her shower, she saw a white robe and matching nightshirt hanging on the back of the door. She slipped them on, then wrapped a large bath towel turban-style around her wet hair. Beside the sink were several unopened toothbrushes and tiny tubes of toothpaste. She brushed her teeth, then opened a drawer, where she found brushes and combs still in their wrapping, plus travel-size bottles of hair conditioner, hair spray, and just about all one would need. Valentina had thought of everything, though Ali couldn't help but wonder why she had all these bedrooms equipped like a hotel. Neither she nor Renée had mentioned having guests often, but again, she'd only just met them. She towel-dried her hair, making sure to leave the bathroom as she'd found it, minus what she'd used.

The bedroom was as luxurious as Ali remembered. The floor-to-ceiling windows faced the beach. She stood gazing at the view, amazed that soon she'd be in her own home, where she'd have almost as good a view. As she watched the ebb and flow of the tide, at the opposite end of the beach that she'd yet to explore, she saw a light, though not a flashlight or the kind of lights fishermen used.

Straining to see, she ran downstairs as quietly as possible. She went out on the deck for a better view. When she realized what she was seeing, it took a couple seconds for her to absorb.

Branches stacked in what appeared to be a pyre-like shape burned bright, the red and yellow flames spewing sparks into the night sky. Ali ran down the three flights of steps. Her cottage was visible, yet far enough away from any danger from the fire. She raced down the path to the beach, then to the public parking lot.

Scrunched down behind a copse of overgrown pygmy date palms, she watched people in gold and red robes circling the fire, chanting, though she couldn't make out what they were saying. This must be the cult Kit was investigating. She knew it as certainly as she knew the sun would rise tomorrow.

Fear trickled down her spine like the touch of tiny spider legs against her skin. Goosebumps mottled her arms and legs. The chanting grew louder, more forceful. Straining to hear, she didn't understand their words, thinking they spoke in another language. She needed to return to Val's to call Kit. Hoping he'd reached Miami, she stayed low to the blacktop, praying no one would see her. As soon as she reached the beach, she ran as fast as she could toward Val's. Once she was on the path leading to the deck, she was relieved she'd made it back without being seen. As soon as her foot was securely on the first step, a hand yanked her back so hard her head hit the pad of cement at the bottom of the stairs.

Fear clutched her. *Scream*, she thought, but no, she didn't want Val hurt. Her arms were gripped above her head by strong hands, her heels dragging through the sand, rubbing against clumps of grass and shell. She felt a knot on her head where she'd hit the pad of cement.

She was unable to see whoever was dragging her, as they had their back to her, but they had to be incredibly strong. Bumping along the wet shore, her hair matted against her face, she took a deep breath, then tried to pull her arms free.

"You son of a bitch! I'll kill you!" she shouted. Knowing Val was out of earshot, and therefore safe, she dug her raw heels into the sand, trying to slow him down. A beast with inhuman strength, he pulled on her arms so hard, she felt a *snap* as her shoulder popped out of its socket.

The world went black.

Chapter Seventeen

*W*hen Alison woke, unsure where she was, a cool hand touched her forehead.

"You're going to be fine, Alison."

Then she remembered. Violet had taken her to the hospital in Cincinnati. She was tired. Though she didn't feel any pain in her arm, she remembered the nurse giving her something that made her feel like she was sleeping on a cloud.

"The doctor wants to keep you here tonight. You've had surgery—a few pins in your arm to keep your bone in place," Violet explained. "You'll be just fine here."

It took a few seconds for her to completely understand what Violet meant. Using her good arm to push herself upright, Alison tried to swing her feet to the side of the bed, when a wave of queasiness hit her.

"Lie down, dear. The anesthesiologist said you'll feel a bit nauseous from the pain medication. Try to relax."

"The bus?" she asked.

"*Another bus comes tomorrow, same route,*" Violet told her.

"*I can't stay here,*" Alison said. "*I don't have any way to pay.*" She turned her face away so Violet couldn't see her tears. Ashamed, she wished Violet would just leave and let her take care of things the way she was used to.

By running away.

"*Let's not worry about that, dear. I've called my son in Atlanta and explained the delay. I've already booked a room at the Holiday Inn across the street. I'll stay there, and tomorrow you and I will resume our trip.*"

Alison turned to look at her. "*Why? You don't even know me. People don't do this,*" she said, because in her world, it was true.

"*Something tells me you haven't been exposed to the good side of this fascinating world. There are good people, Alison, people who help others less fortunate simply because it's the right thing to do.*"

Staring at this sweet woman, Alison wondered if she was an angel. Maybe she had died during the fight earlier, had fallen down the rabbit hole like Alice, and this was Wonderland.

"*I don't know if this is real.*" She waved her good arm around.

"*You want me to give you a little pinch?*" Violet teased. "*This is very much the real world, and today I am going to see to it that you're taken care of. Tomorrow is a new day, a chance for a brand-new start. Now, I am going to let you rest, as I have some things I need to take care of before I go to the hotel. I've given Dr.*"

Grant the number at the hotel, should you need me. Get some rest while you can." Violet placed a hand on her cheek. "I'll see you tomorrow."

Tears rivered down Alison's face. She nodded, then reached for Violet's hand and squeezed it. "Thank you so much."

Alison drifted into a drug-induced, yet restful, sleep. During the night, nurses came and went. She heard their footsteps, the door opening and closing, but she was so satisfied in this half-state of sleep, she didn't care who came into the room. It was so peaceful in spite of the noise, the machines beeping, and voices sounding over an intercom system. It might be nice to just stay here forever.

She was unsure how much time had passed when she woke again, because it was dark outside. The lights in her room were dim. Someone had placed a bottle of Coke and a cup of ice on the bedside table. Filling the cup, she used a straw that bent, which she thought too cool, but no one was here to witness her reaction when she'd figured out its purpose. She was hungry, but she was used to the gnawing sensation. No more had this thought passed through her mind than her door opened, and a girl probably not much older than her carried in a tray. Delicious smells filled the room.

"I came in earlier, but you were sleeping, so I thought you might like something to eat now. It's late," the girl said as she rolled a portable table up to the bed, placing the tray on top. "If you want more, just hit the call button, and the nurses will get you whatever you want."

Alison stared at her. "Another Coke?"

The girl laughed. "Tell you what—my shift is over, but I'll run down to the cafeteria and grab a couple Cokes. You can keep them in your room." She picked up a pale green ice bucket. "And I'll get you more ice. Be right back," she said and whizzed out the door.

In her seventeen years, Alison had never been treated this way. Anything she wished for, and it magically appeared. She used her good hand and reached beneath the cover, where she pinched her thigh as hard as she could. "Ouch!" she said.

This wasn't a dream. She hadn't died and gone to some strange wonderland where people were kind and thoughtful. No, this is what normal people do, she thought as she dived into the mashed potatoes and gravy. She gobbled down all the food, including the small fruit cup. There was a chocolate cookie wrapped in paper beside her plate, so she ate that, too. Taking another drink of her Coke, she'd never been so satisfied with a meal in her life. Closing her eyes, she was content for the moment. When the door opened, she smiled to herself. The young girl bringing her Cokes was fast.

Opening her eyes to say thank you to her, she was shocked when she saw her visitor was not the young nurse.

Her worst nightmare stood in the entryway.

He had found her.

Dried blood stained the gauze bandages wrapped around his neck.

"Thought I was dead, didn't ya?"

Chapter Eighteen

Ali could smell her hair as it burned. Flames scorched her arms and legs, her skin an inferno as the firestorm traveled the length of her body. The flames blazed toward her face. She let out a piercing scream as the flesh fell away from her bones.

"Shut up," said an unfamiliar voice in a harsh whisper.

Ali drifted in and out of consciousness, though in a moment of clarity realized she'd been dreaming. Her hands were tied behind her back. She yanked as hard as she could in order to free them, but only succeeded in deepening the abrasions on her wrists. Her legs and arms numb, she struggled to a sitting position. Taking a deep breath, trying to calm her thoughts. She turned her head left to right, searching for a way out. Not even a sliver of light illuminated the room. Shifting her position, she lay down, lifting her legs as high as she could, flipping her body so that her hands were now in front of her. Her shoulder was on fire. She remembered this pain, its intensity, from another injury in her past.

After another deep breath, she focused on her hands. The rope felt like thick jute, though not so thick that she couldn't bite through the fibers. Bringing her hands forward, her shoulder igniting in pain, she started chewing on the rope. It tasted salty, a slight fishy taste. A fisherman's rope. She bit the fibers until they began to unravel. Using every ounce of her mental fortitude, taking another breath, she managed to yank one hand free. Closing her eyes, pain reverberating throughout her entire body, she removed her other hand from the rope. Feeling the ropes tied to her ankles, she shimmied one ankle loose, then the other. Her body pulsed with pain, her shoulder throbbing, but she managed to stand.

With no visible light, she held her hand out in front of her, touching the walls. The room was much smaller than she thought. Sliding her hands up and down, she touched metal. A door handle. Slowly, she turned the knob, surprised it wasn't locked. Careful not to alert her kidnappers, maybe even would-be killers, she tried to be as quiet as possible. She had no clue where she was, save that it was dark and damp. She pushed the door aside, stunned to find a set of steps above her. Light filtered in through the bottom of the door at the top of the staircase.

She was in someone's basement. No one had basements in Florida. This had to be an underground space, built specifically for reasons she wouldn't even allow herself to imagine. She didn't want to know what had taken place in this room; it was too gruesome. She took one stair at a time, stopping at each step to listen for her attacker. When she reached the top step, she again gently twisted the knob, opening the door to a small room.

Ali was in an old-looking bedroom. Boards were stacked against the wall, and a box spring and mattress, along with junk she didn't have time to identify, littered the room. A broken lamp lay on its side, the shade smashed in. The room looked as though a tornado had passed through.

Fearful of her captor finding her exposed like this, she searched for a door that she could escape through. She had no clue if she was still on the beach or elsewhere. She didn't care; she just had to get out. Scanning the small space, she saw light coming through a dirty window. The sun wasn't completely up yet. She had to get out of here before daylight. Her shoulder was swollen, so stiff it hurt just to touch. She didn't care about the pain. The window was the same sliding style as at the bait shop. Could that be where she was?

She ran her good hand around the edges of the window, searching for the lock. Finding it, she pulled back on the lever, freeing the window. Thankfully, there was no screen. Every second counted, so she placed both legs outside the window, then dropped to the ground below. Catching her breath, doing her best not to focus on her shoulder or the wounds on her ankles and wrists, she spied a dumpster and a rusted boat trailer. It took a few seconds for her to recognize the area. Once she did, she knew all the rumors she had once questioned were true. She was behind the Courtesy Court motel. She recognized the orange building and the green roof. She'd been inside one of the rooms that no one in their right mind would stay in.

Before she had a chance to overthink her situation, Ali ran toward the wooded area behind the hotel. She had to get to a phone to call Kit. Or Val, but she didn't have her cell phone or the slip of paper she'd had with her cell number on it. The only place she knew of that might have a friendly face and offer to help her was the dollar store. Unsure if they were even open, she'd head there and wait. With somewhat of a plan, she weaved in and out of the tall pine trees, glimpsing the backs of dilapidated, rusty mobile homes where people actually lived. Cars without tires were in some of the yards, along with swing sets that'd seen better days and garbage scattered on lawns. This was a bad part of town, just as Val said.

The sun was now up, which gave her a rough estimate of the time. When she reached the intersection of Highway 41 and Pondella Boulevard, she ran across the road, not caring that car horns were blaring at her as she weaved around them at a traffic light. Once she'd made it across, she went to the plaza where, if she were lucky, she'd find Tammy. Hiding behind the strip mall, she leaned against a concrete block, then eased down onto the ground. Safe, at least for the moment, Ali allowed herself to feel every emotion and thought she'd held back since she'd been dragged from the parking lot at the beach.

The fire. The people wearing red and gold robes. The chanting. If she had to guess Betty's part in this sick game, she guessed that she found and drugged victims, then later housed them in the hotel. From there, Ali suspected some sick ritual took place, and its ending couldn't be a happy one. She was unsure of Tank's involvement but positive he wasn't the one who'd dragged her down the beach. That person was strong and definitely a male. Who had it been? And why did they take her? Did she have an invisible target on her head? She'd been struggling most of her life just to stay alive. She'd kept up hope, despite all the horror she'd experienced growing up, in and out of foster care. She'd worked hard, as she truly believed one day her life would be just as she'd imagined, as long as she refused to give up. Not giving in to the cruel intentions of so many people who'd been in her life, Ali was a fighter. But right now, she wasn't sure how much fight she had left in her.

She drifted in and out of a half-conscious state, her entire body pounding with pain. Her surroundings were blurry, though she knew where she was and why. If only she could stand up, she would find help. She leaned against the cement block building, digging her heels in the dirt. Ali managed to stand, using the building for support. Inch by inch, she made her way to the front of the plaza. There were cars in the parking lot, though not many, but enough to let her know someone had to be in one of the shops. As she rounded the building, she saw the dollar store's lights were on, the bright yellow shopping carts already outside for the day.

It took every single ounce of strength she could muster to put one foot in front of the other to reach the store. When she leaned against the glass automatic doors, they opened, sending her crashing to the floor.

Fluorescent lights flickered above her as someone pulled her inside and placed a blanket over her. There was a hand on her forehead, smoothing the salty strands of hair away from her face. A cool cloth blotted the wounds on her wrists.

"I called an ambulance. They're on their way," Tammy said, her voice gruff but soothing.

Ali opened her eyes, making sure she wasn't hallucinating. "You're Tammy, right?"

"I am. I'm gonna take care of you, okay? I don't know who hurt you, but we'll find out. Just relax, kid. I'm not leaving your side."

Unsure how much time had passed when she awakened, Ali knew she was in the hospital. Memories of what had sent her there flashed before her eyes. Ali was mad, enraged by the insane people she'd been exposed to on the island.

"Hey," said Tammy. "You're finally awake."

"Hi," Ali said. Her throat was dry.

Tammy poured water into a cup, adjusting the straw for her. Ali drank as much as she could, then leaned back on the pillow. "Thanks. I can't begin to explain the circumstances that led me to your place, but I'll try."

She spent the next hour telling Tammy what she'd been through the night before, what she'd seen on the beach, and where she'd been when she came to.

Tammy appeared stunned. "My gosh, all the gossip about that place is true!"

"I believe so," Ali replied. There was no other explanation.

"The doctor did a toxicology screen, but didn't say when the results would be in. If you were drugged again, it'll show up. Your shoulder is dislocated. The orthopedic doc took care of it, but says you'll need to ice it, and he's given you a prescription. As soon as they have your paperwork completed, we can go."

"I don't have to stay in the hospital?" Surprised that the extent of her injuries wasn't that bad, she was also relieved she could return to Val's or her own place. She planned to find out who did this to her, and she was going to make them pay.

"Nope, though your wrists and ankles are a mess, nothing was broken, no ligaments torn."

"How lucky am I?" Ali said sarcastically, offering a half smile to her friend.

"Very. Today's supposed to be my day off, but Louise called in sick. I'm glad I was there."

"I hope I didn't cause trouble for you, with your job and all."

"Not at all. I called our part-timer," Tammy said. "He's glad for the extra hours."

"I'm glad I didn't cause any more problems." Changing the topic, Ali asked, "How's Peaches and her kitties?"

"Growing and eating everything in sight. The little critters keep me on my toes," Tammy told her. "Thanks to you," she added.

Had it only been a few days since Ali had found the kittens, then rented a hotel where the owner drugged their guests? It sounded like something out of a horror movie. If she told her story to a stranger, would they even believe her? Probably not.

The doctor entered her room, a smile on his face. "Look at you, wide awake now," he said as he removed a penlight from his pocket. "Just want to check a couple things; then we can let you out of here." He shined the light in each of her eyes, returning the light to his pocket when he finished. "You have some external injuries time will take care of, but I want you to ice your shoulder, get your prescription filled, and rest. Keep your wounds clean. You can use an over-the-counter cream, but I'm going to give you an antibiotic, too, just to be on the safe side. I don't want those wounds to become infected."

She'd heard this before. "I'll be fine," she told the doctor.

"Then I'll let the nurse finish up. She's bringing a set of scrubs and slippers for you. Wasn't much left of your nightgown when you arrived."

Alison felt her cheeks redden. "Thanks."

"Feel better, Alison," the doctor said, handing her his card. "I have a private practice, if you feel you need a follow-up. Just call the office." He stepped out into the hall, then poked his head back into the room. "Should I contact the police?"

"No! This is . . ." Unsure how to explain her injuries, she opted for: "Clumsiness, and too much to drink. I'll call your office if I need to."

The doctor nodded.

"Thank you," Ali said, glad she didn't have to stay the night. She hated hospitals. "For the clothes, and all," she said before the doctor stepped out of the room.

"I can lend you some clothes, if you need them," Tammy offered.

"I have plenty of clothes; they're in the suitcase in

my Jeep. But thanks. The scrubs will be okay for a while. Would you mind giving me a lift to the island?"

"I was planning on it, kid. We're friends now, and friends help each other," Tammy said.

A true Southern girl, Ali thought. "Sounds good," she replied.

Ten minutes later, she was in Tammy's Honda with the windows down, the midday heat even more miserable, since Tammy had no working air-conditioning. "Sorry about the air," she said.

"It's fine; I need fresh air," Ali told her. She debated reporting her kidnapping to the local police. She guessed quite a few knew about the insanity taking place on the island. Maybe some of the police were even involved with the sick cult she'd witnessed. It was difficult for her to accept that there were people who took great pleasure in hurting a human being. She'd had her share of horrific experiences, but this . . . *cult* had to top the list. Why her? She hadn't even moved into the cottage. For the umpteenth time, she questioned her decision. Enticed by the beach and the price of the cottage, she'd allowed her dream to override her common sense.

"I plan on getting a new car next year. Didn't want to spend the money on a new air conditioner. I'm used to the heat," Tammy said. "Been here my entire life. Heck, my parents didn't have central air until I was a teenager. I have their place now, though I don't use the air. Try to keep the electricity costs down."

Ali smiled. It sounded like her new friend hadn't lived a life of luxury. She certainly could relate to that. "It's not a necessity." Food and shelter had always been her main priorities.

When they reached Matlacha Pass, the bridge was open. A trawler at a very slow speed took a few minutes to cross. When the bridge closed, Tammy eased over the wooden slats, then accelerated, heading toward the gulf.

"I can't believe this danged bridge is still working," Tammy said. "You'd think someone woulda modernized it by now. Been this way as long as I can remember."

"That's what I've heard. Quaint, but I'm not too fond of it," Ali told Tammy. "My Jeep is in the public lot. You can drop me off there, and I'll get my things." Pausing, she remembered her purse and keys were at Val's. Had Val already left for Orlando to pick up Renée? If so, Ali would just wait on her deck until they returned.

"I ain't dropping you off and leaving, kid. You're gonna need some help until your shoulder is better."

Not knowing if Kit was back from Miami, she'd take Tammy up on her offer. They could go to her cottage. Kimberly hadn't picked up the key box, as far as she knew. "I appreciate it."

Tammy parked beside the Jeep, then ran around to the passenger side to help Ali. Her shoulder was starting to throb, and her wrists and ankles felt like they'd been scraped with a paring knife. They'd given her a pain pill a few hours before she left the hospital, but its effects must be wearing off. "I should get those prescriptions filled," she said as Tammy helped her.

"I'll take care of that," Tammy said as she closed the door. She placed her arm around Ali's waist, and together, they slowly walked to her cottage.

Ali saw the key box was luckily still there. She

punched in the code, pushing the door open. Expecting some unknown person, or a smell to indicate someone had been in the cottage, she was pleasantly surprised when she saw it was just as she'd left it when they'd rushed to Val's yesterday.

Tammy looked around, a big grin on her weathered face. "I love this knotty pine. You gonna keep it this way?" she asked as she walked through to the kitchen.

Ali followed her at a slow pace. "No way am I going to replace this. It's part of the charm, don't you think?" she asked her new friend.

"Absolutely, girl. This is a rare diamond. I bet this place set you back a couple mil, huh?" Tammy asked.

Normally, Ali didn't discuss financial issues with anyone but Henry. But she didn't see any harm in telling Tammy what a deal she'd gotten. Stuff like this could easily be found out anyway. "A hundred thousand," she said. When she saw the look of surprise on Tammy's face, she couldn't help but laugh, even though it hurt like hell.

"You're kidding?"

"Nope. Paid in full," Ali added. "I've spent my entire adult life dreaming of a home on the beach. When I left your store the other day, I stopped for breakfast, saw this in the paper, had a look, and here I am. It's structurally sound, with a fairly new roof. The air-conditioning is new. It isn't a mansion, but the location is what I've always wanted."

Tammy went to the living area and stood at the windows. "You got the deal of a lifetime. Beautiful view, and sunsets here are the best."

"They are. I saw my first one yesterday," Ali replied. "Do you come here often? To this beach?"

Tammy shook her head, her stiff blonde hair not moving an inch. "Not as often as I'd like. Between working and taking care of the property and the animals, it don't leave much time for a trip to the beach." She stepped away from the window. "You trust me to go after your meds? I can do that and pick up some food if you're hungry."

"You just saved my life. Do I trust you? Darn right I do." She had the paperwork and prescriptions in the pocket of the scrubs they'd given her. "Take this, and as soon as I can get my purse from Valentina's, I'll pay you back."

"Valentina, the psychic lady? She lives in one of these mansions," Tammy stated. "I've had a couple readings from her. She's been pretty spot-on, I can tell you that."

"The one and only," she said. "I was at her place last night when I ran out and left my purse behind. I'd planned on staying the night at her place. The pale blue house is hers." She didn't think it was her place to reveal too much more about Val's living conditions, other than pointing out her house to Tammy, which seemed harmless enough.

"Gorgeous, but your place is a true beach cottage. Lock up behind me when I leave. I'll be back as fast as I can. You gonna be okay here by yourself?"

She couldn't answer with any certainty. "I hope so. I'll keep away from the windows so no one sees me," she said, as this was about the only way she had of protecting herself, since she'd left her gun in the Jeep.

"I'll be back in a flash," Tammy said before she left. Ali locked the doors, then went through each room, double-checking to make sure the windows were locked.

Then she went to the back of her house and stepped outside to the utility room. She peered inside, then locked the door. She wasn't sure if she even had a key for it, or if Kimberly had a separate one. Now it didn't matter. Changing the locks would be her first priority, and she'd change them herself if she had to. At this point, there were only a few folks on the island she could trust.

Not having anywhere to sit, let alone lie down, she went to the bathroom, where the claw-foot tub stood.

"What the hell?" she said to herself. She put one leg in, then the other, careful to avoid bumping her shoulder against the edge. She leaned against the back of the tub, deciding this wasn't all that uncomfortable. With the electricity on, she had hot water, but wanted to wait and take a bath after she'd cleaned the tub. Plus, she didn't want to soak her wounds just yet.

Waiting for Tammy, Ali suddenly remembered Kit had told her to go to The Daily Grind to meet him. Had he tried to call her? She knew he had her cell number, because she'd called him before. Was he looking for her? Or was he still in Miami with this friend, trying to decipher what he'd found on the laptop?

Ali remained unsure if Val was home from her trip. Maybe when Tammy returned, she could ask to use her phone and call. But then she remembered she didn't have Val's number. Her purse, cell, and cash were still in the guest bedroom she'd planned on sleeping in.

She had a thousand questions, the uppermost being: Who the hell took her last night, and why?

Dozing off, Ali startled when she heard someone banging on the door.

"You okay in there, kid?" Tammy called out.

"Yeah, hang on," she said. "Be right there." Easing out of the tub, she limped to unlock the front door.

"Dang, you scared the beejeezers outta me when you didn't answer my knock," Tammy said, both arms full of shopping bags from Publix.

"Sorry. I drifted off in the bath." She laughed. "I've got no other place to lay down."

"I've got some beach chairs in the trunk of my car. I'm gonna bring them in as soon as I get these groceries put away." Tammy took charge, and Ali let her. She really trusted her. She'd proven to be a decent woman, very caring, and Ali would not let her kindness go unrewarded.

"I can't thank you enough for doing this," she said. She thought back to all those years ago, when she'd met Violet on the bus going to Atlanta, and tears filled her eyes. She thought about Violet's kindness, and what it had cost her.

Chapter Nineteen

"*Thought you'd lost me, didn't ya?*" he said, closing the hospital room door, then sliding a chair underneath the door handle.

"*Get out of here before I scream!*" Alison said. "*I'll call the nurse, and they'll call the cops!*"

"*I don't care. Do whatever you want! See what you did to me?*" He pointed to the bloody gauze on his neck. "*You're gonna pay for this. You're lucky I didn't bleed to death. If Dad hadn't found me and doctored me up, I'd be six feet under, and it'd be all your fault. You're gonna be locked up for attempted murder!*" His shrill laughter sounded more like a girl than a nineteen-year-old guy.

"*I wish I had killed you!*" she shouted as loud as she could. The drugs in her system slowed her thinking, but she knew she had to get out of here before he actually finished what he'd been trying to start ever since she came to live with the Robertsons. He was their biological son, dirty-minded and dumb. He *couldn't add two and two if his life depended on it. Alison called him an idiot every chance she got, and for this, he decided she should pay for her words with her virginity. She'd managed to fight him off, but the stupid idiot didn't give up easily.*

He laughed again. "Dad's at the police station now filing charges against you. I can't wait to see your skank ass locked up for the rest of your life. You think you're better than the rest of us, don't ya?" He walked over to her bed. She inched as far away from him as she could without falling out of the hospital bed.

"I am better than you and your trashy family. I hate all of you!" she screamed at the top of her lungs, adrenaline giving her more strength than she'd had a few short seconds ago. She jumped down, nothing but the bed between them.

"We'll see about that," he said before jumping on the bed, then jumping off on the same side. She screamed as loud as she could.

"Alison, dear, I'm here. Open the door," said Violet from the other side of the door. "I've brought clothes for tomorrow."

"He's here! Call security!" Alison yelled at the top of her lungs.

Forcing her against the wall, he yanked her hospital gown off in one swift motion. Naked except for the cast on her arm, she tried to cover herself with her one good hand. He looked at her as though she were nothing more than a piece of meat.

The door flew open. Violet ran toward him, trying to pull him away from her. He tossed her aside, her head slamming against the hard tile floor.

Alison screamed as loud as she could. She was unsure how long it took for security to find her. When they swarmed her room, he tried to run.

"Don't move," said one of the members of the security team. In a matter of minutes, Roy Lee Robertson was handcuffed, then led out of the room by security. Alison crawled across the floor to where Violet lay, blood pooled behind her head. Alison wrapped her one good arm around her, feeling the life leave her body.

Wanting to die with Violet, she screamed until a team of doctors gave her a shot to knock her out.

Two days later, still in the hospital in a state of semi-shock, Alison was able to tell the police what had happened—all of it. What had led her to leave the foster home, and the worst part of all, how much Violet had done to help her. And now Violet was dead.

The only bright light in this dark ending was that Roy would be locked up for a very, very long time.

Chapter Twenty

"It's all good, kid. I'm just glad I was there to help. No telling what woulda happened if you didn't have the guts to crawl outta that horror hotel." Tammy opened Ali's fridge, then stepped back. "I'm gonna wipe this down before I put anything inside," she said.

Ali managed to get the disinfectant and a roll of paper towels, handing them to her one at a time. As Tammy wiped down the inside of the freezer, she told her about the fish guts someone had left.

"That's the sign of the killing bucket." Tammy stopped and turned to face her.

"What?"

"The killing bucket. Redfish, they're bad luck here. You get a load a guts, well, some of the folks say it's the signal for a killing. Meaning whoever finds them is marked for death."

Shocked, yet knowing there had to be a ring of truth to this, Ali asked, "How do you know that? Is it just another rumor? Have you heard of anyone actually living to tell this . . ." She wanted to say, "fish story" but didn't, instead saying, "Rather, anyone who experienced this, and survived to tell their story?" Surely if this were true, Kit would've come across it in his research.

"Not me, but I hear stuff at the store. That's where I heard about the killing bucket. The redfish being bad luck has been known among the locals for years. It's some sick fool who'd do this," Tammy told her. She put the groceries in the now-clean refrigerator, then wiped her hands on her shirt.

"Hey, the water is on, and I have soap," Ali told her.

"No worries. I'm going to get those chairs, and then we can talk, if that's okay."

"Sure," she said to Tammy's back as she hurried out the door. Not wanting to lock her out, she stood in front of the door, waiting for her to return with the chairs. As soon as she saw her, she opened the door. "That was fast."

"Now." Tammy unfolded two plastic lounge chairs. "Have a seat. I'll fix us a bite. You go ahead and talk all you want. I'm a good listener." Tammy found the bar of yellow soap she'd bought, washing her hands before preparing the meal.

Ali was curious as to what Tammy planned to make. She hadn't paid much attention to the food she'd bought. With no pots and pans, no dishes, she'd have to buy all those items when and if she decided to. "First tell me what you've heard about the killing buckets."

"People from the island, mostly the fishermen, I've heard them make jokes about the extra cash they get when so and so is ticked off. I don't have a specific name; as I said, it's mostly the fishermen. Most of them come and go, some are local, others not. I gather when there's a call for redfish guts, it's trouble."

Tammy took a package of some kind of deli meat, cheese, and a small jar of mayo from the fridge, along with a loaf of wheat bread. "Hope turkey is good with you. It was on sale, and it's the good stuff."

Ali nodded. "Yes, that's fine." She really didn't care what she ate. After hearing about the killing bucket, what little appetite she had was gone, though she wouldn't say this to Tammy after all the trouble she'd gone to. Not to mention, she had paid for the food.

Tammy gave her a sandwich wrapped in a paper towel and a pack of potato chips. Alison took a bite of the sandwich, realizing she was hungry in spite of what Tammy had just told her. As soon as she finished, she took a can of soda and downed it. "Would you be willing to tell this to Kit? My reporter friend." She wanted a full explanation for the grisly mess she found, and Kit could get to the bottom of it.

"Absolutely. I'm happy to, if it helps you find out who's trying to harm you. Shit, they already have harmed you! I'll do whatever it takes," Tammy said, wadding her paper towel in a ball, then tossing it in one of the grocery bags. "You need to take these." She whipped out a small white bag from the Publix paper sack. "Antibiotics, and a pain pill."

"Sure," Ali said, taking the dark green Keflex with another soda. "I'll wait until tonight to take the pain meds. I'm okay right now. I need to go to Val's and see if she's home with Renée. You want to walk with me?"

Ali hoped if Val were home, she didn't mind her bringing Tammy along.

"Sure, if you want," Tammy said.

"I want to get my purse and keys to the Jeep so I can change into real clothes," she told her. "I'm slow," she warned as they headed toward the beach.

The sun was still out, yet not a soul could be found on the beach. Birds called, their wings fluttering above them. With a slight breeze, it was just the kind of evening one would spend walking along the beach. Ali took her time, not wanting to injure herself any further. She'd had enough. It was time to find out what the hell was happening on this island. As soon as she saw Kit, she'd let him question Tammy about the killing buckets, if they hadn't already come up in his investigation.

As soon as she saw the blue beach house, Ali spied Renée sitting on the deck with Val and an unfamiliar man. When she reached the steps, she called out, "Is it okay if I come up? I need my purse." She didn't want to interrupt them if this was a private family moment.

"Thank God!" Val said, racing down the steps. "I've been worried to death about you. Come on, there is something I need to tell you." She looked at Tammy. "Do I know you?" Val asked her. "You look familiar."

"I work in town at the dollar store," Tammy said. "You've read for me a couple times, though it's been a while."

"Of course! You'd think I would remember. Come on up, both of you," Val insisted.

They followed her up the three flights of steps. When Ali saw who Renée was sitting next to, she shot Val a questioning look.

"Have a seat," Val instructed. "Before I get started, do either of you need something to drink?"

Both shook their heads.

"Are you okay, Renée?" Alison asked her, though she looked just fine.

"I am fine, seriously. Mom can fill you in," Renée said, giving her a smile that lit up her entire face.

"When I told you about him . . ." Val directed her glance to the still-silent man sitting on the deck with them—none other than John Wilson. "I wasn't completely honest. With you, with Renée, and a lot of other people."

"No, she wasn't, and I should be pissed, but I'm not," John said, then reached over and patted Renée on her leg.

Okay, this was weird, Ali thought. The longer she stayed on this island, the more baffled she felt. Wasn't this guy a freaking pervert?

"John is Renée's dad," Val blurted.

"I . . . see," Ali said, but she didn't. It wasn't what she'd been expecting to hear.

"It's cool, huh?" Renée said. "Mom didn't want me to know about her sordid past, so she made up a story about some French dude being my dad. John . . . Dad suspected I was his daughter, right?" She looked at him, love written all over her face.

Ali waited.

"We had a little romance when we were teenagers," Val explained. "After my parents died, I was lonely, and Andre, my guardian, kept me under lock and key most of the time. When he found out I was pregnant, he forced me to marry *him*, and sadly, I've resented, or rather hated, John since. I thought he'd step up to the plate, take responsibility for his actions. We were both young. Andre told anyone who'd listen that Renée was his daughter. She was just a baby when he passed away. He was way too old for me. I'd convinced myself John was a sexual predator, because he allowed Andre to pretend he was her father. Hurt beyond words, every chance I got to bad-mouth him, I did. Then he told Renée the truth."

"I kinda resemble him," Renée remarked.

Ali looked at John, then Renée. They did resemble one another. She hadn't noticed this before, but there wasn't any reason to, given the fact Val told her he was into little girls.

"John took her out of town for a quick DNA test. That's where they were yesterday," Val finished. "I hope you won't hold this all against me, but I understand if you do. I've given John quite the bad rep with a few islanders."

"Hey, I should've stepped up to the plate and acted like a man instead of a pissed-off teenager," he said. "By the way, Alison, I'm sorry if I scared you. Really. I thought . . . well, it doesn't matter what I thought, but welcome to the island, and all that jazz."

"And to think I was ready to blow your balls off," Ali said, a slight smile curving her mouth.

"Tell them about the killing bucket," Tammy said out of the blue.

All three sets of eyes focused on her.

"I don't think now is the time for this," Ali said, then stood. "If you could just bring my things out, I'll be on my way."

No one said a word when Val went inside, soon returning with her purse and a shopping bag. "Your clothes," she said to Ali.

"Thanks. I need to . . . go home. I'll see you around," she said to Renée. The hurt look on her young face stabbed her directly in her heart, but until she could make sense out of what she'd just learned, it was best she do this on her own.

Tammy followed her down the steps. As soon as they were out of earshot, she asked, "What exactly happened?"

Briefly as she could, Ali filled her in on what Val had said about John. "I suspected there was more to the story, but it wasn't what I thought."

"Tell you what—I'll get your luggage from your Jeep, bring it to you, then see that you're set up for the night before I go home. Peaches and the girls are probably wondering why they haven't been fed."

Ali smiled. "Poor babies. Of course, do what you need to. I'm fine. I have my phone and keys now. I'm all good. There's a sleeping bag in the back of the Jeep. If you could bring that too, I'll be set for the rest of the evening."

"Absolutely," Tammy agreed. "I'll call you when I get home if you want, just to check in."

"No, you don't have to do that. Just take care of the kitties, and don't worry about me. I'm going to take one of those pain pills, call Kit, and pass out."

"I'll get the rest of your things from your Jeep," Tammy said.

Ali nodded. Back in the kitchen, she wiped the

counter down with her good hand, trying to focus on what Val had told her, and why she lied about John Wilson. It made a sort of twisted sense, though she suspected there was even more to her story where he was concerned. What she didn't understand was how Val could badmouth this guy all these years without proving he'd done all the wicked things she'd accused him of. Could it really be that John Wilson didn't give a damn? But that was odd, too. Why would he allow her to spread such vicious rumors? Again, this island and its people baffled her.

Tammy tapped on the door, and Ali hurried over to help her. "You didn't have to bring all of this in one trip," she said, closing the door behind them. "Thanks. Again."

"Glad I can help," Tammy said. "Where do you want me to set this up?"

Ali hated being so dependent on Tammy. She was a good soul and now a friend. It didn't matter how long she had known her; Ali knew in her heart that Tammy was good to the core.

"Just spread the sleeping bag out in the front room. I'll fix the lamp so I'll have a bit of light in there." There were overhead lights in the room, but they were old-fashioned, without light bulbs. She would eventually replace them with fan lights, but for now, all she wanted was to find the person responsible for dragging her away from the beach and dumping her into that hole in the ground. Before she forgot, she went to the kitchen and took a couple one-hundred-dollar bills from her purse. She knew it was more than Tammy had spent, but her time away from work counted, too.

"Take this." She rolled the bills up, tucking them in Tammy's back pocket.

"What's this?" She took the money out of her pocket. "This is way too much. I spent about thirty bucks, kid. I don't take money I ain't owed."

"I know, and I don't either. Your time is valuable. You spent the day at the emergency room with me and lost wages. That counts in my book."

Tammy nodded. "I appreciate it," she said.

"So do I, all you've done for me." With her good arm, she gave her new friend a half hug. "Call me tomorrow," she said, knowing Tammy had her cell number.

"You betcha," Tammy said, then gave Ali another hug before leaving.

Ali stood in the front room of her home, watching the sun as it began its slow descent into the murky green waters of the Gulf of Mexico. And to think, she'd considered giving this up. Palmetto Island was mysterious and inhabited by a few evil souls. She wasn't going to let any of them ruin the life she now had.

Chapter Twenty-one

Awakened by voices outside of her front room window, Ali slid across the oak floors where her purse lay open, her gun's shiny handle waiting for her. She took the gun, checked the clip, then stood up, wincing. Her shoulder throbbed, her wrists and ankles were tender, but it was nothing she couldn't deal with. She eased into the kitchen, staying low, away from the windows.

More voices. She couldn't make out what they were saying. Inching her way along the kitchen floor to the back door, she leaned her head against the door, trying to understand them. Fear crawled up her spine, then settled in the pit of her stomach. Her desire to know who was out there, and why they were on her property, overrode her fear.

Ali was past tired. Over being the object of someone's abuse. Beyond sick of playing the role of victim. "Screw this," she said out loud, not caring if anyone heard her. This was her frigging home, and she was going to do whatever she had to in order to protect it, and herself.

Without a second thought, she yanked the kitchen door open and stood on the back porch, waiting for them to do whatever the hell they had planned.

"Who's there?" she called, not caring. She held her gun in her good hand, her finger on the trigger, ready to fire. Slowly, she crossed the length of the porch, stopping when she heard the voices again. She'd heard them before. It sounded like two, maybe three, men.

A muffled cry came from the front of her house. Voices, then heavy footsteps tromping to the back of her house. Racing around to the back, she stopped in her tracks when she saw Gib. And Hal, holding a young girl close to his large body, his big hands covering her mouth. Then it clicked.

"Let her go!" Ali shouted as she aimed her gun at Hal.

"No, it's okay, Miss Ali. We like her. She's the goodest girl we got, right, Mr. Gib?"

"Shut up, boy," Gib said.

"I am asking you to let her go. Now. I don't want to have to shoot you, Hal." Ali tried speaking as calmly as the situation allowed. "This little girl doesn't want to be with you." She slowly walked down the so-called drive, continuing to point the gun at Hal. "Right, sweetie? You want to come with me, okay?" Ali had no clue who this little girl was, but guessed it was her who she and Kit had heard screaming in the bait shop.

No more than eight or nine, the little girl was rail-thin, her skin a warm brown, eyes shadowed with fear.

Her long black hair was a mass of tangles. "It's okay, Hal. Let me take the girl, then you and Mr. Gibbons can go."

"Okay," he said, releasing his hold on the little girl.

"No!" shouted Gib. "She's mine, you little bitch!"

"Run," Ali shouted to the frightened child. "Hurry, run! Scream as loud as you can!" The little girl finally seemed to understand that Ali was trying to save her, so she ran as fast as she could. "Go to the blue house on the beach! Go!" Ali screamed.

As soon as the girl was out of sight, Ali walked toward Gib and Hal. "What the hell do you think you're doing? You sick son of a bitch!" Eye to eye with Hal, she said, "Get down on your knees."

"I have to ask Mr. Gib first," Hal said, his eyes searching for his father's. "Can I, Mr. Gib?"

"Who the frig calls their dad 'Mr. Gib?'" she said. "On your knees, Hal, or I'm going to shoot Mr. Gib in the head. Blow his brains all over the ground. Like those fish guts you put in my freezer. You want to pick up Mr. Gib's brains, Hal?"

Ali didn't care that her words were cruel. Nothing she said was as cruel as what this man had most likely been forced to do by his sick-ass father.

Hal lowered himself to the ground, tears streaming from his dark brown eyes. Alison almost felt sorry for him.

"You!" she shouted at Gib. "Get over here beside your son, or I promise you I'll do what I said. Your worthless brain will be fish food when I finish with you."

Her hand shook as she continued to direct the gun at Gib. He stared at her, shaking his head.

"You ain't gonna shoot an old man," he said, his mouth widening in a grin so wicked she wanted to stick the gun in his mouth and pull the trigger so he would never be able to smile again.

"This is your last chance," she said, praying the little girl had enough time to reach Val's house. She lifted a foot, then slammed it down on Hal's back. "Or I can shoot *his* brains out," she said.

"Go on—he ain't got none anyway. Stupid boy. He deserves to die for what he did to my Rosa. Woman died giving birth to him, and that devil girl twin. Kill 'im. I dare ya."

It took a few seconds for her to absorb his words. The chanting, the rough Southern twang. Gib had been one of the men wearing robes, chanting in front of the fire the night before. "Why?" she asked, wanting to know what possessed him.

He threw his head back and laughed. "Cause we can!" More laughter; then there was a sharp blast, and Gib fell forward, both hands clutching his chest.

"Don't move, miss," came an unfamiliar male voice. "Put down your gun. We've got this."

Ali slowly eased her finger off the trigger, her arm lowered at her side. A team of men wearing navy blue jackets with the letters FBI in bright yellow scattered around Hal and Gib like ants.

Ali stared at them, wondering where they came from and how they knew to come. She had her answer when Kit Moore, still wearing the same clothes he'd worn when she'd first met him, appeared with Pete and someone else she didn't know.

"You okay?" Kit asked, wrapping his arms around her. He pushed her hair away from her face, tilted her chin up, then kissed her.

"I am now," she said, finally allowing herself to go limp in his arms.

Chapter Twenty-two

Ali laughed at Renée's description of all the extra work her mother was doing since revealing her father.

"I kid you not, she does everything, even folds my clothes. Am I right, Mom? Dad?" Renée teased as John Wilson flipped another burger onto a platter.

"I think Val's got a handle on things," he said, though he didn't try to hide the grin plastered on his face. "She's going to spend the next few years trying to make up for what she did to my reputation."

As odd as she'd found John Wilson, Ali now saw beneath the beach bum attitude, finding he was a very likable guy. Spoiled by his family with too much too soon, he appeared to enjoy being with Val again, in spite of what she'd done, though Ali was pretty sure there wasn't any romance between them. Just Renée tying them together.

The group gathered on the deck of Val's house, the first time Ali, Kit, John, and of course Renée had been together since all hell broke loose. The events of two weeks ago were still in the news. Ali's entire lawn had been dug up and a second set of bones found, along with a few others that belonged to the girl whose bone she'd first found.

"You know how sorry I am," Val told John. "This entire island isn't the same anymore. I'm glad, but so sorry for Hal."

"It's too bad, but he only did what Gib told him to do," Kit said to Val. "He's going to be okay in the group home. It'll be a big change, but he'll adapt."

Ali took a drink of the freshly squeezed lemonade Val had made for the barbecue. "I was beyond shocked when I saw him, and that poor little girl. Gib must've totally lost it when his wife died. I can't believe no one knew about him and his sickness."

"What's going to happen to Gib?" Renée asked. "He seemed like a nice old man."

"Those are the ones to watch for," Kit told her. "I'm guessing he'll spend the rest of his life behind bars. Frankly, that's too good for him; I'm hoping he'll get an ass-kicking in jail. He ruined our family, taking little Jane, who must've trusted him. I don't want to know what he did to her, because if I did, I'm afraid of what I'll do."

John uncovered a plate of chicken, putting it on the grill. The mesquite chips filled the air with their smoky scent. Soft rock played from hidden speakers. The sun was out, the humidity high. Gulls shrieked above the blue-green waters, and the white sand sparkled. A perfect day for a cookout, Ali thought. This is what she'd imagined when she first came to the island. In a million years, she never thought her life would take such a drastic turn, but it had, and she was happier than she'd ever been. Her bad karma turned out to be so much more. Finding that ad in the newspaper was meant to be. Kit had told her this, and she believed him.

They all spent the next three hours eating, drinking, and laughing. A gust of wind, followed by a downpour, sent them running indoors. Ali and Kit eventually said their goodbyes, then together they walked to her cottage.

"You want coffee?" Ali asked when they were inside. She'd made a few purchases since she'd officially moved in, the first being a Keurig coffee machine. Val had given her a small table with matching chairs, which fit perfectly in her little kitchen. She'd decided to keep the old gas stove for now. Later, when she had her friends over for a real dinner, she might consider a new one.

"Yes, please." Kit sat down in one of the chairs, his large presence overpowering the small space.

"Two black coffees," she said as she placed a cup in front of him, then sat across from him.

They spent the next hour discussing yet again the events that had changed so many lives, especially her own.

The story unfolded once Kit's friend read what was on Gib's hard drive. In great detail, he'd written about how he'd come to despise Hal and his twin sister, who died when his wife Rosa gave birth to them. In his mind, all little girls were evil. Little girls like Jane, and little Sofia Carillo, who spent years lying in a morgue, waiting to be identified. When the *Fort Charlotte Sentinel*, along with the *Miami Journal,* published the details of the case, Natalia and George Carillo finally came forward to claim their daughter's remains.

Both were undocumented immigrants who had been working on Matlacha Pass near Ali's cottage. Their daughter had been missing, yet they were afraid to report her disappearance because they weren't in the country legally. DNA testing on the bones that had been discovered proved little Sofia and Jane's identities. Val and John paid for a proper burial for the family. Kit contacted a friend, who was working with the Carillos to gain them legal citizenship. It would take a while. The couple, who had other children born in Miami, agreed to abide by rules set forth in the process, and would begin working legally for Kit's father and stepmom in a matter of weeks. The screaming little girl Ali had almost killed Hal and Gib over was understandably traumatized, but Ali had learned through Kit that she was getting the proper therapy and had been reunited with her family. Gib and Hal had temporarily stashed her at the bait shop, knowing John was away in Orlando, until they could secretly move her to the motel.

So many changes in such a short time. Ali had moments where she didn't believe the evil on this island was truly over. Betty and Tank were part of Gib's cult. Tons of literature on Cyrus Teed's cult and their practices were found on Gib's computer, now in the hands of the FBI's forensics team. Betty and Gib were more than friends. She joined him in his sick mission after Tank was old enough to take care of himself, though Tank denied any knowledge of the cult and their activities.

Soon, Kit left, promising he'd return the next morning. Ali knew it was still hard for him to spend time at her cottage, knowing his sister Jane had been buried there for so many years. They had both agreed to take things slowly, and that was just fine with her.

Ali's thoughts were all over the place. She knew the investigation was just beginning. There were more folks involved in the cult. Ali still didn't understand why Hal and Gib had tried to kill her specifically. Betty had indeed laced her hot tea with Ambien that fateful night. She had used enough to knock out a three-hundred-pound man. Hal had dragged her to Gib's place after attacking her on the beach; they then took her back to the hotel, where Betty gave her another dose of Ambien.

After her arrest, Betty swore Gib had threatened to kill her if she didn't follow his orders. He wanted little girls, and apparently young women, too, so he could torture them, then bury them. At least, that's what she'd told the FBI.

Alison and her ability to know when to run when she felt she was in danger had saved her life again. But from now on, she wouldn't live in the past. She would move forward.

She had two good friends now in Val and Tammy, plus Kit, who'd stolen her heart. Renée was like a little sister. John seemed thrilled now that Val acknowledged him, and agreed the past was in the past. Together, they'd do their best to raise their daughter.

Many of the things that had taken place in such a short amount of time were beyond Ali's ability to explain. Yet she decided that now, all she wanted was to spend time in her little yellow cottage. For the first time in twenty-nine years, she had a home of her own.

Val's Blue Crab Shrimp Salad

1 head butter lettuce or lettuce of choice
1 English cucumber, peeled and sliced
1 beefsteak tomato, cut in half, then quartered
2 pounds of cooked shrimp, chilled
3 pounds of cooked blue crab meat, chilled

Citrus Salad Dressing

¼ cup lime juice
¼ cup honey
3 tablespoons olive oil
1 teaspoon dry mustard
Salt and pepper to taste

Mix liquid ingredients. Pour over lettuce, cucumber, tomato. Top with blue crab and shrimp.

From beloved storyteller and #1 *New York Times* bestselling author Fern Michaels comes a thrilling novel of action and adventure in the Lost and Found series featuring siblings Cullen and Luna Bodman, who must unravel a cold case connected to a mysterious armoire . . .

Luna Bodman always looks forward to a new shipment of furniture at the restoration shop. Her brother, Cullen, has a knack for finding discarded pieces with an intriguing history, and Luna likes to sit with each item to see if she can feel any kind of vibrations. Usually Cullen does his thing while Luna does hers, but the arrival of an old armoire triggers a reaction in Luna that's impossible to ignore.

From the moment Luna wiggles inside the armoire and closes her eyes, she feels an overpowering and disturbing sensation. Emerging, she asks for a flashlight and discovers words scraped into the wood: "Help me!" Hoping to uncover the piece's secrets, Luna contacts her good friend, U.S. Marshal Christopher Gaines, and the group sets out to trace the armoire's origins.

The journey takes them to a military school in New England, and a mysterious, long-ago ransom case. The kidnappers were never found, but decades later the answers may finally be within reach . . .

Please read on for an excerpt from LIAR.

Chapter One

How It Started

1983

Chad Pierce Sr. hit the lottery the day he met Camille. Figuratively speaking, that is. He had been on the sailing team in college and once a year he and his pals would meet up somewhere for their annual bacchanalian reunion. That particular year it was Newport, Rhode Island, during the race for The America's Cup. Even into his late twenties Chad still enjoyed carousing and drinking until the wee hours of the morning. That is until he spotted the lithe, stunning woman leaning on the railing of the yacht club veranda. Her gaze was on the sunrise as wisps of her bangs gently caressed her face. Her white silk scarf floated with the breeze. "Chad was gobsmacked. She reminded him of Michelle Pfeiffer in that stupid sophomoric movie *The Hollywood Knights*. It wasn't because of the character she had played. It was the same striking, understated beauty.

Chad slowly moved off the lounge chair that had served as his bed. He was lucky no one spotted him sleeping, or rather recovering, from a night he could barely remember. He looked down at his rumpled clothes, sniffed at his armpits and jerked his head away in disgust. But that woman. He had to meet her. He looked around for a porter or someone who might know the lady's identity and who might be discreet enough not to run him off the property. He spotted a steward setting up tables for brunch. He rifled through his wrinkled Bermuda shorts, hoping he still had some cash in his pockets. Fortune smiled on him, and he pulled out a twenty-dollar bill. He waited until the steward was within a loud whispering range and he could see the man's nametag.

"Psst. Selwyn."

The man was startled but quickly noticed Chad pressing his finger to his lips, indicating he should say nothing. Chad motioned for the steward to come closer. Once out of the woman's line of sight and earshot, Chad pulled Selwyn to the side. "Sorry, old man, but could you tell me who that lovely young lady is?" Chad made sure to reveal Andrew Jackson's face on the proffered bill. He apologized for his appearance. "A night out with the boys. You understand."

Over the years Selwyn had seen his share of misbehaved, spoiled, and often drunk young men. Newport was rife with them. Especially in the summer duing yachting season. Selwyn also knew to remain invisible, never directly interacting with the clientele unless they needed something. Rarely did any of them offer him money for information. He hesitated but remembered that the young man had been hanging about the night before with several friends dressed in similar regalia. He gently pulled the bill from Chad's fingers.

"That would be Camille Atherton Tindale. A very nice young lady." Over the years Selwyn's Caribbean accent had softened but his sing-song cadence remained refreshing and comforting. When addressed he always made things sound easy, with a nod and an "absolutely" or "no problem" followed by "right away." He continued, "She often comes here early in the morning. She likes to feed the ducks." He grinned at the disheveled young man, eyeing Chad up and down. "If you want to have the pleasure of her company, I might suggest a shower, shave, and a fresh set of clothes."

"Right." Chad was appreciative of the man's kindly straightforwardness. "Can you tell me where she lives?"

"Oh, no. That would not be correct, but what I can do is tell you—she and some of her friends are planning a little party this evening. Some kind of celebration. Six o'clock, if I am correct in my recollection." He pointed to his head.

Chad grabbed the man by both shoulders. He wanted to give him a big kiss. "Thanks, old chap!" Chad patted Selwyn on the shoulders and skedaddled to go clean up his act and figure out a way to meet the very beautiful, very rich Camille. It would take a bit of finesse, but that was something Chad was extremely good at. Charm, poise, and skill. When he smiled, his green eyes sparkled and the dimple on his left cheek made him even more appealing. He could make you believe you were the only person in the room and you had his full, undivided attention. Yes, his demeanor could charm the pants off anyone . . . and it had. Many times. But this time . . . this time it was different. There was something special about that woman, her wealth notwithstanding.

Visit our website at
KensingtonBooks.com
to sign up for our newsletters, read
more from your favorite authors, see
books by series, view reading group
guides, and more!

Become a Part of Our
Between the Chapters Book Club
Community and Join the Conversation

Betweenthechapters.net